WHATEVER IT TAKES

S. JONES

Editing:

Virginia Tesi Carey

Proofreading:

Marla Selkow Esposito

Formatting:

Leanne Clugston at Irish Ink

PROLOGUE

"Hey, Bartender, another shot of Patron," Grant Anderson muttered as he continued his pity party of one. He was at a dive bar down by the river in South Philly. Although his meeting with Dom Scarantino wasn't for another hour, the thought of going home and having to face the very people he continued to let down was too much to bear.

As the burn of the tequila hit the back of his throat, he couldn't help but wonder how his life had taken such a drastic turn for the worse.

From the outside looking in, Grant appeared to have it all. He came from a well-respected family, married the woman of his dreams, and had a beautiful little girl. He even managed to build a career with a promising future.

Everything should have been perfect, but things were seldom as they appeared. His wife was on the verge of leaving him, and his role as an ADA had turned into a sham.

At first, the requests from Scarantino seemed small and insignificant. He would help with a plea here and there, get some inside info when needed, or steer a cop in the wrong direction without suspicion.

Tonight's request, however, was crossing a line. The threats had advanced, and his double life was becoming harder to keep quiet.

About ten minutes before nine, Scarantino walked into the bar, scanned the room, and slid onto the empty stool next to Grant. He removed his suit jacket, rolled up his sleeves, and leaned back.

"Good evening, counselor, what brings you out to our shitty side of town?" Scarantino smirked, the only hint of humor he ever showed. He was powerful and deadly—a man you didn't fuck with.

The amount of alcohol that had built up in Grant's system over the past hour had him forgetting that fact. "Well, Mr. Cartel leader, I'm here because a friend of yours told me that if I wanted my knee caps to stay attached to my legs, that I needed to meet with you."

Scarantino tapped his meaty hand on the bar and ordered two of whatever Grant was drinking.

He waited until they were alone before he spoke. "If you keep running your mouth like that, you'll find your lips will no longer be connected to your face."

Grant clenched his jaw and thought it would be best to not provoke him any further.

"Look, Grant, my father always told me if you're going to dance with the devil, you're going to have to pay the fiddler. I'm here to tell you that your tango with the devil has come to end. It's time to pay up, and I'm here to collect."

Grant wrapped his hand around his drink. "What do you want?"

"I took the liberty of placing a duffle bag in the trunk of your car. Just like we discussed earlier this week, I need you to deliver the package to an associate of mine. Easy peasy, lemon squeezy, my friend.

"I'm not your friend," Grant hissed out.

"No, you're not, Grant. You're a self-centered, drug-addicted prick, that was stupid enough to let his addiction to nose candy get out of hand."

The words stung, but it was the truth.

"My friend is expecting this package to be dropped off at exactly midnight. That gives you plenty of time to sit here and think about all the ways you've fucked up your life." He took a hefty sip of his drink and squinted his eyes. "Or you could spend the next two hours banging your whore that's waiting for you in that swanky hotel room across town."

Grant concentrated on the ticking clock on the wall. He was about to lose everything that mattered to him if he didn't do as he was told. There had been enough implied threats over the last few weeks directed toward his family that he knew he was out of options.

Scarantino pushed back to stand up. "Enjoy yourself, amigo. If I were you, I might switch those shots over to espressos. I'd hate to see you fuck this one up."

"Adios, motherfucker," Grant said under his breath as he watched Scarantino walk away in his well-tailored suit. His goons followed close behind him. After he was gone, he ordered two more shots of Patron. Once he was finished, he dialed up his side piece and told her he was on his way.

Looking back, Grant shouldn't have gotten behind the wheel of a car after downing all that tequila. Maybe then he wouldn't have run the stoplight at ninety miles an hour. Perhaps he should've just stayed at the hotel with his girlfriend. If he weren't so jacked up on coke, he probably would have seen the car in front of him.

But Grant didn't have time to react or second-guess his decisions. He barely had touched the brakes as he skidded through the intersection, tearing the van in front of him in half. His airborne BMW slammed into a tree; the airbag hit his face, and when he woke up, everything hurt like a bitch. He waited a few minutes as he watched the van he destroyed burst into flames.

He didn't have time to call for help; the only thing he could do was save himself. So, he took the duffle bag filled with ten kilos of cocaine and ran...

ONE

CHARLOTTE

"Emery, your breakfast is getting cold," I yelled from the bottom of the stairs and prayed that there wouldn't be any more delays this morning. Who knew that getting a six-year-old ready for school could turn into an Olympic event?

Frustration pushed through me because she was running behind as usual. I brought my hand to the back of my neck, forcing the tense muscles to relax. A part of me just wanted to crawl back into my bed and pretend my life wasn't such a mess.

I glanced around the three-thousand-square-foot house that Grant and I purchased just over two years ago. We sold our little townhouse and bought this dream home when Emery was four. We wanted her to have space to run around and maybe one day grow our family.

I walked to the kitchen window and stared out into the sprawling backyard that backed up to a wooded forest.

When we first saw this house, I envisioned backyard barbeques and princess-themed birthday parties. I pictured little kids playing tag, running around the green open space, and splashing around in the in-ground pool. Grant would walk through the front door at the end of the day, sneak up behind me, and kiss me softly on the neck. We would gather around the table, laugh, and talk about our day. Later in the evening, once Emery was in bed, we would sit out on the porch swing, sipping on a nice glass of Malbec and stare up at the stars, basking in the life that we had built for ourselves.

Unfortunately, my entire marriage was a lie and the life I had built for myself was all wrapped up in this house full of smoke and mirrors.

My hands gripped the granite countertop that he insisted we buy, wishing I could smash it to pieces. I hated what my life had turned into. I liked things calm, steady, and predictable. Instead, my well-organized life has turned into complete chaos in just a matter of weeks.

It only took one bad decision to change everything we had built for ourselves. One fateful night filled with bad choices tainted all the good that Grant had done and destroyed whatever little love I had for him.

"Mom, have you seen my library book?" my six-year-old asked from behind me.

I turned around and forced a smile on my face, not wanting Emery to sense the anger I felt every time I thought about her father.

"I think I saw it on your dresser last night."

She huffed out a deep breath that sent her bangs flying across her forehead and ran back up the stairs yelling something about not getting a piece of candy if she didn't return the book on time. The doorbell rang, just as I was getting the syrup out of the fridge for her pancakes.

I wiped my hands on the dish towel and walked over to the front door and peered through the sidelight window. It shouldn't have surprised me to see Detective Rubin standing on my front step.

I swung the door open to greet him. Only he wasn't alone.

My heart damn near beat out of my chest at the sight in front of me. I blinked once and then twice, feeling my limbs visibly start to shake. I stared at the man, wondering if my eyes were playing a trick on me. The last time I saw Quinn Walker, things did not end well. It had been over seven years since I'd seen him, and he looked to be a far cry from the boy I had once known.

He had on a pair of Ray-Bans that should have shielded his face from my view, but I'd recognize those grayish-blue eyes anywhere. Just like I knew they changed color with the weather. Those intense eyes are what drew me in right from the beginning. Seeing that the sun was out today, I knew they'd be blue, instead of a stormy gray.

I quickly glanced in the hallway mirror, taking a quick check to make sure I didn't look like a housewife that had just rolled out of bed. I could guarantee you there was nothing worse than a surprise visit from your ex-fiancé showing up out of the blue.

"Can I help you, Detective Rubin?" I asked, trying to downplay the panic in my voice, and hoping that Quinn didn't pick up on it. Which was useless, because he was the type to notice everything.

"Good Morning, Mrs. Anderson. This is Detective Walker from the Philadelphia Police Department." He coughed into his hand, like he was trying to choose his words carefully. "I understand that an introduction probably isn't necessary." He scratched the back of his head, looking a little uncomfortable. "We are here to ask you a few questions."

My throat grew tight, and my mind was so overwhelmed by seeing Quinn after all this time, I could barely form a damn thought, let alone words. I shifted my eyes over to him. He was watching me closely, the intensity in his eyes brought a chill across my skin. My gaze cut back to his partner, and I did my best to school my expression. I figured acting indifferent was better than allowing him to see how rattled I was.

"I already told you and the US Marshals everything I

know," I reminded him. "So, unless you have something new to add, or are here to tell me you've found my husband, or the person who left me that threatening note the other day, I'm not really sure what more you could want from me?"

Two days ago, I found a package on my doorstep. It was a small wrapped box with a red bow on top. When I opened it, I found an antique stopwatch with a note attached that said, "Tell your husband that time is running out."

I called the detective on the case and he rushed right over. With the amount of backup he brought with him, you would have thought my house was a murder scene. My neighbors were probably having a field day with the amount of national attention my husband's case had brought to our quaint suburban neighborhood.

Detective Rubin rubbed his hand along his jawline before dropping it. "May we please come in?"

I took a moment and begged my brain to come up with an excuse to send them away. I'd given out dozens of written statements and I've spoken to every law enforcement agency that existed. Answering questions about my husband wasn't what troubled me. It was easy to remind everyone about what a snake I had married. What I couldn't figure out was what Quinn's role was in all this. And when the hell did he become a cop?

A million scenarios ran through my head, none of them making any sense. Last I remembered, he was living the dream out in California. The same dream that ended things between us.

I was just about to invite them inside when a little hand wrapped around my leg. "Mom, I found my book." Emery's head peeked around my side, as her stare alternated between the two men. "Who are these people?"

"They're friends of mine who just stopped by to ask me a couple of questions," I said with a calmness that I was far from feeling. I've been a little shaken up from that little special delivery the other day, but thankfully, she hadn't picked up on the panic I felt every time I opened the door.

"Your breakfast is on the counter. Why don't you eat it before it gets cold?"

Quinn stood a few feet away and stared at Emery with a curiosity that extended way beyond a professional interest. His jaw was clenched, and his hands were balled into fists at his side.

I didn't like how he looked at her. His stare was too focused and too intense.

She rolled her eyes and grumbled, but thankfully, she let go of my leg. The drama queen in her had taken over, and sometimes it felt like she was six going on sixteen.

Heat bloomed in my face, and I pressed my sweaty palms together, trying to hide the fact that they were trembling. "I really don't want to talk about any of this in front of my daughter," I said to Detective Rubin as Emery disappeared into the house.

"We understand and we won't take up much of your time." He gave me a reassuring smile, spotting Emery over my shoulder. "If you want, we can wait until she's taken off to school?"

I looked down and took inventory of what I was wearing. I certainly wasn't dressed to impress in a simple gray top and black leggings. But at least I had showered this morning, so I was thankful for that.

I opened the door and gestured for them to come inside. As soon as Quinn's body got close enough to mine, everything around me stopped, especially my breathing. He paused for a brief second as he passed me; the scent of his familiar cologne caught me off guard. It was the same damn cologne that he always wore. The one that I would put in his stocking every year on Christmas Eve.

He stepped inside, paying close attention to everything as we moved from the foyer to the living room. His eyes seemed intrigued as he studied the photos of Emery lined along the wall. His steps faltered, and he hesitated at my wedding picture on the mantel, a frown formed on his face. I turned my gaze to the ceiling, wishing I had more time to prepare for this. Maybe then I wouldn't be so anxious.

The sound of our footsteps echoed down the hall as the two men followed me into the kitchen. I walked over and placed Emery's lunch in her backpack and zipped the pouch shut.

"All right, sweet pea, you're all set." I turned to put her empty plate in the dishwasher. "Go wash your hands. The bus will be here any minute."

Her nose scrunched up as she looked curiously at the two large men standing in the middle of our kitchen. A little line formed in the middle of her forehead. "You guys are friends of my mom's?"

Detective Rubin's expression softened. "As a matter-of-fact, we are."

She rested her chin in her hands. I could see her inquiring mind working overtime. "What are your names?"

"I'm Marco and this is Quinn."

Emery tilted her head to the side and focused on Quinn. "You know, the sun isn't shining in here. Why do you still have your sunglasses on?"

"You're right. Sorry about that," he said with a wobbly voice as he pushed his glasses up to the top of his head. "Nice to meet you, Emery."

His familiar voice stirred up things inside of me that I didn't want to remember. Memories of broken promises and declarations of love came rushing back, creeping into places where they didn't belong. While it had been more than seven years, it still felt like time stood still. I never imagined that seeing him again would be so painful.

"Emery." I swallowed nervously. "It's time to go. You don't want the bus to leave without you."

"Why does the bus always have to come so early?" she griped while taking one last bite of her toast.

"Maybe if you went to bed earlier, you wouldn't be so tired in the morning."

She gave me the stink eye letting me know what she thought of my suggestion as she stalked over to grab her backpack.

I fastened the strap along her shoulder and pressed a kiss to her head. I could see the bus pulling up at the curb through the window. "You have a good day. I'll see you when you get home."

"Love you, Mom." She smiled and waved goodbye to the two men. "Bye, Marco and Quinn."

Detective Rubin laughed, while Quinn stared at her across my kitchen table with a stoic look on his face. I wanted to know what he was thinking, but then I reminded myself that it didn't matter what the bastard thought.

I walked over and grabbed two coffee mugs out of the cupboard. I turned to Detective Rubin. "Would you like a cup of coffee?"

"Yeah, that would be great. Thanks." He nodded as he made himself comfortable and pulled out a yellow notepad and pen.

Quinn remained standing with his hands bunched along the back of an empty chair. I could feel his gaze on me as I poured the coffee into the mug. My hands shook as I reached over and grabbed the cream and sugar off the counter. I walked around the table and handed Detective Rubin his coffee. Not wanting to be rude in front of his partner, I slid the other mug over to Quinn. The coffee was black, just the way he liked it.

Detective Rubin leaned back in his chair, his eyes were wary. "I know this is difficult for you, Mrs. Anderson, but we need to ask you a few questions."

"I already told you everything I know. I have no idea

where Grant is, and I have no idea what that package was about." I was beyond frustrated with the situation and having Quinn here in my space didn't help.

"We've read over the reports. We have no doubt that you're telling the truth." His body shifted, and I saw his expression change. "We are very concerned about the people he was involved with. Not knowing who they are makes things a lot more difficult on our end. Grant is unpredictable at the moment. So, if he or anyone tries to contact you in any way, do not hesitate to call us."

I laughed, even though there was nothing about this current situation that was funny. "Call you? Hell, I'll do better than that. I'll pay for his Uber ride downtown myself."

"For Christ's sake, Charlotte. Can you be serious here for a second?" Quinn's voice boomed across the table. It was the first time he had addressed me, and his tone set me off. I spent years trying to forget his voice. His smile. His scent. How he made me feel. I was pissed that he thought he could show back up in my life when I was most vulnerable and think that I would be okay with that.

"All right. Let's all take a minute to calm down," Detective Rubin cut in, sliding his chair across the floor. "I know you two have history together. Let's try to keep this conversation professional, okay?"

I glared at Quinn and asked him the question that had been burning a hole in my head since his feet hit my doorstep. "Why are you here?"

He plowed a hand through his hair in frustration. His eyes darted around the kitchen before landing on mine. "Have you ever heard of a woman named Pamela O'Brien?"

His answer confused me because we were clearly talking about something different. I wanted to know how long he's been back for, and why the hell was I just finding out that he was a cop?

Still, his stern expression gave me a bad feeling in the pit of my stomach. "No."

"She's an assistant district attorney from the Philadelphia office."

"Okay," I said, slumping down into an empty chair at the table.

"She admitted to tampering with evidence regarding your husband's case." He blanched. "As well as aiding and abetting."

My eyebrows rose along with the hair along the back of my neck. "Why would she do that? Did she owe Grant a favor?"

Quinn and Detective Rubin exchanged a tenuous look.

"She was with him that night," Quinn replied, looking uneasy.

"I'm confused. There wasn't anyone with him during the crash. The footage from the cameras at the intersection didn't show anyone else in the car with him."

Detective Rubin leaned forward, his gray sport coat strained against his broad chest. "He had just left her at the hotel."

My back straightened. "You mean the hotel bar?"

Quinn ran his thumb along his bottom lip, a telltale sign that he was nervous. I guess some things never change. "Yes, Grant and Pamela were at the bar that night, but they also rented a room together. She admitted to having an intimate relationship with your husband."

I shot up from my seat and stumbled across the kitchen. How the hell was this my life? I should have been furious, angry, and broken, but I was so past it all. There was nothing left to do but laugh at how pathetic my life had become. So, I did. I laughed until tears flowed from my eyes. I hunched over and grabbed my stomach and peeked over at Quinn and Detective Rubin. They looked confused. Join the club.

"Are you okay?" Quinn asked, his brows crinkled with

worry. He started to step toward me, but I held up my hand. I couldn't have him touch me. It wouldn't take much for me to fall into his arms. I was always weak when it came to him.

"I'm fine," I reassured him, wiping a tear from my eye. "I just want this over with."

I didn't know how a man like Grant Anderson could go from being the respected prosecutor who handled all the DWI cases here in Montgomery County to the most wanted fugitive in the state of Pennsylvania.

He was no longer the well-liked son of a local politician. He was now a murderer, wanted for vehicular manslaughter. His reckless actions took the lives of five people when he crashed his BMW into the Dodge Caravan containing a young family who had been coming home from a week-long vacation from the Jersey Shore. He ran from the scene while their minivan went up in flames.

"I'm sorry, Charlotte." Quinn's voice was gruff, almost pained. "My office is now involved in the investigation because the woman in question is from our district. I can't personally handle the case, because it's a conflict of interest."

"So, I'll ask again, why are you here?"

After all these years, I couldn't believe this was actually happening. This shitshow called my life just kept getting better and better.

"Detective Rubin is a good friend of mine. We are both concerned about that package that was left on your front porch. Forensics was unable to retrieve a set of prints which is very alarming. Marco also knows about our history, and we both wanted to check-in and make sure you were okay."

I waved my hands around emphatically. "I'm fine." I didn't want him to think I was weak, because I wasn't. But I also wasn't as strong as I thought I was either. There was only so much I could handle in one day. And right then, protecting my already battered heart was at the top of my list.

My mind couldn't even begin to comprehend the potential

danger Grant left behind. I've watched enough episodes of *Mind Hunter* on Netflix to know that whoever left that box on my porch meant it as a warning.

Quinn's face got serious. "I may not be able to formally investigate this case, but I will do whatever I can to make him pay and keep you and your daughter safe."

This was such a mess. What the hell was I supposed to do? Thank him for being the one to tell me that my husband was having an affair? Thank him for reminding me that there was an unknown threat out there, that my life as well as Emery's, could be in danger?

Just the thought had me petrified. "No, you won't, Quinn. This isn't your business, not official and certainly not personal."

He stared at me in disbelief. "Really, Charlotte? You're going to give me shit when I'm trying to help you."

I crossed my arms over my stomach, trying to get my pulse to return to normal. "I have a lot going on right now. I can't deal with you too. Please, I'll do whatever the police tell me to do, but you can't be the one to help me. I'll deal with anyone but you."

He looked like my words wounded him and that confused me. He was the one who blindsided me when he broke off our engagement. I had to come to terms with the fact that I lost the love of my life. I grieved for him and never quite recovered. I promised him forever, and I meant it. Too bad he didn't.

A stabbing pain hit my chest at the reminder. It was like tearing open a wound that never completely healed.

"Look, Mrs. Anderson..." Detective Rubin's gaze shifted over to Quinn in warning and then back to me. "We're not here to make things worse for you. The US Marshal's office will be reaching out to you again tomorrow. If anything new develops in the meantime, please contact my office. We have officers patrolling your neighborhood looking for anything out of the ordinary. Please keep your doors and windows locked at all times. In other words, be vigilant."

I silently nodded my head as he made his way to the door.

Quinn stood off to the side. He looked torn on whether he should stay or go. His mouth parted slightly like he wanted to say something. My eyes bored into his, pleading with him to give me some space. As curious as I was to confront him and demand an explanation, I just needed a minute to catch my breath.

Detective Rubin clasped Quinn on the shoulder. "We should get going."

It seemed like it was taking every ounce of his self-control to turn away from me. "Yeah." He hesitated on his way out and looked back at me one last time.

We held eye contact for a long, uncomfortable minute. His stare was stirring things up inside me that I thought were long dead and buried. But that's the thing about long-lost loves. Sometimes they return when you least expect them.

I wanted to convince myself that this meant nothing, even though I knew in my heart that this was going to change everything.

TWO

QUINN

MY EYES GLANCED OVER THE REPORTS THAT I SHOULD HAVE BEEN focusing on. My brain absorbed almost nothing. Instead, I switched my iPad sideways on my lap while I scrolled through photo after photo of Charlotte and her daughter Emery.

Even though it wasn't rational, I resented everything about that little girl, because she was supposed to mine, not Grant's.

It was clear from the very first day that he moved in across the hall from us that he wanted her bad. I used to catch him staring at her and stopping by, asking to borrow stupid shit that he didn't really need. As annoying as he was, I never considered him a threat. Charlotte and my relationship was as solid as it could be for two young kids trying to figure things out.

It seemed like just yesterday when she and I made the decision to move in together. We rushed right out to put a deposit down on that little one-bedroom apartment that was barely big enough for one of us, let alone two. It didn't matter though, because it was ours, and we were happy.

Asking her to marry me less than a week after I graduated

seemed like a good idea at the time. I was young and in love and thought I had the world at my fingertips. It took me a while to realize how wrong I was. Not about her, but about my ability to provide for her. I moved out to the West Coast to chase a dream that I thought would secure our future. In the end, it tore us apart.

I set the iPad down on the table and sipped my coffee. I should stay away and respect her wishes. She obviously didn't want my help. But I was going to lose my mind if I didn't get everything off my chest. Not only that, but I needed to make sure she was safe. Even after years of separation, protecting Charlotte was all I knew. It was instinctive.

I snatched my keys off the counter and started walking toward the elevator.

Bree's name lit up my screen just as I stepped inside. "Hey." I smiled while pushing the button for the parking garage.

Bree was a local news reporter in Washington DC. We met when she interviewed me about a local drug dealer I had arrested with ties to some influential Washington politicians. We had an instant connection and have been dating for almost nine months.

"I'm glad I caught you. I'm at Crate and Barrel and wanted to pick up a few things to bring with me to the apartment next weekend."

I slid my eyes shut and tried to suppress my desire to groan out loud. I should have been excited to see my girlfriend after three weeks, but I had this nagging feeling that wasn't sitting right with me.

"Bree, I thought I told you not to spend any more money on me?"

She was always buying stuff for my apartment. While she claimed her reasons were that my place was too boring and needed a little character, my gut told me she was starting to nest like some bird that was ready to take over the place.

"Relax, Quinn. It's just a couple of things. Besides, I'm going to need a better sauté pan and some nice dishes if I'm going to be cooking you breakfast next Saturday morning."

My top lip reflexively curled into a smile as I stepped off the elevator. "Just don't go crazy and keep your receipts."

I pictured her rolling her eyes, and I pressed the unlock button on my key fob. "I'm not making any promises, but I'll try." She sighed. "I can't wait to see you."

I pinched the bridge of my nose, feeling guilty as hell. Here I was talking to my sweet girlfriend while I was on my way to visit my ex. "You too," I muttered, "I'll call you later. Have a good day."

I hung up the phone and stepped inside my truck. Bree was a great girl and things just started to get serious, but it always seemed like her feelings were stronger than mine. I did care about her, but seeing Charlotte yesterday had sent doubts trickling inside my head.

I pushed the start button on my truck and backed out of my parking spot, hoping I wasn't making a huge mistake. I reminded myself on the drive to her house that I had a lot to lose, but when Marco informed me about the package left on her porch, I knew I had to jump in and help. There was no way I could sit back knowing she could be in potential danger.

I pushed my Ray-Bans on top of my head and rang her doorbell. I took a step back, feeling the tension build in my shoulders. I grew more nervous as her footsteps got closer. We really needed to have a conversation about her idiot of a husband and the company he had been keeping.

The door swung open, and I looked down at the little girl with long brown hair and green eyes. She tilted her head to the side with a crooked smile and a missing front tooth. "Hi, Quinn."

I never felt more out of my comfort zone than I did right then. I liked kids, sure, but this little girl wasn't just any kid.

"Emery!" Charlotte's stern voice sounded behind her. "How many times do I have to tell you not to answer the door without knowing who it is?"

"It's fine, Mom. I know who Quinn is. He was here the other day," she said, brushing her messy bed hair over her shoulder.

Charlotte stepped in front of her and stared me down. She didn't look very happy to see me. "It's Mr. Walker to you."

"Quinn is fine," I said, giving them both a friendly wave.

"No. It's not." She narrowed her frosty eyes and reprimanded me right in front of her little girl. "She is six years old and has been taught to greet adults using their last names."

Okay then.

"May I come in?"

She peered around my shoulder. "Where is Detective Rubin?"

"I'm not here on official business," I informed her. God did I miss her smart mouth.

She leaned against the doorjamb and crossed her arms. She was wearing a tight white camisole tank top with a pair of gray cotton pajama bottoms. She looked adorable, despite the scowl on her beautiful face.

"Official business is the only kind of business you have here," she snapped.

"That's not true and you know it."

She stepped forward with a fire in her eyes that turned me on and pissed me off at the same time. She poked her finger in the center of my chest, causing a few strands of her long, brown hair to fall into her face.

"Leave, Quinn. I have nothing to say to you."

"Mom," Emery spoke with surprise in her voice. "That's not nice. You always tell me that I should be nice to others."

Score one for the kid, I thought, while watching her flinch. She swung her head to her daughter; her smile not quite reaching her eyes. "You're right. I'm sorry. Can you give me and Mr. Walker a couple of minutes alone? Your breakfast is getting cold." She pointed toward the kitchen. "I'll be there in a second."

Emery ignored her mother's glare and invited me in. "Do you want to have some pancakes, Mr. Walker?" She batted her innocent green eyes at me. "My mom made extra."

I smiled at the tiny little thing. "Thanks, Emery. I would love to. I'm starving," I said, breezing through the door before Charlotte could stop me.

I heard a grumble and the door slam behind my back. I followed my new friend into the kitchen and sat down at the table, making myself at home. Emery smirked at me as she brought a stack of pancakes to the middle of the table.

"These look pretty tasty." I smiled, running my hands down my thighs.

Emery picked up the syrup, pouring almost half the bottle over her two pancakes and slid it over to me. "They're banana and cinnamon," she announced, and my body physically tensed. "My mom makes them for me every Saturday morning."

"Really." I cocked my head to the side and stared at Charlotte's back. "That's interesting because they're my favorite too. In fact," I said, feeling my mouth water, "I used to eat them every Saturday morning just like you."

Charlotte slammed the spatula in the sink causing the dishes to clatter. Emery leaned over and whispered in my ear, "She's very grumpy this morning."

A burst of laughter popped out of me at her candid and accurate observation. I snatched a couple pancakes off the serving plate. "I haven't had these in a long time. They look delicious."

She looked up from her glass of milk. "I thought they were your favorite?"

"Oh, they are. My girlfriend used to make them for me, but she hasn't been my girlfriend in a long time, so I don't get to eat these pancakes anymore."

Charlotte's shoulders stiffened as I started to dig into my breakfast. Emery picked up her fork and blinked at me through those big green eyes that reminded me of her mother. "My mom makes the best pancakes in the world. You can come over here on Saturdays and eat with me if you like."

Charlotte turned and shot me a look, annoyance was written all over her face. I forgot how striking and bright her eyes were, even when she was pissed. "Emery, I'm sure Mr. Walker has other things to do."

I kept my face impassive, not letting her snide tone get to me. "I'm not sure about next Saturday," I said, remembering that Bree was coming into town on Friday night. "But I would love to come back and have breakfast with you again sometime. Especially if your mom's making my favorite pancakes."

"Okay. Do you have any kids? I don't have a lot of friends my age. You can bring them if you want."

I gave her a sad smile. "No. I don't have any kids."

I wanted to tell her that if I did have a kid, it would look just like her.

"How come?" she asked in between bites of her meal. She was a curious little thing.

"Emery, mind your p's and q's," Charlotte said, saving me from having to answer that question. "Why don't you let Mr. Walker eat his breakfast in peace?"

Emery eyed my plate, but chewed on her pancakes. She was very well-behaved for a little girl. Nothing like my niece, Taitlyn, who was a handful on a good day.

Emery and I sat and made small talk throughout

breakfast, while Charlotte avoided me and made it painfully obvious that I didn't belong in her home.

I was trying to make an effort to turn her anger down a few notches, but every time I would look at her and smile, she would frown and look away.

The cute little munchkin beside me, however, continued to study me like I was an alien from another planet. Her eyes took in every little detail of my face, making me shift uncomfortably. We sat in silence for the next few minutes and finished up our breakfast.

"Was that your bike that I almost tripped over laying in the driveway?" I asked, trying to cut through the silence.

"Yeah." She sighed, pushing her empty plate toward the middle of the table. "My mom won't let me ride it without wearing a helmet, even though I don't need one. I'm a very good rider and I've never fallen off my bike."

I chuckled. "Sorry, kiddo. I'm going to have to agree with your mom on this one. Besides, it's the law."

She didn't look too happy about that. "Well, it's a dumb rule and I look stupid wearing a helmet."

"Emery Rose," Charlotte scolded, and I swallowed, feeling guilty. "Enough. Go upstairs, wash up and get changed."

I expected a full-blown temper tantrum, but the kid surprised me when she brought her plate to the sink and marched up to her room without a word.

"You've done a good job with her, Charlotte."

She narrowed her eyes at me. "Don't."

My body went tight. "Don't what?"

"Don't sit here and make small talk with me. Don't pretend you give a damn about me, when seven years ago you just dumped me to the curb like an unwanted piece of furniture. And don't ever try to use my daughter to manipulate me again."

Okay, I expected the first two slams, but the last comment really got my attention. I shot to my feet and stalked toward her. "Let's get a couple of things straight. Regardless of what you think, I will always care about you." Her eyes widened, not expecting that. "Second, I happen to like your daughter, and I would never use or manipulate her. I was genuinely enjoying her company. And last, we are going to have a civilized conversation whether you want to or not. I'm sick of the attitude."

She folded her arms across her chest defensively. "You've got some nerve." Her green eyes flicked across my face. She was so close, and I knew I should have stepped back. Put some distance between us, but one thing about Charlotte was that I was always drawn to her. "You don't get to tell me what to do. You lost that right a long time ago."

I inched closer to her, and she took a step back. I shouldn't have caged her in against the kitchen counter, but I couldn't help myself. I put my palms on either side of her. "You're correct. I fucked up big-time." Her eyes went wide when I leaned down, bringing us only inches apart. My gaze dropped to her lips with an overwhelming need to bring them to mine. "But I will always care about you, Charlotte. You can't control how I feel about you any more than I can."

She put her hands on my chest and tried to push me away. It was the first time she'd touched me in years and even though it was in anger, I still felt that spark deep in my bones. "I don't care about your feelings. After all, it was pretty clear you didn't care much about mine." She tilted her chin up in defiance. Never in my life had I ever wanted to kiss someone so badly. Even though she was pissed, she was still beautiful and perfect. "You know why I don't care? Because you left me, and my love died for you the second you broke my heart. So you can take that guilty conscience of yours or whatever it is that brought you to my doorstep and get the hell out of my life. I don't need you. I moved on from you a long time ago, just like you moved on from me."

Her words tightened around my chest, making me think

of all the nights I laid in bed wishing I could go back and do everything differently. All the women, all the mistakes, and all the hang-ups I've battled with over the years came crashing down around me.

How was I supposed to tell her that I underestimated how much I loved her? How much it hurt me to stay away from her.

"I lied."

"I'm sorry. Say that again."

"I lied about meeting someone else. There was no one else." I watched her stunned expression and the way her throat rolled when she swallowed. "After I moved out to California, you kept calling and texting me. I couldn't stand to hear your voice. It was too hard. I knew the only way to get it all to stop was for you to think there was someone else. So, I lied."

She squeezed her eyes shut as if my words pained her and then she did something that I least expected. She drew her hand back and smacked me across the face.

THREE

CHARLOTTE

"Let me make sure I understand this correctly," Erica said, holding out her empty wineglass for Mackenzie to take. These two have been my best friends since high school and the three of us have always been close. They were also the first ones I called when "anything" went down. "He said he lied, and then you slapped him across the face and threw him out?"

"That's right," I answered while nodding my head and scrolling through the Facebook app on my phone.

Erica scrunched her eyebrows together, with her long dark hair falling into her face. "How the hell could you have thrown him out without hearing the rest of what he had to say?"

I set my phone down and leaned back in my chair. "You guys don't understand. He hurt me. More than Grant's actions ever could," I told them. "I didn't want to hear his explanations. I didn't want to let my guard down in front of him. I've loved that man my whole life, even when I was married to someone else. And now that I know he blew our life apart for absolutely nothing," I shook my head and felt

26

moisture build up in my eyes, "it hurts even more than I could've imagined."

"You're still in love with him, aren't you?" Erica asked, sitting on the floor and leaning against the couch.

If anyone knew anything about love and heartbreak, it was Erica. She was twenty-nine and had already been divorced twice. She married her high school sweetheart, Zach, at age twenty-one, and soon realized that she married way too young. She then met Jerard, who swept her off her feet. Nine months after they were married, he swept another woman off her feet, and Erica sent him packing.

"I'm not sure how to answer that," I said, bringing my knees up to my chest. The three of us were dressed comfy, in black leggings and casual T-shirts. We were in Erica's living room drinking wine and binging on Netflix when the next episode of *The Office* started. "Quinn was always different for me. You both know that. We have so much history between us."

"You guys were always intense," Mackenzie said, sitting up straighter. She put her wineglass on the coffee table. "I know you loved Grant, but you didn't love him the way you loved Quinn. I never should have kept my mouth shut about what a slimy motherfucker he was." She plucked a piece of cheese off the tray and brought it to her mouth.

Mackenzie never cared for Grant and tried to warn me from day one to steer clear of him. She always felt there was something off about him and that I moved too quickly. Looking back now, there was no denying that she was right.

I knew that what I had with him didn't come close to what I had with Quinn, and I was okay with that. Because let's face it, once you get burned, the last thing you want to do is play with fire again.

"I blindly trusted him over the years, never questioning anything and stupidly allowing him to fill my head with lies."

I shook my head and stared out the window. "I should have picked up on what a lying, deceitful bastard he was."

"I'm going to stop you right there," Mackenzie said as I scrolled through my local news app to see if there were any updates on Grant's case. "He was a practiced liar who had everyone fooled, so go easy on yourself."

Erica patted my knee and refilled my wineglass. "Honey, his own family didn't even know what a piece of shit he was. Although, one would think they should have suspected something considering they raised the little demon."

The Andersons were blindsided, especially his mom, who took the news of what he'd done the hardest. Grant's father was too busy doing damage control and trying to preserve his perfect image. But let's be real, even a well-respected congressman like John Anderson couldn't escape a family scandal without some kind of fallout. And the media was relentless when it came to stories like this.

"Honestly, the only thing I care about right now is making sure Emery is okay."

"She's still young and has plenty of time to adjust," Mackenzie said, trying to reassure me.

She wasn't just one of my best friends, she was also a middle school guidance counselor. I've been leaning on her for advice a lot lately, especially when it came to answering Emery's unending questions. "Have there been any updates on who left you that package?"

Just thinking about it gave me chills. "No, but I'll sleep a lot better when they find out who sent it."

Mackenzie leaned back and folded her hands in her lap. "I bet you will. You are always welcome to stay with me."

"Thanks, but I'm good for now."

The last thing Emery needed was any more change. That move would be a last resort.

"So, where does Quinn fit in all this?" Erica asked. "Other

than being the hot detective on the case? Which is no way a coincidence."

My eyes narrowed as she watched me while casually sipping her wine. "Actually, he's not 'officially' on the case. And what does him being 'hot' have to do with anything?"

"So, you admit that he's still hot?"

Oh, dear God. If she only knew. He was just as handsome as I remembered, but he had matured in a way that made him look even better, and I would bet my house he knew it too. The guy could crawl out of a car wreck and look perfect.

Gone were the tattered jeans and ratty T-shirts. His wardrobe had obviously been upgraded. I wasn't used to seeing him in a crisp white shirt, black tailored dress pants, a gold badge clipped to his belt with a gun peeking out from the shoulder holster. The whole cop thing just added to his sex appeal, and I couldn't help but feel like the universe was poking me in the ribs just to rub it in a bit. It felt like a cruel joke.

I reached over the coffee table and picked up the unopened bottle of Jack Fire and unscrewed the cap, taking a long sip. I was suddenly feeling very thirsty.

I set the bottle down and wiped off my mouth with my sleeve. "He looked all right, I guess."

"If you're trying to convince us that you're not attracted to him and that you no longer have feelings for him, you're not doing a very good job," Erica said while taking pictures of our wineglasses to post on Instagram. That girl loved social media like most parents loved their children. She turned the empty bottle of wine sideways so she could get a decent picture of the label and then snapped the photo to share with all her online friends.

"What do you want me to say?" I shook my head and tried to forget the way he looked at me in the kitchen. "The only thing I see when I look at him is the guy who broke my heart."

"I guess I just don't get it. If he was going to break up with you, he never should've asked you to marry him in the first place," Mackenzie said, as Erica nodded in agreement.

"Exactly," I agreed, and uncorked the next bottle of wine and started to refill our glasses. This was why these two were my best friends. They got me in a way that no one else would.

We all raised our glasses in the air. "A toast…to assholes."

"I sure know how to pick 'em," I said, thinking about how both men turned out to be big disappointments.

Erica waved her hand in the air. "Please, I think I still have you beat in that department."

"I'm starving. I think we should order a pizza," Mackenzie suggested and leaned back into the couch.

"With extra cheese and pepperoni," I added and picked up my phone so I could log into Uber Eats. "Wine and pizza. It's a good thing I wore leggings."

The rest of the night was spent with us laughing and drinking three bottles of wine. I'd like to say that the pizza helped absorb some of the alcohol from my system, but judging by the way the room spun, it was safe to say that I was feeling slightly tipsy.

I reached over to close the pizza box when my phone buzzed on the coffee table. Expecting it to be Grant's mom telling me to come pick up Emery from her sleepover, I was surprised to see the message from an unknown number. I picked it up and swiped the screen. Butterflies fluttered in my stomach when I read the message.

It's Quinn. We need to talk!

Erica raised her eyebrows when she saw my expression. "Who is it?"

"It's Quinn," I answered, holding the phone up to my chest. My heart was beating a mile a minute.

"Shut up!" Mackenzie shouted and leaned forward to get a better look. She was so drunk she practically stumbled into my lap. "Let me see."

I panicked and held the phone out of her reach. "I don't trust you."

"Whatever." She rolled her eyes and grabbed my phone.

"How did he get your number?" Erica asked. "Did you give it to him?"

"Of course not." I looked at her like that was the most ridiculous thing I'd ever heard.

"He's on the fucking government payroll, for Christ's sake," Mackenzie shouted, almost rupturing my eardrum. "Holy shit." She jumped off the couch and ran to the windows. She pulled the shades up to look outside.

"What are you doing?" I asked, watching her press her face up against the glass.

"He probably has a tracker on your phone. He's probably sitting outside in his black town car watching the house as we speak."

Erica laughed. "You've been watching too many *Law and Order* episodes."

Mackenzie walked over and sat next to me. My mind was all over the place. Quinn was slowly invading every little corner of my life. I couldn't even have a girl's night out without him occupying my thoughts.

I wish I could have blamed it on the wine, but his message sat there on the table taunting me. A knot formed in my stomach as I remembered that when Quinn Walker had his mind set on something, there was no stopping him.

"Are you going to text him back?" Erica asked, slipping a slice of pizza out of the box and taking a huge bite.

"And say what? Thank him for telling me about my husband's affair? Or should I tell him how happy I am that he finally confessed to the real reason he broke off our engagement?" I shook my head defiantly. "I don't think so. Quinn Walker can kiss my ass." I rose from the couch, feeling a little tipsy. "I'm going to the bathroom."

I stepped inside and glanced at myself in the mirror. It felt like my whole world was imploding around me. A part of me wished that I could run away and escape all my problems just like Grant did. It had been three weeks since he'd been gone. Three confusing and agonizing weeks. I haven't been able to sleep or eat. All I do is lay in bed and question every decision I ever made.

Seven years I wasted on a man who ended up being the worst mistake I ever made. On top of it all, I now had to deal with the shock of Quinn telling me he lied about being with someone else. That lie was the reason I ended up drinking that night and sleeping with Grant. It was why I was standing in the bathroom of my best friend's condo wondering how the hell this was my life.

I stood there for a full five minutes and contemplated Quinn's text. I would not let the curiosity get the better of me. Whatever he had to say wouldn't change a damn thing.

After washing my hands, I made my way back into the living room and found Erica and Mackenzie giggling on the couch.

"What did I miss?" I asked, causing their laughter to stop.

"Oh nothing." Erica waved me off with a smile in her voice. "I was just showing Kenzie something on my Instagram."

"Come sit down. We polished off all the wine, but we still have the Jack Fire and some snacks to chow on," Mackenzie slurred and picked up a handful of potato chips from the bowl and started crunching away.

I sunk into the couch next to her and plunged a chip in the French onion dip. "I'm going to have to run an extra two miles tomorrow to work off all the booze and extra calories I've consumed in the last three hours."

"Nonsense. You're beautiful," Mackenzie said and started studying my appearance. Then she reached over and grabbed her purse off the table. She took out a hairbrush and started to redo my messy bun until it was smooth with loose tendrils of hair falling along my face. You would have thought we were going out for a night on the town by the way she reapplied a coat of my lip gloss and stroked the powder brush across my cheeks with shimmering powder.

"What are you doing?" I pushed her hand away thinking she was acting weirder than usual.

She muttered something inaudible under her breath and walked away before I could ask another question. I knew I was feeling the effects of the alcohol, but I didn't look that bad. Besides, it wasn't like I was going anywhere other than when I put my drunken ass in an Uber at the end of the night. I wanted to get up early and get a few things done around the house before Emery got home from her sleepover.

Out of the corner of my eye, I noticed that Erica kept checking the time on her phone, which made me wonder where I had put my own. "Hey." I urgently started to search the couch for the missing device. "Has anyone seen my phone?"

I dropped to my knees on the floor to look under the couch when Erica pointed to the kitchen counter. "Oh, I put it in the charger. I noticed your battery was low."

"Thanks." I sighed with relief. I wanted to make sure it was close by in case Emery needed me. "I'm going to order an Uber."

"I'll order you one from my phone. I got a gift card for my birthday, so save your money. Just don't do anything to fuck up my five-star rating."

"Are you sure?"

"Positive," she replied a little too enthusiastically and

grabbed her phone off the table. I watched her tap into the Uber app and order my ride. "If that jerkass of a husband of yours taught me anything through all this, it's to make smart choices."

I touched the hair on top of my head, feeling uncomfortable. She had a point. And I knew I wasn't responsible for what happened, but I was married to the son of a bitch, so it still struck a chord.

As if Erica could read my mind, she reached over and grabbed the bottle of whiskey, took a sip and passed it around. "Stop blaming yourself. Nothing about that night was your fault."

"I'm sorry. I know tonight is supposed to be fun. Sorry to be such a Debbie Downer."

"Hey." Mackenzie reached out and gently touched my arm. "Look at it this way," she said, handing me the bottle of Jack. "At least you're finally free of the asshole."

Free? Is that how I was supposed to feel? All I felt was stuck. The reality was, my husband was gone. I was now a single parent with a mountain of debt, and the small pile of cash that he left behind would run out soon because I had no job.

I applied for a few teaching positions, but the school year had already started, which meant finding a job was unlikely. When I tried to get on a sub list, no one wanted to take me on because of my last name. So here I was, stuck, yet I was supposed to feel free.

"You'll get through this," Mackenzie tried to reassure me. She placed her arm around my shoulder and drew me into her side. "Life sucks right now, but it will get better. Just take it day by day."

"Right," I said, bringing the bottle up to my lips. "I didn't mean to bring you guys down tonight. I'll get there. I promise."

Mackenzie shook her head. "You have nothing to

apologize for. I'm actually proud of you for coming out tonight, even if it was only to Club Erica." She laughed and gestured around.

Erica snatched the bottle out of my hands. "I couldn't agree more, but next time, we are going out clubbing."

I laughed. "You know we're not twenty-one anymore, right?" I reminded her.

Erica swayed to the side a little bit and pointed her bony finger at me. "See, that's your problem. You're at that in-between stage."

"In between?" Mackenzie and I both asked at the same time.

"Yup." She swung her long dark hair over her shoulder. "You're too old to be hooking up with young twenty-somethings, but too young to live your life like a nun. You just need to get laid."

"Erica." I sighed. "I'm still technically married."

She narrowed her eyes at me. At least she tried to. "We are going to fix that problem."

The doorbell chimed, and I watched Erica and Mackenzie glance at each other simultaneously. "Well, speak of the devil."

She swayed over to the door with a shit-eating grin on her face.

As soon as the door swung open, my brain sobered up and my good mood disappeared.

There stood Quinn Walker, and I almost swallowed my damn tongue. He leaned against the doorframe with his lips spreading into that disarming smile that he was known for. He was wearing a white, crisp button-up with the sleeves rolled to his elbows. Who knew that arms could be such a damn turn on?

My eyes did a slow crawl down to his dark, denim jeans, and I calculated in my head how long it would take me to unbuckle the black belt that was clenched along his narrow waist.

A warm feeling bubbled up inside of me and I convinced myself that it was just the alcohol talking. Nothing more.

His intense stare locked on mine and I wanted to squash the trail of goose bumps that broke out along my skin. I hated that my body immediately responded to him. As if he could sense the drool that was about to fall from my mouth, he winked at me. Fucking winked. And it only fueled my anger.

Erica looked amused with herself while holding the door open so he could step inside.

What the hell was going on?

"Why is he here?" I asked, pointing to Quinn and wishing I could make him disappear.

His eyes narrowed. "You asked me to come pick you up."

My voice dripped in sarcasm because it was so much easier than allowing him to see how affected I was. "In what universe do you think I would ask you for anything?"

He pulled his phone out of his front pocket, swiped the screen and held it out. "According to this text, I would say this universe."

I clearly underestimated my friends. I flattened my lips, trying not to let my temper get away from me. "What the hell is wrong with you two?" I snapped, turning my glare over to Erica and Mackenzie who seemed pleased with themselves. So much for keeping my emotions in check.

"Ignore her," Erica said, flinging her hand out and waving me away. She walked into the kitchen and swiped a beer out of the fridge. "How have you been, Quinn? It's been a while." She offered him a bottle of Bud Light, but he shook his head.

"No thanks. I'm driving." He then placed his hands on his hips. His height was so intimidating. He tried to catch my gaze, but I bent my head and looked away. "Does anyone want to fill me in on what is going on here?"

Embarrassment flushed across Erica's cheeks. "Yeah…

Um." She gave Mackenzie a sideways glance. "Kenzie and I texted you from Charlotte's phone when she was in the bathroom."

"Shit," he cursed, never taking his attention off me. "I should've known."

"Yeah, you should have," I scolded him, willing myself to take a deep breath. The air was thickening by the second. The only thing standing in our way was the damn coffee table in the middle of the room. "I'm sorry that you drove over here for nothing. Have a safe drive back to wherever you came from."

I took the last sip of my wine hoping to calm myself down, but I was so pissed at my friends that it didn't help. What they did was not fucking cool and it was going to take me a while to get over this.

He slid onto the couch and completely ignored my request, while I stayed on the other end and refused to talk to him. Erica and Mackenzie spent the next ten minutes getting caught up on the last seven years of his life.

I tried to block out their voices and pretend that I was uninterested, but I could tell Quinn was enjoying himself. He always loved being the center of attention.

I was mortified and felt betrayed that my friends would do this to me. My first night out in a month and I couldn't even enjoy myself.

My life was pathetic.

Erica squeezed my shoulder, trying to bring me into the conversation. "Isn't it great?"

"Yeah, sure. Whatever." I shrugged.

Could I be any more of a bitch?

He deserved it. I reminded myself.

"So." Quinn nervously rubbed the palm of his hands along his knees. "You ready to get out of here?"

I snapped my head up. "I'm not going anywhere with you."

"The hell you're not," he snapped back.

I crossed my arms, giving him a warning. "Don't talk to me like that."

"Then quit acting like a child."

I shot off the couch and got right up in his grill. "I'm far from a child, Quinn. I'm just not stupid. Nothing good can come from me getting in a car with you."

"Oh yeah. Why's that?"

"Because," I huffed. Just when I needed a great comeback my mind went blank. I couldn't think of one thing to say. Not one. Even if I could come up with something, he wouldn't listen anyway.

He sat there with a smirk, as if he could read my thoughts.

"Charlotte," Erica said, cutting through the tension. "He drove over here to see you. He's sober. It's just a ride home."

Quinn pulled on the back of his neck. "I just want to talk to you, Charlotte. That's all. Please."

Damn it.

His voice sounded determined, and I realized this was going to be harder than I thought. I was trying really hard to be strong because everything about him reminded me of the heartbreak I went through. But I knew if I sent him away, he would only be back. Saying no to him would be useless because when Quinn had his mind set on something, he never gave up.

I convinced myself that it would be better to get this conversation out of the way, so I could burn that bridge down between us once and for all. I didn't want to leave it up to chance that I would ever cross it again.

Quinn's eyes never strayed from mine as I said, "Fine. Let's go."

FOUR

QUINN

I DIDN'T KNOW HOW SHE WAS STILL FUNCTIONING AFTER WHAT that asshole did to her.

I stayed away all those years because I thought it was best. I threw myself into my work thinking it would be enough of a distraction. Yet, here I was, right in the middle of the shitshow that had become her current life. Clearly, I was asking for trouble. Charlotte and I were never friends. We were always lovers, so I wasn't sure how to talk to her. The only thing that I was certain of was that she needed to give me a chance to explain myself.

It was obvious that she would rather stick her hand in a blender than talk to me, but there was zero chance of me leaving her alone. Maybe once I apologized, we could start down that road of forgiveness. Maybe with a little bit of trust and understanding, we could try to be friends. Maybe then she would let me help her.

I drew in a sharp breath and tightened my hand along the steering wheel. You could cut the tension in the car with a butter knife. I wanted to crack a joke and make her laugh, but she wasn't in the best mood, and I didn't want to push my luck. So I stayed silent and gave her some space.

We had been on the road for about five miles before she finally spoke. "Am I just along for a nice, quiet, scenic drive? Because if I am, it might be better during the daylight hours seeing that everything is pitch-black. However, if you want to ride in silence the entire way, I'm good with that too."

Her attitude should have pissed me off, and I was half-tempted to tell her that I could pick her up in the morning where she could see things more "clearly," but I didn't think she would appreciate my sarcasm. It was obvious she was uncomfortable, but I took the fact that she was riding next to me as a small victory.

Shifting my gaze in her direction, I asked, "How drunk are you?"

She knotted her hands in her lap. "Unfortunately, for me, not drunk enough."

A laugh tumbled out of me. When I walked into Erica's condo and saw the empty wine bottles strewn around the room, I wasn't sure how things were going to go down. Charlotte and alcohol weren't always friends and her behavior was often unpredictable when under the influence. If my instincts were right, she was slightly buzzed, and I really wanted her sober for this conversation.

As we cruised through town, I spotted a diner up ahead. I took a sharp left and pulled into the parking lot.

"What are you doing?"

"We have some serious shit to talk about and I want your head straight when we do." I unbuckled my seat belt and turned my car off. "Now let's get some food in your stomach and sober you up a bit."

"But I already had pizza!"

I rested my hand on the door handle before opening it. "If you want to get this conversation out of the way, you'll need to convince me that you're not drunk," I said, stepping out of the car.

She scoffed. "So, you're going to force me to eat something? Who died and made you the boss?"

I turned my head sideways as she rounded the car. "We've wasted enough time already, and I'm done waiting."

She huffed while dragging her feet across the parking lot. She was being as dramatic as a middle school teenager, and I felt a smirk spread across my face.

God, I missed that woman.

Luckily, for us, the diner wasn't too busy. We were able to snag a small booth in the back of the restaurant. The waitress came over, poured water into our glasses and paused to take our order. Once she walked away, I leaned back in my seat.

Green eyes studied me from across the table.

"You look like you want to say something to me," I said, taking a sip of my water.

She fiddled with the rolled up silverware. "I'm just curious. When did you go into law enforcement?"

I looked away from her for a minute. She knew that being a cop was my backup plan. It wasn't like my short stint in the security business was a flop. I never considered it a failure. It was also no secret that owning my own company one day was always a dream of mine.

I cleared my throat and gave her a half-truth. "I joined the police force about six years ago. Around the same time my dad got sick. It was enough of a reality check, and forced me to rearrange the priorities in my life."

I also wanted to mention that I was miserable and missed her like crazy, but I didn't think she would want to hear that.

"I didn't know Thomas had been sick."

"He had prostate cancer. It's all good now, though."

Her eyes softened. "I'm glad he's okay."

"Thanks. Me too."

"I'm sure it didn't help being three thousand miles away from your family when they were going through such a tough time."

No, it didn't. It also didn't help that I found out she was marrying that shithead Grant that same weekend I came home to help pops. Talk about a serious kick to the balls.

I pulled on the back of my neck, feeling self-doubt creep into my head. "I hated living out in California," I told her, leaving out the fact that I showed up at her wedding. "That lifestyle wasn't for me. I was making good money, but I still felt broke as fuck living in Orange County."

Traveling back and forth to spend time with my dad, while trying to build the business lost its appeal to me. With every passing day, I became more miserable.

When my brother sent me an email with an online application, I laughed at the irony and the timing. On a whim, I filled out the paperwork, and as they say, the rest is history.

"I'm sorry things didn't work out. I know how bad you have always wanted to open up your own security business."

"That's okay. I still do part-time security work on the side. I plan to use my experience to open up my own business someday. All in all, I guess it worked out."

Our eyes met for a brief moment, and I immediately regretted my words. Did it really work out? If I didn't accept the job, I never would have moved out to California. I never would have pushed her into the arms of Grant. They never would have married, and her life wouldn't be falling apart at the seams.

Her eyes locked knowingly on mine. A funny feeling rattled in my chest. How the hell did we get here? I saw the same question flicker across her face as we both pretended that we didn't know the answer when the truth was, it was my decision to move to California that started the chain reaction.

Our server came over, interrupting the awkward moment, letting us know that our orders would be out shortly.

"So how is that plan coming along?" She sounded genuinely interested.

"I've been working my ass off at the department, picking up as much overtime as I can. I work small security jobs on the side that pop up."

"Doesn't sound like you have a lot of time for fun."

I shrugged. "I manage."

I waited on bated breath to see if she would ask me about my personal life. I was curious how she would react when I told her about Bree. Would she get jealous? God knew it drove me mad thinking about her and Grant. Still did to this very moment.

"How are your parents?"

I guess she wasn't going there. I took a sip of my steaming cup of black coffee that was just dropped off by our server. "Good. Dad still refuses to retire, even though the cancer almost took his life. He tells us all that the only way he's leaving the force is in a pinewood box."

She snorted. It was very unladylike and totally her. "Sounds like him. And Brody?"

I rolled my eyes thinking about my older brother. "Still a jackass."

We both shared a laugh and it felt fucking good. "It sounds like you two are as tight as ever."

She was right about that. There weren't many people in this world that I trusted. My brother was at the top of the list. My family was a close-knit bunch and living out in California made me homesick. Call me a pussy.

Our server came over and placed our meals down in front of us. I hadn't eaten since noon and I was starving, so I started digging right in.

I watched as Charlotte twirled her spoon around in her soup. As much as I enjoyed her company, there was a long-overdue conversation waiting to be had.

We sat in silence as the bustle of the diner could be heard around us. There was something about being here with her that reminded me of simpler times. The years may have changed us both, but she was still my Charlotte. I could still feel her inside me, and when I looked at her, I still saw the young girl I fell in love with.

She snagged a fry off my plate and popped it into her mouth. "After eating all these carbs tonight, I may be asleep before we make it back out to the car." She sighed, as I eyed the remaining quarter of the BLT that she insisted she was too stuffed to eat.

I slid her coffee cup across the table. "You better drink up then."

Her full, pink lips pouted slightly. "I don't want to be up all night either."

For a split second I contemplated not bringing up the elephant in the room. I didn't want to lose the vibe we had going, but subtlety wasn't working. We weren't going to be able to move forward until we laid all our issues on the table.

She looked at me over the rim of her coffee. I focused on her bare ring finger as she cradled the cup in her hands. Even though it brought me great relief to see that, it was a stark reminder that Grant Anderson was still standing between us and I couldn't take it anymore.

"Are you sure you're ready for this conversation?" I asked, my voice low and cautious.

She leaned back and pushed her long hair over her shoulder. "I guess that's why we're here, right?" She laughed nervously.

Tension settled in her shoulders, and I wanted so badly to reach out and grab her hand and comfort her. I hated to see her so upset, and it made me crazy knowing that I had no one else to blame but myself.

"How are you holding up?" I asked cautiously. "I mean really."

I wasn't sure what I expected of her answer. It's been years since our world fell apart. I've accepted that she moved on with her life, but I wasn't going to lie and say that it didn't feel like we made progress tonight.

She set her spoon down and bowed her head. "I'm doing the best I can." Her voice was so low I almost didn't hear her. "It sucks because I'm not sure how I'm supposed to feel. Nothing about my current situation is easy. It's not like Grant and I had this perfect marriage." She looked away, her eyes blazed with emotion. "But my daughter doesn't deserve this. I love that little girl more than anything and there is nothing I wouldn't do to protect her. What Grant did…" She closed her eyes and bit down on her lip. God, it killed me to see her like this. I wanted to kill that fucker. If I thought I hated him before, nothing compared to how I felt now. "He killed five people. He also left my daughter without a father. He destroyed everything."

My jaw pulsed with frustration. "He didn't deserve you," I said, feeling her out. "I'm so fucking sorry." She tilted her head to the side and looked at me. I held her gaze, feeling my throat burn. "I fucked up all those years ago. I walked away from you, from us, when things got hard. I left for California knowing I was breaking your heart. I was terrified of letting you down. God…" I ran my hand through my hair, wishing I had a drink in front of me. I could have used a beer. "Those first few months after we broke up were so fucking painful. There were so many times where I wanted to just pack up and beg for your forgiveness. Beg for you to take me back. Because I knew even then that I had made a mistake. But I was young and stupid and let my pride get in the way. I never should have lied and told you that there was someone else, but it was the only way to get you to stop calling."

"You broke my heart, Quinn." She swiped a tear from her cheek. "You promised me forever."

"And you gave your forever to someone else," I said and immediately cursed myself for allowing the words to leave my mouth. "I'm sorry. That was uncalled for."

Her face looked solemn, but resigned. I knew this conversation wasn't going to be easy, but we couldn't keep avoiding it either. She looked at the floor, her eyes filled with something I couldn't quite pinpoint.

"Say something," I pleaded. The blank look on her face was killing me.

She lifted her gaze to mine. "Do you know how I ended up with him?"

Her question caught me off guard. I've asked myself that same question a million times. He was never good enough for her. It always felt like he stole her out from under me. If I had never left her, there was no doubt that we would still be together. I don't know how I knew that, I just did.

"Only if you want to tell me." I swallowed. A part of me wanted to stop this conversation. I didn't want to hear about her marriage to Grant, but avoiding this topic wasn't going to make the reality of it go away.

"Because on the day you lied and told me you met someone, Grant invited me to go out with him and a few of his friends. I went with the intention of drinking you out of my system. I don't remember everything that happened, but I do remember waking up in his bed the next morning."

I put my hands behind my head and tried to block out that image.

"The second I realized where I was, I regretted it. I told him I was still in love with you and I wasn't ready for another relationship." I drew my eyebrows together and tried to connect the dots on how we got here. "Then I found out I was pregnant a few weeks later."

"So, are you saying you only married him because he knocked you up?"

"Partially, yes."

I gripped the edge of the booth, my fingers digging into the dark wood. "What the hell does that mean, Charlotte? You either loved him or you didn't."

"It's not that simple, Quinn." My gut twisted as I tried to wrap my brain around what she just told me. "He was my friend. I trusted him. He promised to take care of me and give me a good life. I figured it was better than trying to raise a baby on my own."

My mouth hung open. You've got to be shitting me. "Women raise kids all the time on their own. You didn't have to marry him if you didn't love him."

"And you didn't have to move away to California and put an end to our future either."

That one hurt, but I deserved it.

"I don't expect you to fully understand this, but I grew to love him over time." She pressed her lips together and shook her head. "When you left me I was devastated. I did what I could to get through each day. Every night I prayed that you would come back to me. Every damn day I prayed that you would finally answer your phone and talk to me. But you never did." I sat there and watched helplessly as the moisture built up in her eyes. "He took care of me and did whatever he could to make things easier for me." I ran my hands across my face feeling frustrated. I wanted to punch myself for leaving her. I've regretted and second-guessed my decision more times than I could count. "The reason I'm telling you this is because I know you and Grant never saw eye to eye, but he was there for me, Quinn, when you walked away." I wanted to tear that motherfucker in two. He was there all right. Right there to slide in and take my place. "What started out as friendship grew into something stronger. It didn't happen overnight, but eventually my feelings changed. So, yes, I loved Grant. I'm not saying this to rub it in your face, because God knows, if you would have called, came back, I would have been yours. But you never did."

"I did come back."

"What?"

"I heard about the wedding. I went to the lake that day

with every intention of stopping it, until I saw you. I stood in the back. Hiding in the fucking shadows like a stalker and watched you marry the son of a bitch."

I fixed my gaze over her head, remembering how happy she looked that day. Never in my life had I ever experienced such deep and intense emotional pain. For weeks after, I was numb, like someone had knocked me down and I couldn't get back up. Witnessing her marry Grant changed me. I could never quite find my footing after that.

She wiped her face with the pads of her fingers. "I had no idea."

"You looked so beautiful, and when I saw you, all I thought was that I wanted you to be happy." I sighed, needing to get this off my chest. "I've loved you since the first time I ever laid eyes on you, but when I saw that you were pregnant with his child, professing your love and your forever to him, I hated you."

"Quinn," she cried and reached for my hand across the table. I placed my palms inside hers. As soon as our skin made contact, I felt my heart pulsing inside my chest. I watched our joined hands intently, liking the way they still fit together.

"It's okay, Charlotte."

She shook her head. "I hate that you saw that." She pulled her hand back to wipe her cheeks. "I can't even imagine how hard that was for you. But looks can be deceiving, because I may have been smiling on the outside, but I wasn't happy on the inside. I was torn between loving you and trying to find a place for Grant in my heart."

"I'm not trying to drudge up old feelings," I said, searching for the right words, but knew I would only come up short. "I'm not here to hurt you. I just needed to make sure you knew the truth."

Her eyes were soft as she spoke. "I'm glad you did. As much as you hurt me, I wouldn't have given up a single moment with you." She looked sad, and the honesty in her voice hit me hard. "I guess we just weren't meant to be forever."

The years I spent with her, they were the best of my life. There was no doubt in my mind that I still loved her. And knowing that she gave years away to someone who didn't deserve them didn't change a thing. The only difference was that she wasn't mine anymore.

Our server came over and cleared our plates. I looked at my phone to see a missed call from Bree. I turned it over and set it facedown on the table. I haven't thought about her once tonight. I waited for the guilt to hit me, but it never came.

"Look," I said once we were alone again. "Logically, I know I shouldn't get involved in this case, but I can't just sit back and do nothing. I know you want to take care of yourself and your little girl, but please," I pleaded. "Let me help you."

"Quinn, I appreciate the offer, really I do."

I narrowed my eyes, letting her know that this wasn't up for debate. She wasn't going to turn me down. She and I both knew how bad I fucked up by leaving before and there was no way in hell I would make that mistake again.

I was done playing nice. Like it or not, her safety and well-being was not up for discussion.

Grant Anderson was going to stay gone one way or another. I would personally see to that.

FIVE

CHARLOTTE

I SAT ON THE PARK BENCH WATCHING EMERY PUMP HERSELF HIGH on the swings. The sun was shining, and there was a light breeze in the air.

I took her on a walk this morning hoping to clear my head, but my thoughts kept slipping back to my conversation with Quinn and the way he looked at me, the words he spoke, and the impact they had.

My phone rang in my tote bag next to me. I reached in and saw Mackenzie's name flashed across the screen. "Hey," I whispered, fully aware that there were people all around within hearing distance.

"Thanks for picking up my call."

"I almost didn't," I admitted, watching the birds circle over a few scraps of bread that children were throwing into the middle of the grass.

"I guess I can't blame you."

I moved to the other bench where there were fewer people around and could still keep an eye on Emery. I dropped my bag on the ground next to me with the juice boxes and snacks that we had packed earlier that morning.

"Tell me what happened last night after you guys left. I want every detail."

I knew that question was coming which was why I didn't pick up when Erica had called earlier. Even though I loved both my friends equally, Mackenzie was just easier to talk to, and if I was honest, I needed to get everything off my chest.

My eyes darted around the park, taking in my surroundings. There was a dark sedan parked across the street. I squinted my eyes but couldn't see anything because the windows were tinted. When we left the house earlier, I could have sworn that was the same car I saw at the end of my street. I kept a close eye on Emery, ignoring the unease that was prickling along my skin.

"We had a great talk. Even though it was confusing because it still felt like there was some chemistry there. Isn't that weird?"

"No, it's not weird. Just watching you two interact last night. God…" She sighed. "You both grabbed my attention that was for sure."

I reached forward and grabbed my water bottle out of the bag without taking my attention off my daughter. "What do you mean?"

"I could tell with the way he looked at you that there was still something there between you two." She had no idea. "So, tell me everything."

I started from the beginning and told her that he apologized and wanted to make things right between us. How he confessed to being at my wedding. My stomach clenched, and I closed my eyes briefly, dissecting every thought and every word he spoke.

"Wow," she said into the phone. "All this time and you never knew he came back for you. That is…" There was a dreamy sigh in her voice. "So fucking romantic."

I choked on the water I was sipping. "Mackenzie, there is nothing romantic about any of this."

"That's bullshit and you know it."

"I just don't understand how I can feel the way that I feel after all these years."

"Because you never got over him," she said bluntly.

There was probably more truth to that statement than I cared to admit to.

"It doesn't matter how I feel, I'm not even legally separated yet."

"We need to talk about Grant."

"I'd rather not."

I had an appointment scheduled this week with an attorney to find out if there was a way to start the divorce proceedings without Grant's consent. This meeting was a long time coming, and I couldn't wait to get rid of his last name and move on with my life.

My attention immediately shifted to the squeals of laughter echoing from inside the plastic tunnel that Emery and two other girls her age were playing in.

"Okay, we will save that talk for another time. I was actually calling to let you know that there may be an opening for a part-time sub position coming up at my school. We have a handful of teachers going out on maternity leave soon, and my contact at the district office said they are accepting applications."

"Really?" I perked up at the news. I didn't want to get my hopes up knowing that almost every position I had applied for had ended up in a dead end.

"Yes. I know you wanted to stay in elementary, but I have a better chance of getting you in at the middle school where I work if you're interested."

"Honestly, I'll take whatever I can get."

"That's what I thought. The world loves a desperate woman," she teased. "Let me know when you submit the online application and forward me a copy of your résumé. I'll make sure it gets into the right hands."

"Thank you, Mackenzie."

"No thanks required. That's what friends are for. I'll let you get back to Emery. Give her a kiss for me and call me tomorrow."

"You got it." I hung up the phone and walked over to the trash can and threw my water bottle out. I looked up at the blue sky and prayed that my luck was changing.

At the sound of Emery's laughter, I picked my bag up off the ground and strolled to where she was dangling upside down from the monkey bars. I pulled my phone out and probably snapped about fifty pictures, but it made me feel good to see her smile.

The father of the little girl she was playing with wandered through the maze of children and pulled her off the monkey bars. "Time to go, princess," the father said, while the little girl protested at his side.

He looked at me and gave a timid smile. "Sorry, she doesn't like being told no, and I've been trying to get her to leave for the past twenty minutes."

I held my hand up. "Hey, I get it. We're actually going to head on home soon anyways." I turned to the little girl with long blonde hair. "Thanks for keeping Emery company. I hope you guys had fun."

The little girl grinned up at me. "I did. Now I gots to go home and get ready for tomorrow."

Emery came over and took my hand. "Oh, what's going on tomorrow?" I asked.

"I get to go to work with Daddy."

I glanced at the father confused as he ran his free hand along the top of his daughter's head. "Yeah, Maci here gets to tag along with me tomorrow morning for Take Your Daughter to Work Day."

"Oh," I said, looking at Emery. My heart broke when I saw her turn her face away from me. She narrowed her eyes at the ground and bit her bottom lip. The whole situation with

Grant was hitting her much harder than she had been letting on. I wondered how many times she got upset at school when kids would mention doing things with their dads. Things that she used to do with Grant, but she'll never get to do again.

I gave the father a tight smile as we said our goodbyes.

"Are you okay?" I asked, reaching over and dusting the dirt off the front of her shirt.

"Yeah." She sighed.

"Do you want to talk about it?" I was so worried about her and I was trying really hard not to break down in the middle of the park.

"I just want to go home."

I bent over to give her a kiss on the cheek. "Then let's go home."

I glanced over at the road and noticed that the dark car was gone. I let out a sigh of relief and grabbed Emery's hand.

The walk back to our house was quiet. It felt like we were both just focusing on putting one foot in front of the other. I wrapped my one arm around her shoulder, hoping to provide her a little comfort, all the while glancing over my own shoulder to make sure we weren't being followed.

Later that night after dinner, I ran Emery's bathwater and put her bubblegum scented shampoo out on the side of the tub. What happened at the park earlier still stung pretty bad. I wanted to hunt down my no-good husband and strangle him.

"Is my bath ready, Mom?" I turned to see my little girl's head peek through the door.

"It is." I stood up and checked the temperature one last time before I turned the water off. "Hop in and I'll go get your clean clothes."

I walked into her room and started putting some of her laundry away that she had left out. There were a couple of new shirts that were sitting on her bed that Grant's mom had just bought for her. I wasn't sure if it was guilt, or whatever, but I appreciated the gesture. How two good people like John and Laura Anderson could create something so evil baffled the living shit out of me.

I tore the tags off the shirts and was about to throw them away when something caught my attention. I gasped at the picture of Emery and Grant ripped into fours laying on top of the trash can. I picked up the tattered pieces and looked over at the empty frame on the nightstand.

All I wanted to do was help her through this, but I didn't know how. Grant may have been a shitty husband, but he was a good father up until this point.

The school desk that he painted for her sat in the corner of the room, and the monkey he won for her at the school carnival still sat at the top of her bed by the pillows. I stood in the middle of my daughter's bedroom, and I never felt more helpless in my life. There was so much I wanted to explain to her, but she really wasn't old enough to understand it all. Hell, I barely understood it myself.

Emery came in the room in her pink fluffy bathrobe looking so small and fragile. She noticed my puffy eyes immediately.

"What's wrong, Mommy?"

I opened my arms. "Come here, kiddo."

She walked into them willingly. Her skin was still damp from her bath as I stroked her face. "I found the picture of you and your dad in the trash can."

She tried to look away, but I wouldn't let her. "Talk to me," I pleaded, holding her little chin in my hand.

"I'm mad at him."

"Okay." I buried my face in her hair and let her scent wash over me. "Why are you mad at him?" It was a stupid question, but I wanted her to tell me how she was feeling.

"Because he's a bad person, and he doesn't want to be my daddy anymore." Her small shoulders shook and I leaned back, keeping a firm grip on her.

"Emery, no, honey." I squeezed my eyes shut and fought

back the tears that I never let flow around her. The ones that I saved for when I was in the shower, or after she went to bed at night.

"Please listen to me. Your father did some bad things, but he isn't a bad man. I know there is a lot you don't understand, but never forget that your father loves you." I dropped to my knees so that I was at eye level with her. "He did some things that he can't take back. He probably won't ever live here with us again, but wherever he is, I know he regrets what he did and I know he is sorry for hurting you."

"Grandma said he was sick. That he wasn't always that way. That he got a disease when he got older."

That was a great way to put it.

"She's right, but what he did was still wrong. You know how when you do something wrong you get punished?" She nodded her head. "It's the same thing with grown-ups. Your dad broke the law and now he has to be punished."

"Why did he run away?"

"Because he got scared, but once the police find him, they will need to send him to his new home so he can start a very long time-out."

"Will I be able to see him?"

"Don't worry about that right now. Okay?" My heart broke thinking of how much had changed for her. Her life would never be the same again. I wanted that man to suffer a long, slow, painful death. Did that make me a bad person? I couldn't care less.

"I miss him."

I bent over to give her a kiss on the cheek, keeping my thoughts about her father to myself. "I know you do, baby."

"Will you sleep with me tonight?"

"Of course, I will."

She smiled at me as I climbed into bed next to her. I stuck my nose in her neck and watched her sleep until we both collapsed in each other's arms.

SIX

QUINN

"How's my bachelor party coming along?" my brother Brody asked, rounding the corner and squeezing into a small metal chair along the wall of my corner cubical. I clicked send on my document and spun around to face him.

"Isn't that for me to worry about?"

"Actually, no. Ever since you turned down my suggestion, I've been concerned that this is going to turn into a snoozefest."

"I'm not fucking spending twenty-five hundred dollars a night on a penthouse suite at the Four Seasons in Vegas."

I heard a couple chuckles from the cubicle next to mine. That's the thing about working in close quarters with people. There was no privacy whatsoever.

"It's not like you don't have the money in the bank, you tightwad. You've got more overtime accumulated than anyone in the department."

"You know why I'm saving my money, jackass."

"Yeah, well, I don't think a few grand is going to put much of a dent in your savings. You've got to live a little, brother."

Brody was stressed about getting married next month. I

tried not to take offense to his piss-poor attitude, or the way he glared at me. The only reason I tolerated him was because he was my brother.

"God help Gretchen," I mumbled. I was trying to do something different than simply hitting as many bars as we could and visiting seedy strip clubs. I also didn't want to be on the other side of the country and leave Charlotte and Emery as open targets with Grant still on the run. The odds of him doing anything to physically hurt them were slim, but I wasn't willing to gamble with their safety. As far as I was concerned, as long as he breathed the same air outside of a jail cell as them, he was a threat.

"You still planning on bringing Bree to the wedding?" He arched his eyebrow and tossed a stress ball back and forth between his hands. The asshole was fishing, and despite my best efforts to not let my true feelings show, he could see right through me.

"She's coming into town later tonight. I'll ask her."

He smirked, and that cocky gleam in his eye only pissed me off more. Have I been dragging my feet with Bree these past few weeks? Absolutely. He didn't need to know that though. If I was honest, I wasn't sure what I wanted anymore. The only thing I did know was that I couldn't get Charlotte out of my head no matter how hard I tried.

It wasn't fair to Bree that I was hung up on someone else. She deserved better, and I was an asshole because I wasn't sure if I wanted to end things with her either.

"Have you heard anything new on the investigation?"

I rubbed my palm along the side of my neck. "Nothing. Marco is working closely with the US Marshals, but they haven't been able to come up with anything solid."

"Grant Anderson isn't an idiot. He's a smart man with a lot of connections. But eventually, his luck will run out. It always does."

"I'm not letting this go until the bastard is locked up and

doing more time than a ticket taker in a toll booth. This may not be my case, but it's personal."

His phone rang in his pocket. He pulled it out and looked at the screen. "I gotta take this." He stood up and pointed his finger at me. "Be careful."

There was a warning in his tone. He wasn't just talking about Grant.

After following up on a few open cases, I picked up my keys and shoved my phone in my pocket. I wanted to stop by Charlotte's on my way home and check-in on things.

I pulled my car into her driveway and took the two front steps in a single bounce and pressed the doorbell. Something didn't feel right, and the back of my neck tingled. I felt uncomfortable with my back to the street, so I turned around and waited for her to answer.

My eyes scanned the neighborhood. There wasn't anything out of the ordinary. Just a few teenagers walking in groups and a few dogs barking in the background. Normal suburbia. Still in deep concentration, I chalked up my paranoia to just being keyed up.

The sound of the front door swinging open caused me to spin on my heels. "Jesus, Charlotte, you startled the shit out of me. Do you always open the door without asking who it is on the other side?" I snapped.

"Well, hello to you too." She smirked, her voice was thick with sarcasm.

I brushed past her, taking in the lingering scent of her perfume. "Just don't ever open the door without knowing who it is, okay? It's not smart."

"Yes, Dad," she replied and closed the door behind her. I walked into the house, noticing that it smelled like clean linens and lemon.

"Where's Emery?" I asked once I reached the kitchen counter.

Charlotte walked over to the sink and poured a glass of

water. "She's upstairs getting changed. We're going out for pizza to celebrate."

I took a seat on one of the barstools at the counter and asked. "Celebrate what?"

She smiled, a blinding smile that almost knocked me out of my chair. It was the first genuine smile I'd seen from her in years.

"I got a part-time substitute teaching position at one of the middle schools a couple towns over."

"That's great!" My eyes met hers with pride. I was glad to see her putting that degree that she worked so hard for to use.

"Hi, Quinn," a familiar little voice called from across the kitchen. I turned around in my stool, thankful for the interruption.

"Hey, Peanut."

Emery giggled. "Why do you call me Peanut? My name is Emery."

I feigned a surprised look and brought my hands to my chest. "It is? I guess I thought your name was Peanut because you're so tiny."

She breezed into the room in a little pink and purple dress, holding a doll with a matching outfit. She walked over to the fridge, grabbed a juice box, and took a seat next to me at the counter.

"You know my name, silly," she said, handing me her drink so I could push the straw through the pouch for her.

"Who's your friend?" I asked, pointing to the doll that looked like her.

"That's Samantha. She's my American Girl doll that I got for my birthday." She took a sip of her drink and placed the doll in my lap. "You can hold her, but she's very expensive," she warned, and I felt my eyes crinkle in the corners.

"I'll be careful," I promised.

I knew how much those damn dolls cost. My niece, Taitlyn, had a couple of her own. The first time my brother-in-law got the credit card bill in the mail, he just about ended his marriage.

She folded her hand under her chin and looked at me. "Are you going out to eat pizza with us?"

I cleared my throat. "No, I'm sorry. I'm not."

"Why not?" she asked innocently while swinging her legs out in front of her.

"I have a friend who is visiting me this weekend."

She looked up at me with familiar green eyes. "Your friend can come if he wants to. My mom always says, the more the merrier. Right, Mom?"

"Actually." I felt my throat close up. This wasn't how I wanted Charlotte to find out about my relationship. "My girlfriend, Bree, is coming to stay with me this weekend. She lives in Washington, DC and we don't get a chance to see each other very often."

Charlotte whipped her head around, her questioning green eyes locked with mine. I wasn't prepared for the hurt I saw or the heaviness that rested over my chest.

"Your girlfriend?" Charlotte asked with a shaky voice. "How come you didn't mention that before?"

"Never seemed to come up in conversation." I eyed her cautiously and decided to test the waters a bit. "Is that a problem?"

Her hand went to her throat. "Of course not. I'm just surprised, that's all." She looked like she needed a few minutes to collect herself.

"You're surprised that someone would want to date me?" I was trying to make light of the conversation and lessen the shock for her.

"Quinn, stop it. You know what I meant."

She was right. I knew exactly what she meant. It was petty of me to drag this out and make her feel uncomfortable, but I wanted to see if it made her the slightest bit jealous.

"Bree and I have only been together for a few months," I said, feeling guilty for not telling her this the other night.

"That's nice," she said, turning her back to me.

She leaned over the kitchen sink and pretended to wash dishes that were already clean. I snuck a glance at Emery who was coloring in a notebook.

Sliding off my barstool, I made my way over to her. Her back went straight when she felt me approach from behind. I leaned in and whispered in her ear, "Talk to me, Charlotte."

"What are you doing here, Quinn?"

"I wanted to check on you guys." That was partially true, but I couldn't tell her that I haven't been able to stop thinking about her. Or that I needed to see her. I'd gone seven years without her, yet I kept manufacturing reasons and coming up with excuses just to be near her.

She turned the faucet off and spun around. She looked over my shoulder to where Emery sat, oblivious to our conversation.

"We are fine. Thank you for the concern. You don't need to check-in on us." She looked at the clock on the microwave. "Thanks for stopping by. Have a great weekend with your girlfriend."

Her tone was cold and distant, and not entirely unexpected. The lines between us grew blurrier as each day passed. I couldn't simply pretend not to care about her any more than I could stand there and have her dismiss me just because her feelings were hurt.

It's been over seven years for Christ's sake, so I didn't feel like I owed her an explanation. I was free to do whatever the hell I wanted, wasn't I? She had no right to be pissed at me, did she?

I backed away, hating how we were leaving things. "You don't need to be like that."

She jutted her chin out. This woman was so fucking stubborn. "Like what?"

"Jealous," I said, searching her face for a reaction.

She scoffed and tried to nudge around me. "You always were full of yourself."

I grabbed her by the elbow before she could walk away. I angled my head so I could whisper in her ear. "Stop the bullshit. You feel this between us. I'm still in your head just like you're still in mine. I'm not sure what that means, but it means something and we're going to figure it out, one way or another."

I let go of her elbow and walked over to where Emery was still coloring in her book. "Hey, Peanut. I'm really sorry I can't go out to dinner with you and your mom tonight."

She had no idea how much I wanted to go. I was half-tempted to call Bree and tell her not to come, but I couldn't do that to her. She deserved better.

Emery set her crayon down and handed me the piece of paper she'd been doodling on. "Okay, Quinn, but I want you to have this." She handed me a picture of a giant pepperoni pizza. My lips pulled up to the side. She was absolutely the cutest thing on the planet. I could easily fall in love with this girl.

I reached over and stroked her back. "I'm going home and putting this on the fridge."

"You are?" she squealed, clearly liking that idea.

"On one condition," I said, holding back my laughter when her nose scrunched up. "You save me a piece of pizza tonight. Deal?" I held my hand out for her to shake.

"Deal." She smiled and shook my hand in return.

I took the picture and walked to the front door. Charlotte stood in the entryway with her arms crossed. I snuck a glance over my shoulder and winked. I wasn't going to say goodbye, because I had every intention of coming back. I just didn't know when.

———

"I can't believe you brought all this shit for one weekend," I told Bree as I carried her enormous suitcase into my bedroom. My apartment was small; barely big enough to hold my own junk, let alone a steamer trunkful of God knows what she brought with her.

"I wasn't sure what the weather was going to be like, so I brought a little bit of everything with me."

I laid the big black suitcase tagged with the orange heavy sticker from the airlines on the floor and unzipped it. She probably had twenty pairs of shoes and three makeup bags and God knows what else. Bree was a beautiful woman, the kind that had any man noticing her when she passed them by on the street. She didn't need all the extra bells and whistles, but they were important to her, and what the hell did I know about women's fashion?

"I'm gonna grab a beer out of the fridge. Can I get you anything?"

"You don't by any chance have any wine, do you?"

"No, but we can stop at a liquor store on our way out to dinner."

If I was a better boyfriend, I probably would have made sure I had her favorite bottle of Merlot when she visited, but the truth was, I was too preoccupied with everything going on with Charlotte to think about anything else.

I fetched a bottle of Labatt's Blue Light out of the fridge, feeling on edge. My girlfriend was in the other room, curling her hair, getting all dressed up to impress me for a night out, and there I was thinking about my ex and staring at a picture that her daughter drew me.

When the bathroom door swung open, I was blown away by how gorgeous she was. I'd be lying if I said I wasn't a little nervous about how the weekend was going to turn out.

I ran my hand through my hair and stared at her. My stomach was in knots, it felt like I was on the verge of throwing up. She had on a little navy dress with a pair of dark brown boots that looked hot as hell on her. Her long blonde hair was falling over her shoulders and her lips were painted a bright red. I waited for my body to react to her, but nothing happened. She looked like just another pretty face to me. Not the one that I wanted.

"Are you ready to go?" she asked, grabbing her purse off the counter.

"Yeah," I said, not having a fucking clue what I was going to do, but knew I had to be smart. I reached for her hand and led her out the door. This weekend was going to be a huge test for us.

Once we were in the elevator, Bree stared at me as if she were trying to figure me out.

"Is everything okay, Quinn?"

"Why are you asking me that?" I asked, pressing the button to the ground floor. I snuck a quick glance at my watch. Charlotte and Emery were probably eating dinner right about now. I wondered where the ended up going and what time they would be home?

She worried her bottom lip between her teeth. "You seem distracted."

"I've got a lot going on at work," I commented, knowing that the truth was that I needed to get my head out of my ass and stop thinking about Charlotte while I was with Bree. Clearly, this wasn't the best way to start off the weekend.

"You also haven't kissed me once since I've gotten here."

If I was going to make this work, I needed to put in a little effort. I ran my hands up and down her back and pressed my lips to hers. "I'm sorry," I said, keeping the kiss light.

"You can talk to me, you know." Her big blue eyes told me that she knew there was more going on with me than I was letting on.

The elevator doors opened, and I reached for her hand. There were a couple of guys in suits stepping in as we walked out. I noticed them staring at Bree. It should have bothered me or at least made me jealous, yet I didn't feel a fucking thing.

When we got to my truck, there was a folded-up piece of paper stuck to my windshield under the wiper blade. I snatched it off the window and unfolded it, expecting it to be another annoying flier from the Mexican restaurant down the street. All the color drained from my face when I read the handwritten note.

Stay away from MY wife and daughter!

My eyes frantically searched the parking lot, looking for the piece of shit that had left me the message. My blood ran cold, and it felt like the world had come to a stop. I shoved my door open as Bree rounded the hood of my truck. "Get in," I barked.

"What's going on?" she asked cautiously, her gaze flashing around the parking lot.

I grabbed my phone out of my pocket and dialed up Marco. He answered on the second ring. "What's up, Quinn?"

"Get to Charlotte's house now. That motherfucker is here in town. He left a note on my windshield. Call it in. I have no idea when he left this, but I was only inside for an hour or so. I'm going to forward you the number to the management company that owns my building. See if they have anything on the security tape."

My stomach twisted as I peeled out onto the street. Every decent law-abiding part of me left my conscience as I sped toward Charlotte's house. I knew I had to keep calm, but I was freaking the fuck out.

"It's going to be fine. Calm down," Marco said, sensing my panic.

I gritted my teeth. "No, it's not fucking fine. As long as that son of a bitch is still out there, it won't be fucking fine."

I didn't give a damn what Marco thought he knew about Grant Anderson. Everyone on the planet was looking for him. He'd gone to a lot of trouble to keep out of sight. It took tremendous balls to pull a stunt like this, knowing what might happen if he got caught.

I ended the call and dialed Charlotte's number. The call went straight to voicemail. I gripped the steering wheel, refusing to believe that he had gotten to her in some way. She wanted to believe that he was harmless, but after this stunt, I wasn't taking any chances. He was a man with nothing left to lose and my experience taught me that was never a good thing. Suddenly, the only thing that mattered was making sure she was safe.

"Who's Charlotte?" Bree asked, interrupting my thoughts.

I kept my eyes on the road and a firm grip on the steering wheel. My windows were fogged up from my intense breathing, and I knew this conversation was going to happen eventually. This wasn't my case, but there was no question that I had inserted myself so deep, there was no end in sight for me.

I weaved through traffic and merged onto the highway. "I know you want answers Bree, but my mind is going a million miles a minute."

She deserved so much better than what I was giving her. She was gorgeous, kind, affectionate, and everything I could ever want in a woman. But I didn't realize it until then that she wasn't the woman I wanted. The one I spent the last seven years trying to forget but couldn't. "Charlotte and I have a past."

"She's the one you told me about? The one you were engaged to marry?"

"Yes." I drew in a shuddered breath.

I saw a tear drop from her eye as we drove toward Charlotte's house without any more words between us.

SEVEN

CHARLOTTE

"MOM, WHY ARE ALL THOSE POLICE CARS IN OUR DRIVEWAY?"

I slowly waded my way through the three unmarked cars and the two patrol cars sitting in front of my house. *This couldn't be good*, I thought as I pulled in behind Quinn's truck.

Quinn was talking to a group of uniformed officers who were camped out on my front porch. When he saw me, he leaped over the railing and ran to my car. Before I even had a chance to unbuckle my seat belt, he flung the door open.

His eyes were wild, and his hands shook as he pulled me out of the car. "Where the hell have you been?"

"What happened?" I asked as he planted me firmly down on the pavement. I looked behind him to where Emery was sitting in the back seat. Quinn's gaze followed mine and he let go of my arm and rushed over to grab her.

"Hey, Peanut." His voice was strained, and every possible scenario raced through my head, and not one amounted to anything good. "Sorry to scare you. I tried to call your mom and got worried. I sent a few friends of mine over here to check on you guys and make sure you both were okay."

Emery smiled up at Quinn completely oblivious to the chaos around us. "We were at the movies."

I reached into my purse and pulled my phone out to see the missed calls. "I turned my phone off when we got into the theater," I explained.

Quinn helped Emery out of the car, by pulling her up and wrapping her little legs around his waist. A female officer with shoulder-length dark hair and a warm smile walked over. "Hi, Emery, my name is Joanne. Would you like to go inside and color with me while Quinn talks to your mom?"

Emery's hands folded around Quinn's neck, holding on for dear life. He pressed a hand to the back of her hair and kissed her forehead. "It's okay, Peanut. Joanne is a friend of mine. Will you go inside with her while I talk to your mom for a few minutes?"

She looked unsure and worried her bottom lip between her teeth.

He ran his hand across her cheek trying to ease her anxiety. "It's okay." He eyed the pizza box in the back seat and pointed to the leftovers we brought home with us. "Did you leave me a piece like you promised?" Emery nodded her head. "Good girl. Would you mind putting my pizza on a plate and wrapping it up for me, so it doesn't get cold? I promise, your mom and I won't be long. As soon as we're finished, you can watch me eat and tell me all about your movie. Sound good?"

Her green, trusting eyes flickered across his face. "Okay."

My heart did a funny little thing while I watched the two of them together. It made me realize that I made a monumental mistake by letting him back into my life. She was already getting attached to Quinn. It was going to be hard when this was over and he was no longer around.

I watched as he handed my daughter over to the friendly lady in uniform. I gave her my key ring as she held hands with a bouncing Emery, who was clearly excited about spending time with Quinn after.

"Did you find him?" I asked as he stepped in front of me.

Quinn roughed a hand over his face. "No. He fucking found me." He dug deep into his back pocket and pulled out his phone. "I found this on my windshield."

With a shaking hand I looked at the photo of a note with the familiar handwriting. What the hell was Grant up to? I couldn't for the life of me understand how he'd gotten himself into this situation.

"The note was turned over as evidence," Quinn explained and stepped uncomfortably close into my personal space. He angled his head to the side, looking as angry as I've ever seen him. "Have you heard from him?"

I hated that he even had to ask me that, but I understood that it was his job. Now was not the time to feel insulted. "I swear on my daughter's life I haven't heard from him, but…" I shook my head. "It's probably nothing, but when Emery and I were on a walk the other day, there was a dark car with tinted windows parked at the end of the street. Then, later at the park, I thought I saw the same car, but I can't be sure."

"Why is this the first time we are hearing about this?"

"Because nothing happened. Am I expected to report every unfamiliar car I see?"

It seemed like he was debating something in his head as he looked at me for a long moment. That should have been my first warning, because Quinn never gave his emotions away. "I wanted to put this conversation off, but there is something you need to know."

I swallowed thickly. "Okay."

"The security footage from my apartment complex was able to get a picture of the license plate of the car he was driving."

"What are you saying?"

"You really have no idea of the things he's done or the people he's involved with, do you?"

My eyes narrowed. "Obviously not, if we're having this conversation right now."

He cursed and started to pace in front of me. "Your husband isn't the kind of guy you think he is, Charlotte."

I stepped forward and lowered my voice. "If you've got something to say, just say it."

The vein in his neck pulsed, as his eyes glanced around my yard to make sure no one was listening. "Grant was delivering drugs on the night of the accident. That's why he ran." His eyes studied mine while my chest heaved up and down with heavy breaths. "The amount of cocaine in his briefcase that he took off with was worth more than he would ever make on his measly public servant salary. Our informants on the street have confirmed that the Philly PD aren't the only people looking for him," he said with a delivery that sent my world spiraling.

How the fuck was this happening? This couldn't be right. Grant was many things, but a drug dealer? No. I wouldn't accept that.

I shook my head, refusing to believe what he was saying. "This has to be a mistake."

"I wish for yours and Emery's sake, it was."

I always knew that there was something off about my husband, but thinking it and knowing it were two completely things. Him running from the scene of the accident never made sense to me. There were things that I suspected, but nothing to this level. "How long have you known this?"

He took a deep breath, pushing his hand through his hair. "We've had our suspicions, but nothing solid until tonight. I know you have a ton of questions, but I don't have all the answers right now."

I stared at him, feeling my mind twist and turn with a panic like I've never felt before. "You've got to give me something."

He looked at me carefully, like he didn't know what to say. "We still don't know all the facts, but he was dealing with some pretty shady people. I wish I had more to tell you, but it seems that we are just scratching the surface. You didn't happen to get the license plate of the car yesterday, did you?"

"No. I didn't get close enough. I never saw that car before. I couldn't even tell you the make and model. Do you think it was Grant?"

He clenched his jaw. "I have no clue. But I've got a bad feeling about this."

Marco quietly approached, his eyes bouncing between Quinn and I. "I'm going to have a patrol car stationed outside your house, and make sure there is someone watching you and Emery twenty-four seven."

"Do you really think that's necessary?" I asked, glancing between the two men, almost afraid of the answer. "Are you trying to say that my daughter and I are in some kind of danger?"

Marco shook his head, his face was filled with sympathy. "It's too early to rule anything out. That's why we need to take extra precautions."

Quinn gripped the back of his neck, his biceps flexing with each pull of his hands. "You don't need to send anybody. I'm going to stay here with her until things settle down."

Marco quirked an eyebrow. "When you say stay until things settle down, do you mean tonight, or…"

"As long as it takes," Quinn hissed out.

I stumbled backward. "Um…excuse me. I don't remember us discussing this."

Did hell freeze over? Because last time I checked he had his own place. Not to mention I don't remember inviting him to crash at my house.

"Quinn." I closed my eyes and shook my head. The idea of him staying with me was not even a possibility as far as I was concerned. He was always a weakness for me, and I was only human. This brave front that I like to put on for show would only last for so long. "You are not staying here. I'm perfectly fine with having whoever Marco assigns to watch over us."

He stared at me, looking cool and unfazed by my rejection, while I felt like I had stepped into an alternate universe where pigs could fly.

He put his hands on his hips. "You got a problem with me staying here?"

I looked at Marco for help, only he backed up and held his hands out. "Don't look at me. This is between you two."

"Could you please explain to Detective Walker that this is highly inappropriate?" I asked nicely, hoping I could bring him to my side of thinking. There was so much to unpack from tonight, I wasn't sure where to begin.

"It's only temporary, Charlotte." Quinn sighed as if that explained everything. "I just need to sleep under your roof until Grant is behind bars and you and Emery are both safe. That little fucking weasel put a target on both of your backs."

I scoffed. "You're being irrational. Grant may be many things, but he would rather swallow broken glass than allow anyone to harm a hair on his daughter's head. And even though our marriage has been strained, he would never allow anyone to hurt me either."

He loomed over me, his strong jaw ticked like it was ready to pop through his skin. "Christ, woman. You are so fucking stubborn. He killed five fucking people. Did you ever imagine him doing that? No, you didn't. You also didn't know that he was dealing dirty on the side either. So, let's face it, you don't know what he's capable of." His face turned to stone as he continued his rant. "And I can't believe that you're seriously defending that piece of shit."

"Can you back the bus up for a second, please?" He needed to take a step back. He was too close to me. I couldn't think with him breathing down my neck. The more he pushed, the more my anxiety peeked.

"You and Emery are all he has left in this world that are of any value. These scumbags that he was involved with will use whatever means necessary to get to him, and I'm not taking any chances."

He had a point, but I didn't want to admit that to him. What he said was scaring the shit out of me. It had me questioning everything. "I don't know what you all want from me." I looked over at Marco thinking he was the safe one to focus my attention on. "I've never been in this situation before, but I know that Quinn can't stay here with me."

There is no way I could handle having Quinn rooted that deep in my life. He was already way more involved than he should have been. The thought of him edging in any deeper terrified me.

"Charlotte." Quinn's voice grew soft and it only made matters worse. "If anything ever happened to you or to Emery, I would never be able to live with myself. You don't have to agree with me, but I need you to trust me to keep you and your girl safe. I'm a professional. This is my job. I know you don't like this, but no one will protect you like I will."

His words were enough to convince me that I didn't have much of a choice in the matter.

Just then a woman who I could only describe as a human Barbie doll stepped up to join the conversation. She was stunning, and no amount of envy I was feeling could deny that. She was dressed in designer clothes that made her look like the classic beauty she was. The one he deserved to be with.

I pulled on my thin jacket and was grateful that I had wrapped a wool scarf along my neck because it helped hide my ratty long-sleeved T-shirt. When she took in my holey jeans and black ankle boots, I wanted to crawl into the pavement and die.

She swept her questioning gaze over to Quinn, the emotion I saw pass between them made my stomach squeeze.

He cleared his throat and moved his eyes over to me. "I'm sorry, Bree. I forgot you were here."

So, this was the girlfriend he told me about. She wasn't what I expected, and trust me, I spent plenty of time wondering what she looked like. Jealously edged its way through me even though I had no right to feel that way. Things were about to get a whole lot more fucking interesting.

She rubbed her hands along her arms looking more hurt than pissed off. "Yeah, I can tell."

"Quinn." I stood off to the side, keeping my distance. "You mentioned that you had plans this weekend. Please, don't feel obligated to stay here. Emery and I will be fine."

"I'm not leaving. End of discussion, Charlotte."

His girlfriend's mouth fell open, and she did a slow blink. "You want to tell me what the hell is happening right now?" She folded her arms across her chest. I guess she was done playing nice. "You're seriously going to move in with her?"

I stared at him in disbelief. I wanted to step in and say something, tell him that he was handling this all wrong, but it wasn't my place. She had every right to be upset, hell, even I was pissed off, but I didn't want to make matters worse by pointing that out in front of her.

Marco cleared his throat and spoke up. "Why don't I take Charlotte into the house, while you two hash things out?"

Quinn pressed his lips together in a firm line. Things were stressful as it was, the last thing I needed was an unhappy girlfriend thrown into the mix.

"That's a good idea. I need to get Emery ready for bed." I gave them both a tight smile as Marco and I rounded the hood of the car. He spoke to a few officers as he ushered me up the front steps to my house.

I caught a few of my nosy neighbors standing at the edge of their driveways and spied a few peeking through the windows of their homes. I could only imagine what they thought of me now.

There was a time when I was friendly with most of them, but after the accident that all changed. Some no longer wanted to be associated with me, while the others I simply didn't trust. It was one of the drawbacks when your husband was a wanted fugitive.

Marco greeted the uniformed officer at the door. "Are you guys done checking the perimeter?"

The officer tipped his head to the side. "Mickey is just finishing up in the back. No sign of him."

Marco patted him on the shoulder. "I'm not surprised. Good work. You guys are clear to go."

The rest of the officers shuffled toward their patrol cars as we walked into my house. Emery was sitting in my big overstuffed chair in the corner, coloring while a Nickelodeon showed played on the TV.

"Mommy!" she yelled, jumping off the chair and running toward me like it had been days since she'd last seen me.

"Hey, sweet girl." I kissed the top of her head and held her close. She was all I needed at that moment to remind me of what was important. "Are you having fun with Officer…" I paused and looked up, trying to remember her name.

"Joanne is fine." She smiled down at my daughter. "We've had a great time, right, Emery?"

Emery shook her head and looked over at the door. "Where's Quinn?"

I fixed her headband that had slid down her forehead and pushed it back in place. "He's outside talking to his friend."

"Okay. I put his pizza in the microwave."

"Pizza?" Marco said with way too much enthusiasm. "I hope you saved a piece for me?"

Emery tilted her head all the way back to look at him.

She crinkled her nose up. "You can have a piece of cheese because I saved the pepperoni for Quinn."

Joanne snickered in back of me. "I see Quinn's charm doesn't discriminate. Even the little ones are allured by his good looks."

"Please." Marco rolled his eyes. "He's got nothing on me."

Joanne and I both laughed.

"Emery, why don't you go upstairs and get your pajamas on?"

"Okay, but make sure Quinn knows where his dinner is." She looked at Marco. "Do you want yours now?"

He patted his flat stomach with the two dimples dancing in his cheeks that probably had all the single ladies speeding through town, hoping to get pulled over. "Do you think I've got room in here for pizza?"

"Oh, Lord," Joanne groaned. "Fishing for compliments from a six-year-old, really, Marco?"

"What?" He laughed. "Do you know how hard I work for this eight-pack?"

She rolled her eyes and looked at the time. "You know what? I'm out." She walked over to Emery and kneeled down so they were at eye level. "It was nice meeting you, Emery."

She grabbed her coffee cup that was sitting on the end table. Her dark eyes met mine. "I hope they find him soon," she whispered so only I could hear her. "You and that little girl deserve some closure. I've dealt with your husband a few times over the years. I'm just sorry this all happened. He always seemed like a decent guy."

Just when I thought my day couldn't suck anymore, she had to go and remind me that Grant wasn't always the bad guy that people perceived him to be. Deep down, I knew that to be true, but somewhere along the way he changed. I wasn't sure if it was because of greed, power, or anger. It could have been any or all of those things. Maybe if I were a better wife and paid closer attention, I wouldn't have been so blindsided.

Emery waved as we said our goodbyes. Once the door was shut I walked over to the couch and started to fold a few throw blankets that were laying around. I tried to keep myself busy and distracted as I moved around the living room, picking things up and putting them where they belonged. I was on autopilot, trying to make sense of my husband's double life. I wanted to demand answers from him and ask him who he really was, because he sure as hell wasn't the man I married. Or was he, and I just didn't know it?

I snatched the remote off the end table and turned the television off. It was getting late, and with all the excitement that went on tonight, our bedtime routine was going to be a challenge.

"Emery, go fix Marco a plate and head upstairs please."

He shot me a wink over his shoulder as the two of them scampered into the kitchen. He was so damned likable sometimes I forgot why he was actually here.

I could hear Marco's big throaty laughter and Emery's little giggle all the way through the house. I shook my head and spent the next few minutes tidying up the living room. After fluffing a few pillows I padded over to the window and pushed the curtains back.

I watched from afar as Quinn held his girlfriend against his chest. I wanted to look away, but something about that moment had me rooted to the spot. I pressed a hand to my neck, trying to ease the growing tightness in my throat.

"Cute kid," Marco said as he walked back into the room. He lingered to my left as we watched Emery bounce up the stairs. When I turned to fully face him, his expression softened in concern. "How are you holding up?"

"I'm fine," I lied, stepping away from the window, hoping I didn't look like a stalker.

He eyed me warily, and I could tell he didn't believe me. I was a mess on the inside, I could only imagine what I looked like on the outside. "We're going to find your husband. I promise you that." It was almost laughable that Marco thought my stressing out was all about Grant. "And once we do, maybe then you and Quinn can get your shit figured out."

I scooted around him, not liking the fact that he could read me so easily. But then again, wasn't that his job? "There is nothing for Quinn and me to figure out."

He looked like he didn't believe me.

"Quinn's a good guy," he pointed out, glancing over my shoulder and looking out the window. "We've known each other for a long time. He's one of the finest investigators we have. He always does what's right no matter what the cost."

"Why are you telling me this?"

"He will do whatever it takes to get your husband off the streets. This may not be his case, but he's the most motivated person I have in my corner. He doesn't need his mind fucked with right now. So, if staying here and watching over you and your daughter is going to keep him sane, then you let him do what he needs to do."

I swallowed and turned away, trying to hide any emotions that would give me away. The thought of Quinn here in my house, sharing my space did funny little things to my heart.

"Are you speaking as a friend or coworker?"

He laughed. "Both, I guess. We all have the same goal in mind. I want Quinn to be smart about this and not let his personal feelings get in the way. He's got a keen sense for justice, but the second your husband stuck that note on his car..."

I held my hands out. "You don't need to finish that sentence. I know. I feel terrible that Quinn's been dragged into this mess."

He smirked. "Trust me, Quinn can hold his own."

"I'm not just talking about that." I pointed out the window to where Quinn's girlfriend appeared to be crying against his neck. "That doesn't look good."

"Ahh..." He nodded his head and shifted his eyes away

from me. "Why don't you let Quinn worry about that. He's not going to do anything he doesn't want to do."

"I know that," I snapped, feeling frustrated. For some reason it felt like I had to defend myself, and he just happened to be the poor guy standing in front of me. I knew the kind of man Quinn was. I knew that he still cared about me and wanted to keep me safe. But at what cost?

"Let's be realistic here for a second. You want to catch my husband. Do you honestly think he's going to come near this house if he knows that Quinn is staying here? I mean come on, that would be stupid."

"As Quinn said earlier, it's not just Grant we're worried about. But if your husband thinks that another man is moving in on his life…" he whistled, "not just any man, but a man that he hates, that's going to cause him to lose his shit and do stupid things. Things that will make it easier for us to catch him. Tonight is a perfect example of that."

Damn it. He had a point. Now if only I could convince my foolish heart that this didn't mean anything.

EIGHT

QUINN

"Let's be honest here. You're obviously on Grant Anderson's radar," Marco said, as Charlotte sat silently in the recliner with her knees folded underneath her.

She was sipping a hot cup of tea waiting for Emery to finish up with her bath. She'd been quiet, listening to Marco and I go back and forth. I knew she wanted to ask me about Bree and why I sent her home.

What could I say other than breaking things off with her felt like I had no choice? Not with my heart making the decision for me.

Things were changing with me and Charlotte, and with Grant now out of the picture, I didn't want anything standing in my way. In my mind, I was reclaiming what should have been mine all along.

"Hey, Quinn, are you listening to me?" Marco asked, rapidly snapping his fingers to draw my attention back to him. I gritted my teeth, not liking the fact that I was distracted. I'd been spaced out for almost a minute, lost in thought when I should have been focusing.

"I just want some fucking answers," I replied. "It seems

like we're glossing over something. This doesn't make sense. Somebody with resources is protecting him, but who?"

"I agree. That's why we don't want to rule out any possibilities, no matter how unlikely they may be," Marco explained while finishing off his pizza. The two slices of pepperoni that Emery had left out for me sat untouched. My appetite was shit. "You need to be extra careful because word on the street is that those drugs belonged to Dom Scarantino. You know, King Dom who owns the drug trade in Nicetown and Hunting Park." Marco eyed me carefully. "According to my friends in Narcotics, he's one step away from the big boss. Which means whoever is helping Anderson is in a much more powerful position with a lot more connections."

Didn't I know it. We have exhausted every fucking lead. Used every goddamned government database at our disposal. Ran background checks on everyone associated with Anderson and his family. I've been online looking at every social media site out there and called in favors to every law enforcement agency available to me. Only to come up with nada.

I was desperate for answers, but without knowing who was helping him, I was simply wasting my time on a case that technically wasn't even mine.

Marco stood up and started pacing the living room. He was just as pissed off as I was that we weren't getting any closer to finding that son of a bitch. "As your friend, I'm telling you to keep your eyes open and to be safe. As a fellow cop, I want to remind you that this isn't your case. You are not on official police duty, but I do expect you to stay armed at all times. We've got everyone out there looking for him. We're going to find him."

I blew out a deep breath. "He's right under our fucking nose. I can feel it."

Marco nodded in agreement. "I agree. You would think

his ass would be parked on a beach in Mexico drinking tequila by now."

"What about the woman he was with?" Charlotte asked as I eyed her carefully across the room.

Marco gave her that famous grin that he loved to brag about. "Already checked that one off the list. He hasn't been in contact with her as best as we can tell. I appreciate the help though," he added with a wink.

My eyes narrowed.

"I'm sorry," she apologized. "I feel useless just sitting here. I wish I could be more help."

I could feel the angry scowl form on my face. "Stop apologizing."

I hated that she always felt like she had to apologize for him. As if any of this fiasco was her fault. Grant Anderson was an idiot. He had it all. A successful career, a beautiful wife, and an adorable daughter. Yet for some reason, it wasn't enough for him. Well, his loss was my gain. I probably sounded like a hypocrite, but Charlotte and I were in a different place back then and I wasn't stupid enough to make that mistake again.

"I've got a few tips I've got to follow up on," Marco announced and swung his head to Charlotte. "You're in good hands, sweetheart."

She smiled, and I scowled. He really needed to quit the fucking flirting.

"Quinn!" Emery squealed from the bottom of the stairs. She sprinted across the room and landed right in front of me.

I laughed at her enthusiastic greeting. "Hey, Peanut."

She had on a blue and yellow pajama set that had monkeys from top to bottom and a pair of brown bunny slippers that looked way too big for her small feet. Her dark, long hair was soaking wet and looked like it was in need of a good comb through. When I noticed the tiny dimples dancing in the middle of both cheeks, I knew I was in trouble. For such a little thing, she sure could cause a huge rattle in my chest.

Marco clapped his hands as he walked toward the door. "You guys have a good night."

"I'll walk you out." I stood up and followed him out to the front porch.

The second the door closed behind us he asked, "What happened with Bree?"

I blew out a deep breath and looked up at the night sky. "I sent her home."

He studied me for a minute, leaning up against the porch railing. "To whose home?"

"I sent her back to DC."

He whistled. "I can't say I'm surprised. Don't get me wrong, she's a nice girl and all, but you and Charlotte obviously have some unfinished business."

"That's the understatement of the year, brother."

Love was a bitch. Whoever said it was easy never loved anyone before. I should have been upset about breaking up with my girlfriend after nine months, but instead all I felt was a sense of relief. Up until recently, I thought I was happy. That all changed the second that fate brought Charlotte and I back together again, and it was becoming more obvious with each passing day that things between us were far from over.

He patted my shoulder. "Just go slow with her, dude. She's got a lot of shit going on at the moment."

I wanted to tell him to mind his own fucking business, but he was a friend and he meant well. He knew how important Charlotte was to me, but he also had an obligation to solve this case. He was just as much a part of this mess as I was.

I watched him walk down the driveway and hop in his cruiser. Once he was gone, I took a minute to survey my surroundings, looking for anything that was out of place. I widened my stance and crossed my arms over my chest. If that fucker was watching, I wanted him to know that I wasn't leaving anytime soon.

I made a mental note to call the security firm where I worked part-time to have them come out and wire up the house with door and window sensors, cameras, and motion detectors. The security system that Grant had set up would be replaced by morning.

Whether she wanted to admit it or not, Grant Anderson and his lifestyle were a threat. My biggest struggle, however, was getting her to acknowledge that fact.

I walked back into the house and noticed the front living room was empty. The hall light was on, so I rounded up the stairs and followed the sound of two soft voices. I stopped at the second door on the left and peeked my head inside.

Charlotte laid next to Emery on her bed, reading a book in her hands. I rested my weight against the doorframe, watching as the two girls giggled.

"That must be some funny book you're reading."

They both lifted their heads in surprise at the sound of my voice.

"We're reading Junie B. Jones," Emery stated as if everyone in the world should know who that was. I wandered into her small room and glanced around. It wasn't what I had pictured in my mind. The walls were light blue with no pink in sight. The only girlie things she had were a couple of American Girl dolls and a gigantic dollhouse. She had board games, puzzles, and an old-fashioned school desk in the corner with a big chalkboard on the wall.

"What's the book about?" I asked, slinking down on the edge of her twin-sized mattress. Charlotte moved her feet up to make room for me.

"It's a about a stinky, smelly school bus and a dumb girl who is trying to save a seat for her friend."

"Sounds like the bus I rode when I was in school. Is it good?"

"It is," Emery replied. "It's my turn to read the next chapter. Do you want me to read it to you, Quinn?"

"What?" I feigned shock. "You can read already? You're only six."

Emery sat up proudly and rested her body against the headboard. "I'm almost seven and I can read better than anybody in my class."

"Emery," Charlotte spoke in a sharp tone. "It's not nice to brag."

She shrugged her shoulders. "I'm not bragging. I'm telling the truth."

Charlotte and I both laughed as Emery started reading the next chapter all on her own. I was surprised that they used words like stupid, dumb, and hate in a kid's book, but was impressed when Charlotte would follow up and ask, "What should she have done or said differently?"

Watching her interact with her daughter was an experience all on its own. She was an incredible mother who was doing a good job at hiding the internal battle that she struggled with. The love for her daughter shined through her big green eyes. You could hear it in her voice. See it with her actions. It made me angry every time I thought about the heartache that they both had to endure. Things were far from over, and it was going to get worse before it got better. I closed my eyes, wishing I could make this all go away for them. It was weird feeling so connected and protective over a little girl that wasn't even mine.

Emery closed the book once she was finished and placed it on her nightstand. I stood from the bed, ready to say good night when Emery's question surprised the hell out of me.

"Are you going to sleep in my daddy's room tonight?"

My back went straight. "What do you mean, *your daddy's room?*"

"My daddy had his own bedroom, but he's not using it anymore. My mom said he has to go live in another house so he could start his time-out, so you can sleep there if you want."

My eyebrows rose in confusion. I was dumbstruck on the beginning part of that sentence. "Your mom and dad didn't sleep in the same room?"

"Nope," Emery replied. "My mom's room is across the hall. My daddy's room is the one on the end."

Well, wasn't that fucking interesting. There was no way in hell that I was going to sleep in Grant Anderson's bed. But I couldn't say that to the sweet little girl who was simply trying to offer me a warm place to rest my head at night.

I stepped forward and reached for Emery's shoulder and brushed a piece of hair to the side. "Thanks for offering me your dad's room, but I already have my stuff downstairs and planned on sleeping on the couch." I dropped my arm and took a step back. "Good night, Peanut. I'll see you in the morning." I dropped my arm and took a step back.

Charlotte turned her head when I looked at her. "I'll be down soon," she said, and then walked over to Emery's dresser to turn on her night-light.

I walked out of the room feeling more confused than ever.

After eating leftover pizza, I kicked my shoes off as Charlotte and I settled on opposite sides of the couch. I was feeling on edge instead of relaxed. She'd been quiet since she came downstairs and was pretending to watch some stupid home improvement show.

"So." I paused briefly, trying to think of what to say and decided, fuck it. My curiosity was killing me, and I couldn't focus on anything other than the fact that she and Grant were sleeping in separate rooms. "Are you going to talk to me or keep avoiding me all night?"

"That seems to be our thing, wouldn't you say?"

"Yes, and I don't like it. I want to know why you and Grant were sleeping in separate bedrooms."

She crossed her legs and pulled her shirt down, a clear

sign that she was nervous. "That's really none of your business."

I pressed my hands into the armrest of the couch, trying to bury my frustration. I couldn't stop staring at her. Couldn't help but wonder what the hell would have led them to stop sleeping together. If she were mine again, she would be lying next to me every night. Never, ever, ever, would she sleep anywhere but my bed.

"Charlotte, I'm going to be blunt here for a second. I just broke up with my girlfriend less than an hour ago. Your estranged husband left a threatening note on the windshield of my car. We just found out he is associated with some dangerous people that I wouldn't even trust with my dog if I had one. I've put my life on hold and moved in here to keep you and your daughter safe. I think we are past all this shit."

My hands were shaking by the time I finished my rant. I was done tiptoeing around our issues. Done playing games.

She leaned forward, appearing calm and resigned, but I knew she was feeling the exact opposite. "I'm sorry to hear about your girlfriend." I cocked an eyebrow. She didn't look sorry, not one bit. "And I feel horrible about that note, but I never asked you to move in here. In fact, I told you no, but like always you go ahead and do whatever the hell it is you want."

She shot to her feet and stormed toward the bathroom. I was right behind her. We were dealing with this crap tonight.

She pushed the door open, and I stepped sideways and edged my way in. Her eyes widened in panic as I backed her up against the wall. Her feelings were just as strong as mine, I could feel it.

I placed my hands on either side of her head and flattened them against the cool gray tile. I was determined to get an answer out of her.

"Why were you sleeping in separate bedrooms?" I demanded, leaning into her face.

She stared at my lips. I recognized that look. It had been too long since I'd seen it. Maybe we were finally getting somewhere.

She tipped her chin up, bringing those lips that I was starved for even closer to mine. "Why does that answer matter to you so much?"

I tried to soften my voice even though it felt like I was about to come out of my skin. "Answer the question."

Her one hand went to my shoulder while the other went to my hip. "I asked Grant for a divorce last year. He refused to give me one." I just blinked at her as she continued. "It was a mistake to marry him, but I was stuck. I thought if I moved out of our bedroom that it would force his hand, but he was determined to stick it out."

"That's why you weren't so torn up about his cheating."

She swallowed. "Right."

I hooked a hand around her waist and stared into her eyes. "Why did you want a divorce so bad?"

"Because I didn't love him."

There was no denying how I felt about her, I'd made myself clear. Now it was time for her to do the same. "What about me? How do you feel about us?"

Her hands slid along my sides, leaving a trail of heat in their path. That familiar spark came to life. "I've never stopped loving you, Quinn. That was always the problem, I loved you too much. But I can't do this with you now. My life is a mess."

I battled with the urge to kiss her. To claim her. To remind her she had always been mine. But she was right, we had a mountain of issues to work through. When I asked her to marry me, we were both young and naïve. It didn't matter how much love and passion there was in our relationship. Whatever hope for a future we had, I thoroughly destroyed. And that asshat capitalized on it. Now it was my turn to try to fix it and get us back to where we were meant to be.

Together.

"I'm going to do whatever it takes to make you see that I'm checking back into your life. I know you think I left you, but I never really let you go." A tear fell from her eye and I pushed it away with my thumb. "I'm here to stay this time. I promise you."

"Don't make promises you can't keep. The last time you did you broke every single one, including my heart."

"I'm so sorry, baby." I brought my hand up to the back of her neck. "I'm right here. One hundred percent." She shook her head like she was trying to reject my words. I saw the doubt in her eyes and it killed me. "I know I broke your heart, but please let me be the one to put it back together."

"It's going to take some time, Quinn. Our problems can't be fixed overnight. Plus," she threaded her fingers along the top of my hair, and I closed my eyes, loving the feel of having her hands on me, "we can't ignore the fact that I'm still technically married."

I groaned. "Don't fucking remind me. But we're going to fix that." I pulled her mouth to mine and brushed a slow kiss to her lips. They felt familiar but new. So soft and inviting. Seven years of regret melted in an instant.

Kissing her was better than I remembered. Everything seemed more intense and profound as our tongues lashed together with an urgency that matched the beating in my chest. My hands wrapped around her ass and her fists grabbed my shirt. My restraint was fleeting, and I found myself grinding into her because I couldn't help myself. No matter how many years had passed or where life had taken me, nothing compared to having her back in my arms.

I didn't know how long we stood in that bathroom and made out like two teenagers, but eventually, she pulled back and placed her palms on my chest. I brought my shaking hands up to cradle her face and ran my thumb along her jaw.

"We'll figure this out," I promised and kissed her

forehead. "I'm going to go lock up. Why don't you get changed and come lie on the couch with me? I'll pour you a glass of wine and you can just relax."

She looked up at me and nodded. "Okay."

I gave her one last kiss and walked out of the bathroom, feeling like someone had just pressed the reset button on my life.

After locking all the doors and closing all the blinds, I flipped through a few movies on Netflix. I smiled when I saw one of her all-time favorites. I strolled into the kitchen and poured a glass of chardonnay like I promised. I grabbed a few throw blankets and relaxed back into the couch. I stripped down to my white T-shirt but left my jeans on.

Charlotte came down the stairs holding a few pillows and a phone charger. She'd changed into a comfortable pair of pajamas that did nothing to hide her figure. I patted the space next to me and saw her face light up when she saw the movie that was about to start.

She cocked an eyebrow. "*Pretty Woman.*"

"It's still your favorite, right?"

She twirled the ends of her hair around her finger. A bright smile lit up her face. "I appreciate this whole seduction thing you've got going on here, but let me give you a tip: I'm a sure thing."

I threw my head back and laughed. "I forgot you knew the whole movie, line for line."

She shrugged her shoulders and padded her way over to me. "Something's never change."

I pulled her tight up against my side and gave her a small kiss on the lips. "You're absolutely right."

We sat and laughed throughout the whole movie as I quizzed her about every scene. She could tell you word for word what Richard Gere and Julia Roberts were going to say before they even said it. As soon as the credits rolled across the screen, she was out like a light.

I knew I should have brought her upstairs and laid her down on her comfortable bed, but I liked having her in my arms. So much that I sat and watched her sleep. She looked so peaceful. The last thing I wanted to do was wake her up. So, I selfishly pulled her tighter against my chest and had the most restful night's sleep in years.

NINE

CHARLOTTE

I STRETCHED MY LEGS OUT ON THE COUCH AND SHIFTED MY BODY to the side. My eyes darted around the living room, noticing that the blinds were still down. The house was dark and quiet. The smell of Quinn's familiar scent was on the empty pillow next to mine.

I reached for my phone and looked at the time, but that wasn't what caught my attention. My phone chirped and beeped, alerting me of multiple missed calls and text messages all from Erica and Mackenzie. I threw my phone back down and stared at the ceiling. Those two were persistent and would no doubt keep calling, but I had zero desire to explain my current situation to them. As if on cue, my cell started to ring again. I groaned and sent it straight to voicemail.

I pinched my eyes closed as the memories from last night played on repeat in my head. My disgust with Grant was still front and center in my mind. Yet, sleeping in Quinn's arms brought me a peace that I desperately needed. Now, I was left wondering what I was supposed to do next.

He made it very clear last night about what he wanted. And as much as a part of me would love to just throw caution to the wind and say the hell with it, there was another part reminding to slow my roll. My life was in shambles, and the last thing I needed was more complications than I already had.

I threw the blanket off and gave up on trying to make sense of something that I would never understand.

My steps slowed on the way to the kitchen, not prepared for the sight in front of me. Quinn and Emery were sitting at the table eating breakfast while watching cartoons on his phone. She said something to him and he reached over and tickled her side, causing her to giggle.

My heart ached while watching the two of them interact. Seeing the softer side of Quinn and how at ease Emery was with him, had me wishing for another life.

One where Quinn was my husband and Emery was his daughter.

"Good morning," I said, glancing around the kitchen and taking inventory of the mess that they made. There was a stack of dirty pans piled in the sink, and the stovetop was painted in yellow pancake batter. But there was no way in hell I would point that mess out. Especially not with Quinn sitting at the head of my kitchen table, looking like he belonged there, and my little girl smiling up at him like he hung the moon.

Emery lifted her head, her big green eyes full of innocence that I was desperately trying to preserve. After all the stress of last night, it was nice seeing her so relaxed.

"Well, well, if it isn't Sleeping Beauty," Quinn teased with a grin that was nothing short of irresistible. He looked like he didn't have a care in the world, while I was trying to ignore the butterflies causing havoc in my stomach. I wanted to talk to him about what happened last night, and about where we stood because boundaries needed to be set and lines needed to be drawn. In other words, I needed to guard my heart.

"I see you guys made breakfast," I said casually while swiping a piece of bacon off the plate.

Emery grinned while wiping the syrup from her mouth. "Quinn made banana pancakes and bacon."

"I hope he made enough for me," I teased, feeling a smile break across my face.

"I wanted to wake you up," she said as I was reaching for my coffee mug. "But Quinn said you needed your beauty rest."

My eyes found his as I poured the cream into my coffee. He scanned me from head to toe with a smile. I was feeling a generous amount of happiness, almost to the point where it didn't feel like I deserved it.

I cleared my throat and grabbed a plate off the stove. "This looks delicious. Thanks for cooking and for letting me sleep in."

"It was the least I could do seeing that you and Emery are letting me stay here."

I rolled my eyes; it wasn't like he gave me much of a choice.

Emery cocked her head to the side and studied me. "Mommy, your hair looks really messy this morning."

Quinn covered his laugh with a cough, while I attempted to tame my wild hair with my fingers. Sometimes I hated having naturally curly hair.

"Thanks for pointing that out," I grumbled and took a sip of my steaming hot coffee.

Just as I started digging into my pancakes, the doorbell rang. It was followed with loud, obnoxious knocking.

Quinn jumped from his seat, but I grabbed onto his arm. I knew I should have answered their text messages as soon as I got them.

"Relax. It's Erica and Mackenzie."

I stood up to go answer the door, but he pushed me back down in my chair. "I got it."

"Quinn, it's ten o'clock on a Saturday morning. I can answer my own front door."

His eyes went hard, and he shifted his gaze to Emery. I knew he was going to lay into me later, but I didn't care. He was being ridiculous and completely over the top.

I threw my napkin on the table and walked out of the room. I could hear the girls talking as I approached the door. I wasn't prepared to deal with them right now, but there was no way of avoiding them.

"Good morning." I smiled, as they both stopped talking at once.

"What the hell is wrong with your phone?" Erica pushed past me with Mackenzie right on her heels. "We've been texting you all morning long and why the hell did it take you so long to answer the door. Are you trying to give us both a heart att…" Her voice stopped when she entered the kitchen.

Quinn greeted them both with a grin.

"Quinn. You're here awfully early." Mackenzie's eyes moved around the kitchen, taking in the current mess and inspecting everything that her eyes landed on.

"He spent the night last night," Emery's sweet voice offered up, basically hanging me out to dry.

Erica was leaning up against the counter. I thought her jaw was going to hit the floor.

Mackenzie pushed her sunglasses on top of her head as she walked over to Emery. "Quinn spent the night, huh?" Her eyes narrowed on mine. There was no doubt I was in for a round of interrogation.

Emery's smile grew wide. "He's moving in with us. We are going to his apartment to get his stuff today."

A collective silence fell over the room. Both of my friends snapped their heads to mine so fast, they were in danger of detaching from their shoulders.

"I'm sorry," Erica said, finally finding her voice. "Did you say Quinn was moving in?"

The man in question rose from his seat and placed his dirty plate in the dishwasher. "Why don't I take Emery with me to my place to pick up a few things? You girls will stay here with Charlotte while I'm gone, right?"

They both nodded their heads without saying a word.

"Great." He grinned. "Hey, Peanut, want to take a ride with me, so your mom has some time alone with her friends? There is also a cool playroom in my building that I want you to check out."

She tilted her head to the side. "What kind of playroom?"

"It has a jungle gym and playmats with books and toys. I've never been in there. I thought we could check it out together."

"Okay." She jumped off her seat. "I'll go get my coat and shoes."

And just like that she was gone.

Quinn walked over to where I was leaning against the kitchen island. He placed a possessive hand along my hip, leaned in and brushed his lips along mine. "I won't be long. Make sure they stay until I get back. I don't want you alone."

He couldn't have been any more obvious, and it dawned on me that we were really going to need to have a conversation. My stomach was in knots from all the events that unfolded last night. From learning that Grant was involved with some very dangerous people. To the possibility that Emery and I could be at risk because of his involvement with those dangerous people. And then there was that moment that Quinn and I shared last night in the bathroom. I should have known that the peaceful feeling of falling asleep in his arms would be short-lived. I stared at him and wondered how this would all work out. Talk about whiplash.

He gave me one last squeeze before he let go to retrieve his keys off the counter.

Both of my friends stood off to the side, stunned stupid.

"It was good seeing you both." He shot them both a wink and sauntered away.

Erica slammed her purse on the counter. "Okay! What the actual fuck just happened?"

"Hold that thought," Mackenzie said and padded over to my wine rack and grabbed a bottle of Moscato. "You've got orange juice, right?" she asked while pulling out three champagne glasses from my cabinet.

My voice was scratchy as I pointed toward the fridge. "Yeah, top shelf on the right."

She handed the bottle of wine over to Erica to open while she assembled the glasses on the table. Once the glasses were filled, I sat and stared at my drink and tried to think of what to say.

"Start talking."

This was the tricky part. How much did I want to tell them? There were so many questions that I didn't have answers to and too much uncertainty about where we stood. My life was a mess, and while last night proved that Quinn and I still shared a connection, I wasn't convinced that starting things back up with him was the smartest thing to do.

"Charlotte." Mackenzie's voice was gentle. "Tell us what's going on in that head of yours." She reached her hand across the table, sensing my struggle.

I let go of her hand and took a sip of my mimosa and gave them the rundown of everything that happened last night. Their jaws went slack when I told them about the note that Grant left on Quinn's windshield and about the drugs and the potential danger. They both sat on the edge of their seats, hanging onto every detail. I thought their eyes were going to fall out of their sockets when I told them about the encounter in the bathroom.

Erica leaned back in her chair. "Okay, so what's the problem? You both obviously still love each other. He explained why he left you. He's able to look past you marrying someone else. He broke up with his girlfriend. The list goes on."

Everything in Erica's mind was simply black and white. You were either good or bad. Right or wrong. You were either her friend or her enemy. And based on her words, it was obvious how she felt about my ex.

"I asked Quinn to give me some space, but he won't give me an inch," I protested. "I feel like he's bulldozing his way back into my life and there isn't a damn thing I can do about it."

Mackenzie leaned back in her chair and watched me. "Listen." She cleared her throat. "You've been through a lot. It's understandable why you would be hesitant. What I want to know is how do you feel about Quinn?" She waved her hands around in a circle. "Forget about everything else. What's in your heart?"

Tears started to prick my eyes. "I'll always love Quinn, but I feel like if we do move forward, we would need boundaries."

"Are you afraid he will hurt you again?"

"That's part of it." I swiped a tear from my eye, hating that I was getting caught up in the moment. I just wanted to curl up in a ball on my couch and sleep forever. Yet here I was exposing my soul to them. "I barely survived losing him the first time."

"But you did," she reminded me in a soothing, encouraging voice. "I'm not going to tell you how to live your life, but you need to live your life. Does that make sense?"

"What about Grant?"

Erica watched me. I sensed that she wanted to say something but was biting her tongue.

Mackenzie leveled me with an annoyed glare. "Grant is a piece of shit who doesn't deserve you. He never did. You have every right to be angry with him. You have every right to hate him. He's already stolen seven years of your life, don't let him take another day."

"I'm still married to him."

"You have an appointment this week with an attorney, right?"

"Yes, but this could drag on forever."

"And yet Quinn knows this and still wants to try with you anyway." She cocked an eyebrow, knowing she had me at that moment.

I sat back in my chair and crossed my arms. "I didn't realize that I had signed up for a therapy session today."

She chuckled and leaned forward. "Your life was turned upside down because of someone else's actions. Grant will be brought to justice for his crimes, eventually. Your marriage is over in every way that matters. It has been for a long time," she reminded me. "You have someone that loves you in a way most of us will never know. Do what makes you happy."

If only everything was as simple as she believed it was. Unfortunately, I was a mother first and my focus needed to be on my daughter. I stood up and started pacing the room. "You have no idea what a relationship with Quinn Walker could cost me. I'm not some young, single twenty-two-year-old girl anymore. I have a daughter that needs me."

"Who says you have to choose?" Mackenzie asked, before chugging the rest of her mimosa. "And why do you view him as a threat?"

"Because he makes me feel weak." I rubbed my forehead, feeling like my life was spinning out of control. "I hate that he knows me so well, that he can get under my skin."

"I bet that's not all he's planning on getting under." Erica giggled.

I narrowed my eyes and continued my rant. "He's distracting and bossy. He pushes my buttons and makes me feel things I don't want to feel."

"Okay," Mackenzie said, holding her hand out. "Let's

tackle one thing at a time. You've already established that you're afraid he will hurt you again. I'm here to tell you that playing it safe is no way to live your life. It's not going to fulfill you. You deserve the kind of passion where a guy will push you against the wall and kiss the hell out of you."

Why did it feel like I was going to regret telling them that?

"I've seen you with Grant. You never had that with him. You've only ever had that with Quinn. Let that thought guide you. But don't let one bad choice that he made all those years ago define who he is today. Everyone makes mistakes, but that doesn't mean he has to pay for that mistake for the rest of his life. Now let me ask you something."

"What?" I asked, picking up my drink.

"Do you have any regrets when it comes to Quinn?"

I didn't even need to think about my answer. "I've never regretted anything about my relationship with Quinn. I'm just still a little bitter about how he ended things."

She smiled smugly. "Well, then I guess you have your answer."

Erica slammed her hands down on the table. "Damn you're good."

"What about the fact that he told me he was moving in? He never even asked."

I shook my head and tried to focus on all the reasons why this wasn't a good idea. Now that I had a little bit of space and the fog in my brain was clearing, I was convinced that this would be a disaster.

"We all know that if you really didn't want him here, he wouldn't be."

"I don't want to complicate my life any more than it already is."

"You're running out of excuses."

"I just gave you one." I tucked my hair behind my ear and looked away.

"It's not good enough."

Jesus. When did she become such a hard-ass?

"I get it, okay? You guys are team Quinn. Excuse me for feeling like I should get my shit together before I start something back up with him."

"I think it's too late for that. Things have already started back up," Mackenzie said while pouring more Moscato into her glass. Seriously, I'm not sure why she even bothered with the orange juice.

I laughed bitterly. "Like I'm strong enough to stay away from him."

"Well, I can't say I blame you," Erica said as she rummaged through my pantry closet looking for a snack.

I rolled my eyes. "I'm overwhelmed. I know you guys think that I'm not living my life, but I'm doing the best I can."

"You're allowed to be happy, Charlotte." Erica smiled sadly. "I've been married twice, and I've never come close to having the kind of love that you and Quinn have. I know you have shit to work through, but you deserve a second chance. Who knows, maybe you'll both get it right this time."

That thought made me smile. There was nothing more I wanted than to spend more time with Quinn. I was anxious to get acquainted with the grownup version of him and learn every little detail about his life. I was curious to find out how much he's changed and hoped that there was enough of him that was still the same.

Mackenzie grinned. "I saw the way you just smiled, you're obviously thinking about him."

I should have been embarrassed, because just a few minutes ago I was trying to come up with a million reasons why I shouldn't move forward with him, but they were both right. I couldn't put my life on hold forever. I wanted to be sensitive to Emery and her needs, but Quinn was helping me through a very difficult part of my life. He's been amazing with both of us so far.

"Since he's been back, I feel different," I confessed.

Mackenzie tilted her head to the side while Erica nibbled on a granola bar. "How so?"

"I feel safe and less stressed, because I know he would never let anything happen to me."

Mackenzie leaned forward in her seat. "Then focus on that and the rest will figure itself out."

I was getting uncomfortable with all the attention on me. "Okay." I slid into the chair next to her. "Enough about me. How are things with you guys?"

For the next hour, we carried on about Mackenzie's love life and Erica's lack of one. Mackenzie had been hooking up with a seventh grade English teacher in her building. It was actually kind of scandalous for her because casual hookups were never her thing. Erica, on the other hand, I worried about her. She worked hard and partied harder. She wanted us all to believe she was doing it all in fun, but she wasn't fooling anybody.

After a quick phone call with Grant's parents and a much desirable shower, I walked back downstairs to see my two best friends still sitting at my kitchen table.

"You guys don't need to stay and babysit me all day."

Erica put her phone down and gave me a once-over. "You clean up nice, and we're not leaving. You can stop trying to kick us out."

"How was the phone call with the in-laws?" Mackenzie asked while she rinsed out our wineglasses.

"I feel bad for them." I sighed. "They love their son and I can tell their hearts are torn."

Erica opened up the fridge to put the orange juice away. "Are they still trying to help you out with bills?"

"Yes, and I appreciate it, but I really need to get this shit figured out and learn how to stand on my own two feet."

"One step at a time?" Mackenzie smiled as she dried her hands off with a towel.

I nodded my head. "After my meeting with the attorney, I

have an appointment with the branch manager at Citizens Bank later in the afternoon. I need to get whatever money we have in one place."

It's been weeks since he's been on the run, and the bills were still coming in. The part-time job would help, but I needed to come up with a plan B.

The front door slammed shut and nervous energy started to fill me up. Would it always be like this whenever he was near? Yes, I reminded myself, because it had always been like this.

"Mommy!" Emery's sweet voice squealed. She rushed into my arms and held on tight.

Quinn stepped into the room with a black duffel bag around his shoulders and a rolling suitcase behind him. "Thanks for staying with her," he said, setting his belongings off to the side.

Erica smirked and glanced in my direction. "Someone needed to make sure she took a shower. She cleans up pretty well don't you think, Quinn?"

I shuffled on my feet, trying to avoid the intensity of his stare. I put more effort into my appearance than I normally did on a Saturday afternoon. I had on a pair of dark washed skinny jeans and a black cashmere sweater that hung off my shoulders. My hair was in loose waves, and I finally got to break out my new Urban Decay makeup palette.

"You look pretty, Mommy."

I brushed a hand through Emery's hair. "Thank you, baby."

Quinn closed the distance between us and reached for my pinky that was dangling at the side. "Very pretty indeed."

I swallowed. Whatever doubts I voiced to my friends earlier went out the window.

One touch. One glance. And I was done.

TEN

QUINN

I LAID ON THE LIVING ROOM COUCH AND LOOKED AROUND, hating that Grant was practically everywhere. It was impossible to ignore the fact that this was his house, and I wanted to erase every single trace of him that was left over. His face was in the family pictures on the wall. His golf clubs were in the garage. His leather recliner that I wanted to burn sat in the corner.

It pissed me off that the selfish bastard had the family that should have been mine.

Charlotte appeared at the end of the stairs and looked around at the scented candles that I had lit while she was getting Emery ready for bed. "She's finally out."

I rubbed my own bloodshot eyes, feeling physically worn out from our afternoon outing. We spent most of the day out in a farm field, picking our own pumpkins to decorate the house. That little girl was a ball of energy as we chased her through the corn maze, visited every goat and chicken at the petting zoo, and spent the better part of the afternoon jumping on and off the circular bales of hay. If Emery wanted it, she got it. She had a unicorn painted on her face, ate Shake Shack for dinner, and somehow managed to sucker me into overpaying for her sixty-dollar cowgirl costume for Halloween.

I didn't know how Charlotte did it on her own. She had to be exhausted, but she couldn't look any more beautiful to me. She wasn't wearing anything special, just a pair of navy sleep shorts and a simple ivory top that clung to her waist, but it suited her.

A smile came to life on my face, noticing her hair hanging loose down along her shoulders. The naturally curly, wild untamed look was always my favorite.

I got off the couch and made my way over to her. I was feeling anxious, everything inside of me was overflowing with anticipation. I wanted to pick up where we left off last night in the bathroom, and I hoped to God that she wanted the same.

I wasted no time pulling her against my chest. "Does that mean I finally have you all to myself now?"

"Quinn." Her voice was shaky as she peered up at me with those big, green emerald eyes that I wanted to get lost in. "What are you doing?"

I grinned down at her, my lips ached to kiss her again. "Exactly what you think I'm doing."

The moment we had last night had been on my mind all day. I was ready to take it up a level, but I needed her to be comfortable with the idea of us. And if I was reading her right, she seemed a little on edge around me.

She lifted her chin to look at me. I could see the hesitation in her eyes. "I don't want you to fight me on this, but we need to take things slow."

My jaw clenched in frustration at the word "slow." I managed to pull back and look at her. "I hate that you're having doubts about us."

Her hands moved up my arms and landed in my hair. "You're taking this the wrong way."

"So, explain it to me."

She sighed as if she was frustrated, but her body still leaned into mine. Such a contradiction. "I lost myself in you once before. I don't want to make the same mistake. If we are doing this, I want to do it right."

I brought her hand up to my chest and placed it over my heart. "You never lost me, Charlotte, because I never let you go. You're still in here."

Moisture built up in her eyes. "Saying things like that only makes this harder for me. Don't you understand that?"

I wrapped my hands along the back of her neck until our foreheads were touching. "I know you're scared, but I refuse to deny what is happening between us. I'm not taking things slow, not when I can finally feel my heart beating again after seven years."

The tears that she was trying to hold in began to flow freely down her cheeks. "Quinn." She swallowed; her fingers trailing lightly across my chin. "I don't know what to say." She paused. "Of course, I feel this connection we have too, but I'm still scared."

I pulled on her hand until we were falling back on the couch against the window. "Come here," I commanded, sliding her up my chest so we were nose to nose. "Just relax."

Her fingers drew small little circles along my chest. I've lost track of how many times I've wished for moments just like this. Where I could just hold her and protect her. This content feeling had me wondering how I ever could have settled for anything less.

Her arms slipped around my waist; she gave me a quick smile. "We really need to get you a bed while you're here."

I pushed her hair off her shoulder. "Are you offering yours?"

Her eyes closed like she was conflicted. When she opened them I held her gaze, not wanting her to look away. "It's not that I don't want you there. I just need to be respectful of Emery and how she perceives things."

Both of my hands slid up to her face and I pressed a kiss to her mouth. "We'll figure it out, but, sweetheart, you need to understand something. Whatever walls you still have up guarding your heart, I want them gone. Or I will shatter every single one of them. Don't be afraid to give into your feelings. Not tonight. Not ever. You're always safe with me."

I was probably pushing her too hard, but I didn't care. The reality was that I finally had my hands on everything I ever wanted, and I wasn't ever going to her let go again.

If I could go back in time and kick my own ass for breaking her heart, I would. Earning her trust back would take time. Until then, I'd just keep on trying and reminding her that I wasn't giving up.

I brushed my mouth against hers, waiting for her to open up for me. She seemed timid at first, so I took my time going soft and slow until she was ready. I placed tender kisses on the corner of her mouth, down her delicate jaw and made my way to her neck where I gently nipped under her ear. I smiled remembering that was her favorite spot.

Her hands disappeared in my hair as she started to relax into my touch. My kisses were light and lazy and nothing like the powerful and passionate moment we shared last night. This was more tender and unhurried because I knew she was overthinking, and I wanted her comfortable and less nervous.

She let out a soft sigh, and I tilted her head back. My eyes searched hers, looking for any doubt or hesitation. "We don't have to do anything that you're not ready for."

Her hands rested on my chest and she stared at me with the weight of my words hanging between us. I brought my hand to her face, letting my fingers trail along her jaw. Her long hair slipped over her shoulders, and she never looked more beautiful to me.

She drew in a shaky breath, letting the reality of what was happening sink in. I saw the exact moment that something shifted in her eyes. When they changed from uncertainty to lust.

Her mouth crashed down to mine. Our hands began to explore on a journey all of their own. Our tongues began to move against each other's in perfect rhythm. Our hearts were beating in sync as our familiar sounds spoke the words that didn't need to be spoken. Each touch and each caress helped awaken feelings that had been forgotten. Reminding us of who we were.

"Is this okay? Will Emery wake up?" I asked while adjusting her on top of me.

She wrapped her legs around my thighs. "Actually, this is more than okay. And I wouldn't be here right now if I thought Emery would walk in on us."

My hands slid up her leg, and I knew right then, without a shadow of a doubt, that we would find a way to make things work.

I brought my hands up to her breasts and rolled my fingers around each nipple, feeling them harden underneath the fabric of her thin top. Intimacy with her was as natural as breathing to me. Knowing that I still knew how to work her body into a frenzy caused a familiar hunger to race through me.

Her moans filtered through the air, spurring me on like nothing else. I moved farther back on the couch, letting my fingers and my tongue do all the talking because, with Charlotte, no words were needed, and when her touch started to trail south, it spoke volumes. Her small, delicate hands reached my erection and she started to stroke me through my jeans. I lifted my hips up so she could undo the zipper and pull me free. God, please let this go where I prayed it was going.

She got on her knees in front of me and the second her warm, wet tongue swirled against my crown, I had to pinch my eyes shut and concentrate on not exploding right then and there. My cock started to twitch as she eagerly ran her tongue from the base all the way to the tip before taking me in the back of her throat. I threw my hands in her hair and guided her up and down as if my hips had a mind of their own. The sensation was too much and no matter how much I tried to hold it in, my release was going to break free way sooner than I wanted it to. She brought her hands up to my balls and squeezed them gently sending a string of curses to fly from my mouth.

"Fuck," I hissed out and closed my eyes as everything in my body tightened up. I leaned my head back against the arm of the couch when all I wanted to do was lift my head up and watch her take me. I didn't want to go off in her mouth. Not for our first time together after all these years. I pulled her head back and noticed the tip of my crown glistening with precum.

I rolled her to the side and stood up. I was done being patient. Done waiting. Done taking things slow.

"Take your clothes off," I commanded.

She didn't look shy or nervous anymore. And thank God, for once in her life, she didn't argue with me. Her hands went to her top and she pulled it over her head. Next, she slid her shorts down her legs taking her black thong with them.

Jesus! When did she start wearing those? I shook my head and made quick work of removing my clothes. It took me seconds to strip everything off.

Suddenly, it was like I was standing in front of her for the first time. I took a moment to look her over and appreciate what was laid out before me.

"You're beautiful," I whispered.

Her body had changed over the years and I couldn't wait to reacquaint myself with every inch of her.

She bit her lip and smiled, as her eyes traced over me. And then she said the words that every man loved to hear. "I don't remember you being so big." I gripped my cock and started stroking, showing her how long and thick I was capable of getting. She laughed and shook her head. "I was talking about your muscles."

I laid over the top of her and brushed my nose against hers. "I'm about to refresh your memory on a lot of things."

I trailed my mouth down her neck, sucking and nibbling as I went farther south. Everything felt soft and her curves felt like they were made just for my hands to roam. I spread her legs apart, opening her up nice and wide for me.

"Gorgeous," I whispered with a smile on my face.

I placed my head in between her legs and plunged my tongue inside. I licked and swirled around sucking up her juices. Most men thought of this as a chore, or like something they had to do. I genuinely loved having my mouth on her, it was always a favorite of mine. She tasted better than I remembered, and I wanted to lick her from the inside out. I could die a happy man right there in between her legs.

After a few minutes of working her clit, I pulled back and sunk my fingers inside. I gently guided them in and out, watching the look of pleasure grow on her face. With every strangled cry I would add a little bit more pressure.

Her hips arched into my face, and her legs wrapped around my back, like she wanted to anchor her body to mine. I was starved for her and showed no mercy. She squeezed and pulled my head forward, my name was on her lips as she rode her orgasm out and released herself on my tongue.

I didn't even give her a chance to come down. She looked surprised as I positioned myself at her entrance.

She grabbed onto my shoulders and tried to push me back. "Quinn, we need a condom."

"No," I told her sternly. "I'm not fucking using a condom with you."

She started to protest, but I wasn't having it. I brought my thumb down to her clit and moved in a rhythm that I knew drove her crazy.

"Oh God, Quinn." I watched her head fall back as I brought my mouth down on her nipple and flicked my tongue. Her hands fisted in my hair. I could feel her body begging me to fuck her.

"Tell me, Charlotte. Tell me you want me just like this."

"Fine," she huffed out.

I pulled back and arched an eyebrow at her. I wasn't letting her win this one. We never used one before because she used to get the shot. She told me she stopped getting them after we broke up, which would explain how Emily was conceived. Normally, having sex without protection wasn't something I did. But Charlotte wasn't just anybody and I was willing to leave whatever was meant to be up to fate.

"I don't want anything between us. I promise I'm clean."

Her hand clutched my shoulders. "Okay. I trust you."

I squeezed my way in slowly, moving in and out with ease. My movements were deep, long, and slow. The feeling of our bodies connecting had me feeling at peace for the first time in forever. This was where I was always meant to be. This was my home.

Her body along with her heart had always belonged to me.

"I want to fuck you all night. We have a lot of time to make up for," I whispered, as a single tear flowed out of the corner of her eye. "I'm going to make you remember how good we are together." I pushed into her deeper. The feeling of her warm heat wrapping around me had me wanting to blow my load right then. "It's always been you. No one else has ever made me feel this way."

"I've missed you so much." She cried out, meeting me thrust for thrust.

"I've missed you too, sweetheart." My mouth went to her neck, tasting and sucking and biting with each stroke. Her hands tightened around my ass making me push harder as she arched her back. I sucked her nipple into my mouth, licking and flicking it with my tongue. Her arms squeezed around me painfully tight as she moaned my name.

The tension that built up inside my balls was begging for a release. My strokes became faster and relentless. The tip of my shaft was hitting the deepest parts of her. Every second I was inside of her felt like I was unraveling. My thrusts got rougher, pushing the limits of my strength as I pounded into her.

My hands grabbed her tiny waist and clenched down. I was fucking her so hard; it felt like I was tearing her apart. Everything started to tighten as my orgasm rippled through me. I grunted and pulsed, feeling her clench around my shaft. It felt like she was going to squeeze the blood flow right from my cock.

I collapsed on top of her, my bones aching in the best possible way.

My eyes met hers, she held my stare for a moment. I could practically feel every emotion and hear every unspoken thought. That's how connected we were.

No memory I had could ever compare to the real thing.

Her head fell back, revealing red cheeks and swollen lips. My eyes traveled down to her breast, noticing the bruises and bite marks I left. She was going to have my balls when she saw the hickeys on her neck.

We laid there for a few minutes trying to catch our breath. She threw her hand over her eyes and sighed. "God, I'm so easy. I can't believe I caved that quickly."

I chuckled, shifting to my side and slowly pulled out of her. "You put up a good fight."

We both knew that was bullshit because she never stood a chance.

Her eyes rolled into the back of her head. "I appreciate you trying to make me feel better about my moment of weakness."

I brought my free hand up to her face and trailed my finger along her cheek. "You won't hear me complain."

She moved to sit up a bit, bringing her tits up to my face without meaning to. I took advantage and swirled my tongue around each one.

"Stop that." She laughed, trying to wiggle away from me.

I positioned myself on the side and propped my face in my hand. "I'm insatiable when it comes to you."

She blinked at me. "I forgot how good it is between us. It was never like that with…"

I put my palm over her mouth. "Do not finish that sentence. I do not want his name brought up while my dick is still wet from being inside you."

She threw her head back. "God, you're so crude."

"No." I glared at her. "I'm serious."

She cleared her throat. "We're going to have to talk about him eventually."

I reached out and brushed a wayward strand of hair from her face. "I know, but can we wait until tomorrow? I just want tonight to be about us."

She ran her hands down my chest, her eyes were growing misty again. "What happened to us?"

The sadness in her voice pulled at my heartstrings.

"I fucked up, big-time, and I've regretted it every moment since."

She sighed and buried her face in the curve of my neck. "You're here now. That's all that matters."

I kissed the top of her head. "That's right, sweetheart. And I'm here to stay now," I promised.

ELEVEN

CHARLOTTE

The law office of Daniel & Smith was easy enough to find in downtown Philly. I stepped off the elevator, entering on the eleventh floor and told the receptionist with white hair who I was looking for. She barely looked up at me from her computer monitor when she pointed down the hall and said, "Conference room on your right."

I started in the direction where she had told me to go when she grumbled, "Never mind, I guess I'll show you." She slid out of her chair and rounded the desk. She seemed about as friendly as a porcupine as I attempted to make small talk with her as we walked down the long hallway.

Swallowing hard, I stared at all the desks littered with folders and law books as interns and paralegals buried their heads in paperwork. I pulled on the sleeves of my white top when we reached the conference room where I would meet with my divorce attorney, Jason Daniel.

Thankfully, a few of Grant's colleagues and I were on friendly enough terms where they recommended a few divorce attorneys that they thought would be a good fit. My situation was complex and finding the right person wouldn't be easy. The publicity around my husband wasn't good, and the local news was still reporting details about him on a daily basis. Basically, I didn't know what to expect, but I was preparing myself for the worst and hoping for the best.

Day by day. That's all I could do.

Mr. Daniel's receptionist tapped on the door to announce that I had arrived. I didn't know what I expected, but it wasn't this. Mr. Daniel was much younger than I had pictured. He looked to be close to my age with a warm smile and a small build. Calling him short would be an understatement of his five-foot-two frame.

"Mrs. Anderson." He rose from the chair and walked around the long conference table to meet me. The wood was dark, and it was everywhere. From the tables, paneled walls, built-in bookcases to the credenza in the corner. The smell of leather-backed chairs and desk blotters tickled my nose as I adjusted to the room. The long-paned windows were draped with red floor-length curtains, and books filled every available inch of space on the shelves.

"Mr. Daniel." I accepted his hand in greeting. "It's so nice to meet you."

"Please take a seat." He gestured to the chair in the middle of the table. "This is my paralegal, Mary."

Mary waved from across the table while she sipped her tall Starbucks coffee. She was a middle-aged woman with bleached blonde hair, who looked like she spent all of her free time in a tanning bed.

"Would you care for something to drink?" he asked on his way to the cart set up along the window, holding an array of refreshments.

I sat in the chair and folded my hands in my lap. "No, thank you."

He nodded, poured himself a water and took a seat at the head of the table.

"I reviewed your case thoroughly." He opened up a file and glanced up. "I'm fairly confident we can start the proceedings without the consent of your husband. In most cases, the spouse would need to be served with divorce papers. But there are circumstances where you can file on your own. With your current situation as it is you definitely fall into that category."

This all seemed too good to be true. I licked my dry lips and asked, "How long does that take?'

Mary chimed in, "Typically it takes up to six months for everything to be finalized."

I let out a breath. I could be free in six months. I wanted to cry. I stared out the windows and studied the view while the two of them got all the paperwork ready to go over with me. The downside to all this was that if Grant were to be found before the divorce was granted, we might have to start the whole process over again. He could fight me and drag this out as long as possible. The fact that he was still out there somewhere unknown made it hard for me to hope for anything.

Mr. Daniel leaned across the table. "We will get you through this, Mrs. Anderson. It's going to take a little bit of time, but no matter what, you'll be a free woman in six months. I'll make sure of it."

I crossed my legs and tried not to get too excited. "What if Grant is found before then and tries to stop the divorce?"

These past few weeks had been filled with endless stress, resentment, and constant worrying. Sometimes it felt like the universe was giving me the middle finger, but I'd like to think that my luck was changing. It had to, right?

"I'm not going to lie." He folded his hands in front of him and stared me in the eyes. "There will be issues, but in my opinion, your husband won't have a leg to stand on."

"Thank you," I said with a shaky voice. There was a reason why this man had such an amazing reputation. I wasn't sure how he was going to deliver on his promise, but his confidence was growing on me. I was ready for this all to be over with.

He pushed paper after paper in front of me and told me to sign my name next to the little yellow sticky note attached at the bottom of each document. The tension in my shoulders lifted with each stroke of the pen. By the time I got around to signing my name on the last legal document, I was exhausted but filled with relief. This meeting went better than I expected. I knew the process wasn't going to be easy, but I somehow felt lighter walking out of that conference room.

I turned down the hall until I reached the two individual bathrooms. My bladder was protesting thanks to the two extra cups of coffee I had this morning. When I stepped inside, I felt someone behind me. I turned and gasped as Grant pushed his way in.

"Oh my God," I shrieked as he slammed the door and clicked the lock in place.

I concentrated on taking in deep breaths through my nose. My heart raced so fast I could feel the room spin. I didn't know what happened to him, but the man standing in front of me was not my husband.

There was definitely something wrong with him. My eyes scanned the small restroom looking for a way out. I was never afraid of him before, yet when I looked at his shaking hands and the dark circles around his eyes, my gut told me he was either on something or coming off his high.

"Grant." I was breathless and on the verge of yelling, but my voice was lost. Goose bumps prickled along my skin. The man that I married had never hurt me, but after these past few weeks, I wasn't sure what he was capable of.

"Jesus, Charlotte." An impatient sigh left his lips as he studied my reaction. "You're afraid of me now?"

He looked disheveled, like he hadn't slept in weeks. My eyes darted across the room, wondering how he got in here without anyone noticing. Curious as to why he would risk getting caught when he'd gone to so much trouble to stay hidden.

He crossed his arms in front of his chest and looked me over. His forehead creased in the middle as he stepped toward me. "Don't." I held up my hand trying to keep him at a distance.

Sweat trickled down his eyebrow from under his UPenn baseball cap, he wiped it away with unsteady fingers. "Charlotte, you have no idea how sorry I am."

I ignored his apology and gripped the back of the sink. I glared intensely at him. He couldn't possibly be serious. "You don't deserve to still be able to walk this planet after what you've done." I looked him straight in the eyes and continued with a strength I didn't know I had. "You left those people for dead. Do you have any idea the amount of pain you have caused? What you've put your family through?"

"I had no choice." He removed his cap and grasped his hair, tugging on the ends. "I panicked, and by the time I realized what I had done, it was too late."

My fist clenched at my side as I stared into his eyes, trying to see if he was telling the truth. "You panicked? You are a fucking prosecutor! You know more than anyone that excuse means nothing!"

"Charlotte, I've had to live with what I've done every damn day. Every day I've had to wake up alone, in a strange room, without my wife and daughter. Every night I go to bed and fight the sleep that my body needs, knowing the nightmares will take over my head once I close my eyes. I know you and Emery aren't there. I don't know what to do."

"You need to turn yourself in, Grant. That's what you need to do."

He shook his head. "I won't survive prison, Charlotte. You know that."

"So, what? You're just going to hide out until the police

find you, or whatever drug dealer you were dealing with finally catches up to you? Because mark my words, you will be found one way or another. Dead or alive."

He flinched even though he knew that was the truth. Seconds stretched into minutes as I watched the tension in his jaw become more pronounced. "I know one police officer in particular who would love to see me caught."

My back went straight, and I narrowed my eyes. "Excuse me?"

"I know that Quinn Walker has been playing fucking house with my family since I've been gone." His voice vibrated in anger across the small space. "Care to explain that one?"

His bitterness and callousness made me furious. I wasn't the one who up and ran like a fucking coward without a second thought about anybody but themselves. He was the one who left those people to die. It was him who was living a double life at the time, not me. Dealing drugs and having affairs on the side. And he had the nerve to judge me after everything that he's done.

"How dare you?" I folded my arms in front of me. His indifference had my stomach in knots. Did he even have any humanity left in him? "You left a clusterfuck behind. Quinn is there to protect me and Emery."

"I'm sure." He rolled his eyes and let out a disbelieving laugh. "I would never lay a finger on you and you know it. He would do anything to get back in your pants."

I narrowed my eyes. The implication was clear, and I wasn't going to address that comment with a response. Really, what would be the point? He had much more important things to deal with than Quinn fucking his old lady.

"Maybe you should be more concerned about the drug dealers you're running from, and what that could mean for me and your daughter."

He closed his eyes and swallowed hard. "I'm doing everything I can to make sure that nothing touches you and Emery. You have my word."

I shook my head in disgust. His word was about as useless as a politician's campaign promise. He had to understand that his word meant shit right now.

"Did you know that your new buddies left a present for me on our front porch?"

"I'm aware. The situation has been handled," he replied without even looking up from the floor.

I was so stunned, I almost couldn't speak. Anger swelled inside me. I narrowed my eyes, trying to figure him out. What I wouldn't give to get inside that twisted head of his.

"I don't even know what to say to you right now." I was at a loss for words on how to deal with him.

"I'm doing everything I can to make sure this shit doesn't touch you guys, okay? And I sure as hell don't need another man protecting what's mine," he snarled. "You and Emery are my responsibility to keep safe. Not fucking Quinn Walker's."

"What about your mistress? Are you protecting her too?" His eyes widened in surprise. "Did you think that I wouldn't find out about her?"

He was such an ass.

"She's nobody." He ran a hand over his jaw, leaned back and looked at the ceiling. "I swear. She means nothing."

I sighed, resisting the urge to throttle him. "That's supposed to make it acceptable? You are unbelievable." I squared my shoulders, willing my tears to stop, remembering all the times where I felt trapped in a loveless marriage.

He claimed to love me, but he didn't. He just wanted to prove to himself that he could have me. "You've been sleeping with the woman for months! All the while I begged you for a divorce. I told you repeatedly that I wanted out. You manipulated me into staying by using our daughter against me. Telling me we needed to stick it out for her sake. All for what? So you could have your sidepiece because I refused to sleep with you? I'm sorry that you don't have feelings for her." And I really was. In fact, I was hoping that he did because it would make my life a hell of a lot easier. "I'm done, Grant. I'm moving on and I don't want you to fight me on this and make things harder than they already are. Save your energy because you're going to need it."

His nostrils flared. "It's because of him, isn't it?"

"I don't want to talk about Quinn."

He leaned his hips against the counter and crossed his arms. "So, you're not denying it."

"I don't know what you want me to say, Grant. I would want this divorce whether I was with him or not. You're a wanted fugitive," I pointed out. "Your days of freedom are numbered. You have to understand that you are in a no-win situation here."

He froze as if my words struck a nerve. I wasn't trying to purposely hurt him, but he needed to understand that his actions had consequences. This was all on him. He's the one who made the decision to run. He is the one who set this train wreck in motion. He was a dead man walking. He had to know that. One way or another, his mistakes would catch up to him.

"I guess I never really stood a chance." The disdain dripped from his voice. "All I've ever done is fight for you, but you never fucking loved me. It didn't matter how much I gave you, all you ever did was want him."

I was seething in anger, because, of course, this was all about him and his feelings. I swear this man brought out the worst in me. "If you want to put the blame on me, fine. Blame me for our failed marriage, and I use that term loosely. Our marriage was a sham. We both know that we were simply roommates sharing space and raising a child. And you can deny it all you want, but I'm pretty sure the only reason you wouldn't give me a divorce was because you wanted to protect your precious image. And well…" I shrugged. "I guess we don't have to worry about that anymore, do we?"

He brushed an errant piece of hair off his face. I'd never seen him look so out of sorts before. "Charlotte, I was under a lot of stress. I fucked up. You and Emery were the only good things in my life. I wasn't giving that up, no matter how badly you wanted out. Shit was going down that you didn't know about. I made mistakes and they cost me more than you could ever imagine." He ran his hand through his hair and looked over his shoulders at the locked door. "Now I've lost my family, my career, my fucking freedom."

A tiny part of me felt sorry for him, and the other part despised him for destroying so many lives. I wanted to ask him what drove him to all this madness, but I knew he would only give me excuses, and nothing he said would make me understand anyway. He's told so many goddamned lies that I wasn't sure if he was even capable of telling the truth anymore. Would he even tell me where he's been all this time? Probably not, but I still had to ask because that question had crossed my mind more times than I could count.

I looked him over for any sign of physical injuries. Other than his unkempt appearance, he seemed fine. "Where have you been hiding? Who's been helping you?"

He nervously shifted his eyes away from me. "I can't tell you that."

My mind screamed at me to run. To get the hell away from him. Yet I couldn't seem to get myself to move. I was too angry and still needed answers even though I knew he wouldn't give them to me. "Are you going to turn yourself in?"

"I can't." His eyes dropped to the manila folder I had in my hands. "I'm also not signing anything until you let me see my daughter."

"You've got to be kidding me. You're going to use Emery

like she's some bargaining chip? She's not some pawn that you can sacrifice in order to get what you want."

He had a set of balls on him. I'd give him that.

"I want to see my daughter. I want to hold her in my arms instead of watching her from afar like a fucking stalker. Do you have any idea how hard it was for me? To watch you both laughing and having fun on that playground, living your life as if nothing has happened. Do you have any idea how badly I wanted to snatch her off of that swing set and take her away with me?"

I surged forward and pushed on his chest. My vision blurred and it felt like my heart was going to explode. "Don't you even think about taking her away from me you selfish bastard."

He grabbed on to my wrist and held me back with a bewildered expression on his face. "Relax. Just because I said I wanted to doesn't mean I would. I wouldn't do that to you."

My chest heaved up and down. A sense of loathing spread through me. I crossed my arms over my chest and pinned him with a death glare. "Don't ever threaten to take her from me again."

"You need to calm down," he said, staring at me as if I was the crazy one. "I'm not going to take her with me."

His words stalled in my brain. What the hell was he talking about? Take her with him? Oh my God. He really was messed up in the head. He had no intention of turning himself in.

How could someone as smart as Grant possibly think he could get away with this?

"Do you honestly think you can survive on the run forever? How will you live?" I folded my arms and glared at him. "Are you fucking crazy?"

He looked completely undone. It was hard to see a man who was usually so put together fall apart before your eyes. "I'm living in hell. My life is a fucking nightmare." He exhaled, clenching and unclenching his fists. "Things had been spiraling out of control for months. I keep getting dragged deeper and deeper into a life that I never wanted."

"That's no excuse," I shot back.

He looked at his feet, his voice was barely a whisper. "All I wanted was for you to love me. To be a good dad to Emery. For my parents to be proud of me. I failed at every turn. Nothing I did was ever good enough. Everything was a constant struggle. My job was the only place where I felt like I was in control. When that started to unravel, I started doing things that I'm not proud of. And at that point, I knew it was too late to turn things around."

I stared at him in disbelief. He had life so damned easy; he didn't know what real struggle was. Sure, he worked hard to prove himself, but opportunities that most people only dreamed of were always at the tip of his fingers, whenever he needed them.

"Don't turn yourself into a martyr, Grant. You need to get beyond yourself and think about what this is doing to Emery."

He slowly shook his head. "She's the only reason why I haven't ended it already."

A small part of me wanted to help him, but looking into his lost, helpless eyes, I saw a man backed into a corner with no way out. I couldn't help someone who wasn't willing to help themselves.

"So what, you're just going to keep running?"

"For as long as I can. Besides," he looked down at the floor, "it doesn't seem like I have much more here waiting for me."

Bile rose in the back of my throat. Every part of me silently begged him to come to his senses and turn himself in. The tears in my eyes pleaded with him to do the right thing. I couldn't let him keep running. My chest was tight because I knew what I had to do. I swallowed hard and tried to take hold of my emotions. With shaking hands and a heavy heart, my free hand slid into my purse. Grant's gaze followed. He closed his eyes and rushed to the door.

His face crumbled when I pulled my phone out to call 911. "Please tell Emery I love her."

And then he was gone.

TWELVE

QUINN

My frustration was evident as I hopped up and tried to smack the ball out of Brody's hand. His reach was longer, his jump was higher, and his body thicker. He thunderously dunked the ball and threw me a smirk that only riled me up even more. We've always been competitive, but basketball was my sport and football was his. I would not let him beat me. I didn't care that we were just horsing around, trying to burn off a few calories from the cheesesteak that we had at Jim's for lunch. Winning was what mattered. After all, I had a reputation to protect. I was the one who brought my high school team to the state championship during my senior year.

I ran down the court, spun around, and laid the ball up underneath as Brody tried to block my shot. The ball swished through the net as my brother jumped up to grab the rebound. On defense, I pressed him so hard he was unable to make his last three baskets.

Finally, he stopped running and threw his hands on his hips, trying to catch his breath. "All right, hotshot, I'm done."

I dribbled the ball between my legs, taunting him, because why the fuck not. "You owe me lunch on Friday."

He shook his head and walked over to his duffel bag.

"Yeah, well, you owe me a fucking bachelor party. My wedding is in a couple weeks."

I frowned, wiping the sweat from my face. "I told you I got it handled."

Brody passed me a water. "Yeah, you going to fill me in?"

I took a huge sip of my water, practically guzzling the whole bottle in one sip. "Sorry, dude."

The only thing he knew was that I had a block of rooms reserved at the Marriott Convention Center on Saturday night. He'd been kept in the dark about the weekend plans that included a nice meal at his favorite restaurant, a private room reserved at an upscale club, and an evening full of poker and cigars. Then to top the weekend off, I organized a tailgating party and a post-game pub crawl for the Eagles game that Sunday. Brody would go out in style.

He threw the bottle in his bag and zipped it up. "Did you figure out what you're going to do about Charlotte this weekend?"

I pulled my phone out of my bag and turned it on. My battery was running low when I got to the gym, so I was trying to save as much juice as I could. "Her friends are spending the weekend with her and Emery."

My phone turned on and I paused when I saw all the missed calls from Marco. It had only been a half hour since Brody and I had been horsing around. A knot formed in the pit of my stomach.

I swiped his name and hit send.

"Where the fuck are you, Quinn?"

My blood ran cold as I held my phone in a strong grip. "Brody and I are at the gym. What's going on?" I tried to keep my voice steady and ignored that crushing weight on my chest.

My brother looked over and raised his eyebrow.

"Grant approached Charlotte at her lawyer's office inside the girls' john."

I was already running out the door with my brother on my heels. "Is she okay?"

"She's a little shaken up, but otherwise okay. She just left, you might want to meet her at her place."

"Did you get him?"

"I wish. He was gone before she could even tell us he was there."

"Where the fuck is he now?"

"That's the million-dollar fucking question."

I slammed my hands on the steering wheel as soon as I slid into my car. "Find that fucker," I yelled into the phone.

My brother held my door open as I started my car. "What's going on?"

"Grant made his move on Charlotte. I gotta go."

His eyes widened. "I'll head to the station now and see what I can find out."

I nodded, slammed my door, and sped away like a bat out of hell.

The traffic on I-76 was a bitch (as always), and I couldn't catch a break to save my life. I somehow ended up behind every fucking Dudley Do-Right driver and caught every stoplight on my way to her house. I broke every traffic law imaginable, and by the time my truck made it to her driveway, I was ready to come unglued. Thank God she picked up the phone when I called and was able to fill me in on my drive over. Hearing her voice helped, but I needed to see her with my own eyes.

I sprinted into the house and found her sitting at the kitchen table. The second she saw me she rushed into my arms.

I reached out, touching the side of her face. "Are you okay?"

There were a whole lot of what-ifs flowing through my mind, drawing up every conceivable scenario. None of them amounted to anything good.

She leaned her cheek into my palm. "I am now."

I just wanted to close my eyes for a few minutes and wrap her up in my arms, be her anchor in the storm. The overwhelming need to protect her was stronger than anything I ever felt before. I wiped a tear falling down her cheek. "I never should have let you go there by yourself."

She placed her hand on my shoulder. "Quinn, he would never hurt me."

I looked at her as if she had lost her mind. Didn't she understand how ridiculous that statement was? "You don't know that. You told me yourself on the phone that he looked strung out on drugs. You have no idea what he's capable of."

"Yes, I do. I'm not going to fight you on this. I know my husband."

My eyes narrowed. "Oh, so now he's your husband?"

"Technically, yes, he still is."

"Only on paper," I shot back.

"At this point, I'm pretty sure that's the only place that matters."

I stumbled back, her words were soft but the impact was hard. She might have well sliced me open. I leaned my hip into the counter and tried to act like she wasn't grinding a knife through my heart. My anger was rising, and I knew I should just shut my mouth. My temper wasn't going to do me an ounce of good, but I was ready to lose my shit.

How the hell did we just go from her clinging to my arms to her wanting nothing to do with me?

I was seething. "Okay, Mrs. Anderson. Explain to me how this works going forward."

She squeezed her eyes shut and pulled in a deep breath. "What am I supposed to do? Tell me. You want me to pledge my loyalty to you? Want me to tell you that I hope he rots in hell? I can do that, but it won't change the fact that he's the father of my daughter."

I winced and turned my head away from her so she

wouldn't see the hurt in my eyes. "Why do you always feel the need to remind me of that? You don't think I understand he's Emery's father? That is no excuse for the shit he pulled today."

"I just need you to understand that it doesn't matter if he's sitting in a padded cell in Philadelphia, or sipping tequila under a palm tree in Mexico, we will always be connected somehow. This is my life now, Quinn."

She threw her hands up in her hair as I silently watched a single tear fall from her eye.

"I promised you I would keep you and Emery safe. I know today messed with your head, but you don't have to go through this alone."

Charlotte has always been stubborn and strong-willed. It was one of the things I always loved about her. But she needed to understand that there wasn't a chance in hell of me backing away. She could try her best, but I wasn't going anywhere.

"I appreciate all you've done for me. I'm very lucky—"

I cut her off. My pride was taking a huge hit. I could not let her continue. My sanity was at stake. "I don't want your fucking gratitude."

"I know." She sighed. "Today was hard for me. I just need some time to process all of this."

I didn't know what was going on in her head. Things were perfect when I said goodbye to her this morning. These past few days had been the best I'd had in a long time. I had no idea what Grant really said to her, but it felt like whatever it was, it was going to set us back a bit.

My arms itched to reach out to her and shake some sense into her. I didn't want to go backward, not after all the progress we made.

My gut told me to keep my mouth shut and just give her some space. But I felt threatened, and I needed to know where we stood.

"Have your feelings about us changed?" I asked with a calmness I was far from feeling.

"Quinn, I love you. That hasn't changed. But how can I even think about a future with you while I'm still married to another man?" Her words gave me comfort and tore me apart at the same time. "These past few weeks have been difficult for both of us. Maybe we should press the brakes for a little bit and take some time to let all this drama play its way out."

Her words threw me. What in the fucking hell was she talking about? It felt like our relationship was deteriorating right before my eyes.

I clenched my fist at my sides. "I know things are complicated, and I know this isn't an easy situation for anybody. But I'm trying here. Really trying. I'm trying to be the better man here, Charlotte. For you and Emery. I'm trying my best to take care of you. Don't shut me out. Not after you finally let me back in."

"I'm not shutting you out." Her tear-filled eyes held mine. "I feel guilty. I feel confused. I feel like I need to stand on my own two feet before I can move forward with you."

I haven't been able to bring myself to admit that maybe Grant was a bigger obstacle than I had originally thought. I knew she loved me. There was no doubt. But as long as he was out there, she wasn't going to be able to move forward with me. She needed closure and until he was caught, he would always be in the way. I didn't want to push her too hard, but the fear of losing her again was too much to comprehend. Walking away from her was the last thing I wanted to do, but maybe it was time to do what was best for her and put my own personal feelings aside.

Giving her what she wanted as opposed to what she needed was one of the hardest things she could ever ask of me. My fucking heart felt like it had been yanked out of my chest.

I snatched my keys off the counter and started to race out of the room.

Her eyes widened in panic. "Quinn, wait." Her arm rushed out to grab onto mine, but I pulled it out of her grasp and walked right past her. I went straight to my duffel bag that was sitting on the living room floor. All I could think about was getting the hell away from her.

The television was on and I quickly grabbed the remote when I saw the news report. I turned the volume up so I could listen.

The US Marshals Office has just released an updated photo of local District Attorney Grant Anderson who is wanted for the vehicular deaths of the young family from Upper Marion County that were killed on the night of August 30th when they were struck by Anderson's SUV. The photo today was taken outside of the law offices of Daniel and Smith. US Marshals believe he made his getaway in an unmarked 2018 Black Lexus Rx 350. Investigators said that Anderson has been on the run since the deadly crash. Investigators don't believe he is armed but encourage anyone with information to reach out to the US Marshals Office or the Philadelphia Police Department.

Charlotte was bunched over, staring at the TV as the news reporter switched to the local weather.

I grabbed my duffel off the floor and studied her face. Words could not express how much this was tearing me apart, how much I hated every second of this. The pleading look in her eyes did nothing to quench the frustration coursing through my veins.

After a few tense moments ticked by, it was obvious that her mind was made up.

My free hand reached for the door and I did everything I could to hold in what I really wanted to say. Because believe me, I had a lot to fucking say.

She looked down at her feet and wiped her hands across her cheeks that were soaked with moisture.

I swallowed hard and shook my head. "I need to stop by my apartment and grab a few things before I head back to work. I'll be back later. Don't wait up."

I didn't give her the chance to respond; I shut the door and made my way down to my truck. As I got on the highway, I cursed myself for believing that things were good between us and that we had finally moved past our issues. One little visit from Grant changed everything.

I was in a foul mood when I got back to the precinct. Every little noise or question set me off even more. Just thinking about the two of them alone in that fucking bathroom had me wanting to throw my fist up against the wall. I swear when that motherfucker was found I was going to tear him apart limb by limb.

My phone chirped with a text from my brother asking for an update. I slammed my phone down on my desk, feeling too irritated to respond. I made my way over to the break room to pour myself a shitty cup of coffee.

Marco stepped in and came right for me. I turned around, gripping the cup in my hands. "I hope you're here to tell me he's downstairs in lockup."

I was pretty sure I sounded like an asshole, but I could have given zero fucks at the moment.

"This is a shitshow," he admitted, knowing damn well that Grant Anderson was making a mockery of the police department. "Captain is breathing down my ass. The Feds are poking their nose in my business and I don't like it. I want this asshole behind bars. I promise you, I'm going to end this shit soon."

I scooted back in my chair and brought my hands to the back of my neck. "Someone is helping that fucker, and I would sell my left kidney to know who it was."

Marco combed his fingers through his hair. "Agreed. Which is all the more reason why you staying with Charlotte is a good thing. I know she wants to stay under the delusion that Grant is just some lost soul who made a bad mistake. But this is something else. I can feel it in my gut."

He had no idea how true that statement was.

"You need to find out who owns that Lexus that he got away in. I don't give a fuck how much red tape you have to cut through, just do it. If there is shit you're not comfortable doing, let me know. I have no problem getting my hands dirty on this one."

"You my boss now? Did someone promote you and forget to send me the memo?"

"No. I'm just a man who is trying to take care of the people I care about."

Marco whistled and rocked back and forth on his heels. "I know you want his ass locked up. Just don't go jumping the gun in search of answers when you're this angry. You need to think about the repercussions. We will find him. Focus on taking care of your girl."

"I'm not really sure she's even my girl right now," I blurted out.

I hated how we left things earlier. There was nothing worse than feeling like you were on rocky ground, knowing it could crumble at your feet at any minute.

Now that I've had time to cool down, I probably could have handled things better. But I wasn't thinking straight, and as usual, my anger got the best of me. I wanted her to feel the same amount of hurt and pain that I felt.

"Don't be stupid." He glanced at the clock on the wall. "I gotta head back and comb through those files. I promise you, between the Marshals and the Feds, we'll get his ass."

He slapped me on the back, turned, and walked away.

I forced my thoughts aside and concentrated on doing my job. I had a murder case that was coming up to trial. I needed to spend the rest of my day going through my notes. Then I had to go out in the field and gather more evidence into a missing person's case that had captured national attention. Speaking of which, my phone dinged with a text message.

Bree's name lit up the screen.

I'm going to be in Philly later tonight doing a piece on the Goodman case. Any chance we can get together? Maybe grab dinner or a drink? I have a few things of yours that I'd like to return.

I stared at the message, debating on how to respond. Would Charlotte even care? She said she wanted space, well, she was going to get her space.

I quickly tapped out my reply.

Sure, I can meet for a quick bite to eat. Where do you want to meet?

I set my phone down and booted up my computer so I could log into my Word document.

I'll text you which hotel I'm staying at as soon as I book it.

I stared at the message, my thumb hovered over the send button before I clicked on it.

Sounds good.

THIRTEEN
CHARLOTTE

"CAN YOU PLEASE STOP PACING? YOU'RE MAKING ME DIZZY," Mackenzie said as I continued to walk in circles across my living room.

I turned and glared at her. "I think I really fucked up."

When I received the text from Quinn telling me he was going to be late getting home, and that he was sending Mackenzie over to sit with me until he got here, I assumed it was because of work.

Imagine how stupid I felt when he told me he was meeting Bree for dinner. At her hotel! Bree, his ex-girlfriend. Bree, the one who looked like a blonde Barbie doll.

I didn't even know what to say, so I said nothing. I've checked my phone all night, stared at the clock, and prayed that he would actually walk through my front door tonight.

What if I pushed him too far? God, I was so stupid sometimes.

"Charlotte, you need to stop getting yourself so worked up."

I sighed and flopped down on the couch next to her. "I just got him back after all this time. If I lose him over this, it's my own damn fault."

She casually sipped her wine, like she didn't have a care in the world. "It's been an emotional day." She set her wineglass down and reached for my hand. "Just calm down and take a deep breath. You've been through more than most people could ever comprehend. Was your reaction perfect?" She paused, picked her wine back up and brought it to her mouth. "No, it wasn't. You're allowed to have bad days. You're allowed to make mistakes. Quinn knows how you feel about him. I'm sure he probably just needed time to cool off. You guys will get through this."

I prayed that what she was saying was true. I just wish he wasn't with *her*.

We haven't spoken since he left here earlier today. He was so angry with me, but more importantly, I hurt him. I was pissed at myself for letting Grant slide under my skin so easily. For making me feel weak and questioning my loyalties.

The second Quinn walked out the door, I knew I had made a mistake.

"Why don't you call him or text him?" She gestured to my phone that was sitting on the table.

My leg was bouncing with nerves as I picked up the phone and sent him a text. Thirty minutes went by, and I still hadn't heard from him.

Mackenzie gave me a weak smile and poured me a glass of wine. It felt like my life was unraveling right before my eyes. The situation with Grant was already stressing me out, and I hadn't realized how much it was impacting my relationship with Quinn until now.

He wasn't even back in my life for a hot second and I had already pushed him away. Quite possibly into the arms of another woman.

Another hour went by, maybe more. I lost count.

There was a commotion outside my front door. I thought I was prepared for this, but I was wrong. Guilt and a mixture of nervous energy formed in my gut. I paused the TV and opened the door.

I wasn't prepared for the sight in front of me. My eyes slid from the intoxicated man who had stormed out of my house earlier to the familiar giant in the red plaid shirt, who was trying to fit them both through my doorway.

Brody had his hand hooked around Quinn's waist, his head struck the doorjamb as they stumbled into the living room. "Watch my fucking head," Quinn mumbled.

I rushed over to help Brody keep him steady. I placed a hand on Quinn's back and wrapped the other around his middle.

I was thankful that Brody was on the other side, considering he was a heavy son of a bitch. There was no way I would have been able to handle him on my own.

Quinn rolled his head to the side and squinted his bloodshot eyes at me. "You don't look happy to see me," he slurred. "Were you expecting someone else? Like your husband maybe?"

Brody slapped him on the stomach with his free hand. "Don't be an asshole, Quinn."

"You're drunk?" I asked the obvious.

He stumbled, almost sending me crashing to the floor with him. Brody's grip was strong enough to pull us both back. "I needed to forget about our problems for a few hours. What can I say, you drove me to drink."

I tried not to let his comment get to me, but it was hard. What hurt the most was thinking of him and Bree together. They obviously did more than just share a meal tonight. He was with her for hours doing God knows what. I could practically smell her perfume on his clothes.

There wasn't anything I wouldn't do for Quinn, but if I found out they did more than just talk tonight, I might end up sharing a cell with my estranged husband.

The three of us moved up the stairs, while I held Quinn

close to my side. Mackenzie started to clean up the living room while I directed Brody to my room and helped him plop Quinn down onto my bed.

"Jesus. I haven't seen him this trashed in a long time," Brody grumbled as he ran his hand over his jaw. His long fingers scratched the stubble of his well-trimmed beard.

It's been years since I've seen Quinn's brother. He was always big, thanks to the many years of playing football. But the man standing in front of me looked like he had muscles on top of muscles.

Brody and Quinn had many similarities, but their distinct differences set them apart. They had the same color eyes, except Brody's were kind and expressive, where Quinn's were dark and intense. Brody looked more rugged, unlike his brother who was more masculine. Everything else about the two of them; their lips, noses, and chiseled features were exactly the same.

He smiled when he caught me staring.

"Thanks for driving him and getting him home safe."

His eyes softened with sympathy and understanding. "It's good to see you. Sorry it's not under better circumstances." He paused and looked over to his bother. "I know you guys hit a rough patch today."

"Yeah, although it ended up being a lot bumpier than I had thought. He ran to his ex-girlfriend after our first fight. I think that says it all."

He stood taller, seeming more authoritative. "I wouldn't be so quick to judge. Please be understanding. You guys haven't had an easy journey. It would be a shame to let Grant and a simple misunderstanding come between you guys. Especially with all the progress you've made."

My shoulders drew back. I couldn't help feeling defensive from his comment. "It's not like that. My marriage is over, it has been for a while."

"I know things are messy right now, but you hurt him

today. Believe me, I know he can be a pain in the ass at times, but if you're not ready to move on then you need to be honest with him."

I nodded my head and looked over at Quinn. I really didn't want to talk about this, but Brody needed to understand what was at stake. "You've got it all wrong. Quinn's the one I never moved on from."

He blinked slowly and shook his head. "I really hope you two figure your shit out," he said and started to walk away. "I'll leave my cell number with your friend. Call me if you need me."

His heavy boots thudded down the stairs. That was an awkward reunion. It shouldn't have surprised me that Brody had his brother's back. After all, I was just the ex with all the baggage.

I turned and stood in the doorway of my bedroom. Quinn was sprawled out on my white comforter. His one arm rested over his eyes as his other arm hung at his side. I walked over and untied his shoes. He mumbled something but I couldn't make it out. Once I had the other shoe off, I started to pop the buttons of his shirt.

I felt pathetic as my eyes traced over his neck and face, looking for lipstick stains. *He wouldn't do that to me*, I thought while sliding his jeans off. Once I finally had finished undressing him, I walked over to the chair and grabbed a blanket and threw it over the top of him. I didn't even attempt to get him under the covers because I didn't want him to wake up. I flicked the dimmer switch on and quietly closed the door.

Mackenzie was folding a dishtowel when I made it back downstairs. "How's he doing?" she asked.

"He's out cold," I said and poured myself a glass of water from the sink.

"Do you want me to stay?"

"No, I'll be fine." I looked around the kitchen and noticed that she had picked up. "Thank you."

She squeezed my shoulder. "You're welcome. Are you sure you're going to be okay?"

I took a huge sip of the water and set the empty glass in the sink. I tilted my head back and stared up at the ceiling. "I just want a normal life," I admitted. "I hate this."

"Oh, sweetie." She came over and placed her arms around me. I buried my nose in her shirt, letting the events of the last twelve hours finally get to me.

I pulled back and grabbed a tissue off the counter. "I told him we needed to take a break." I sniffed. "He ran to Bree the second we had our first fight."

"You don't know all the facts. Don't go jumping to conclusions. He's upstairs in your bed, not hers."

I knew that should have brought me comfort, but how was I supposed to feel an ounce of peace when everything felt unsettled? How was I supposed to feel secure when the ground beneath me was constantly moving and shifting?

After she left, I shut off all the lights, activated the top-of-the-line security system that Quinn had installed, and made my way upstairs.

I checked on Emery like I always did and quietly shut her door. I was thankful that she was such a sound sleeper.

I walked into the bathroom and got ready for bed. After wiping my makeup off, I leaned my head against the wall and wondered what my life would have been like if we had stayed together. Would it have been as perfect as I imagined? Or have I just been fooling myself all along?

After changing into my pajamas, I hesitated at the foot of my bed and gazed down at Quinn who was snoring loudly. So much was happening and changing at once. In my heart, I had to believe that he came back to me for a reason. I had to have faith that we would get through this.

I slid under the comforter, angling my body away from his, and brought the sheets up to my chin.

As conflicted as I was, it felt nice having him here next to me. I still wasn't exactly sure what happened between him and Bree tonight, but he was here with me. That's all that should matter. So why was I focusing on their meeting up tonight? Why did the thought of the two of them together leave such a bitter taste in my mouth? He ended things with her. It was me he wanted. Me he loved.

He settled deeper into the mattress and I felt the gentle pressure of his hard length against me. My thighs were a quivering mess.

His hand slid underneath my shirt, and a large palm rested over my breast. I closed my eyes at the feeling of his hot breath on my neck.

"You feel so good," he murmured, shifting closer. His fingers kept pressing into my skin. This was reckless, so damn reckless. But whenever Quinn's hands were on me, I couldn't help but get turned on. "I need you, baby. Let me make you feel good."

He started to kiss the back of my neck, with his thumb grazing across my nipple. My body jumped and I turned my head. His eyes looked glossy in the soft glow of the light from my nightstand. I reached my hand out and stroked my thumb along his chin. As much as I wanted to feel close to him, my heart was too heavy. I needed to think with a clear head, and I knew if we had sex that all my thoughts would get muddled up again. We needed to talk before we moved forward.

"Go to sleep, Quinn. We'll talk in the morning."

I heard him grunt in disapproval and expected him to move away, but he stayed close and kept his hand right where it was. "I love you, Charlotte. I'm sorry it took me so long to find my way back to you." He nuzzled his face into my shoulder and pressed a kiss. "I'm never leaving you again. I'm so sorry about what happened with Bree tonight. The kiss didn't mean anything."

FOURTEEN
QUINN

MY HEAD WAS POUNDING AND I HAD TO FORCE MY EYELIDS TO open. Where the hell was I? I rolled over to the side feeling the plush down comforter underneath me. That's when I shot up and started rubbing my eyes.

The events of last night slowly came back to me. The last thing I remembered was going up to Bree's hotel room to get the box of stuff she had of mine, after drinking way too much at the bar downstairs. She basically threw herself in my arms and started crying after I told her how sorry I was for hurting her. I thought I was doing the right thing by giving her comfort. But then she leaned in to kiss me goodbye. Even though my brain was clogged from all the alcohol, her lips felt wrong and I pushed her away.

Damn it! I sat up in the bed and looked around. I let out a sigh of relief when I realized it was Charlotte's bedroom and not Bree's hotel room. I ran my hand through my hair and cursed myself for almost messing up big-time. Thank God I didn't actually do something stupid.

I swung my right leg over the side of the bed and started to stand up. Emery's teddy bear fell in front of my foot. I leaned on the edge of the mattress and rested my arms on my knees.

I can't believe I boozed it up with Bree knowing she still had feelings for me. Why the hell did I have to go and do something so stupid? I picked my phone off the nightstand and was thankful that Charlotte put it in the charger. There was a bottle of Tylenol and a glass of water sitting next to it.

I folded up the blanket and went downstairs to get my bag. I needed a shower and a change of clothes. Living out of a suitcase was getting old, but I was here and finally in her bed, so at least I had that.

As soon as my feet hit the bottom of the stairs, I wasn't expecting to see Emery sitting on the couch, eating a bowl of cereal while watching cartoons. I frowned, wondering if something was wrong.

"How come you're not at school?"

She looked up at me and smiled. "I have a doctor's appointment today. I'm going to school when I'm done."

I swallowed hard and slipped my hands in the front pockets of my jeans. She just caught me coming down the stairs from her mother's bedroom. Charlotte was going to have my ass. She had rules in place, and I had crossed a line.

"Is your tummy feeling better?" she asked, swallowing a bite of her Lucky Charms.

"What do you mean?"

"My mommy said she let you sleep in her room because you had a stomachache. She lets me sleep with her when I don't feel good too."

"Yeah." I ran my hands through my hair. "I'm feeling better, Peanut."

"Mr. Bear probably worked. He always makes me feel better. You can keep him for a while if you want."

That explained why I had a stuffed bear laying on my chest when I woke up.

"Thanks. I appreciate that. Where is your mom?"

"She's in the kitchen."

"I'm going to get a drink. I'll be back in a few minutes."

I walked into the kitchen and stopped dead in my tracks. Charlotte was bent over the dishwasher, her perfectly round ass was a sight for my sore eyes. Her long dark hair was hanging over her back like a silk curtain. She was already showered and dressed. If you considered that short, black skirt she was wearing clothing. It was showing more skin than I was comfortable with.

I stood there and watched her like a stalker. I took a deep breath when she turned to face me.

"You're awake," she said in a cool tone and pushed the dishwasher tray in and shut the door. "I was hoping we would be gone by the time you woke up."

My body leaned against the wall and my eyes begged her to look at me. She acted like she could barely stand to be in the same room as me.

"Charlotte. We need to talk about yesterday."

She spun around and kept her gaze over my shoulder. I kept telling myself to calm down and let this conversation play out. But she couldn't even fucking look at me. "Not now," she snapped. "I need to get Emery to her appointment and then I have to run a few errands."

I touched my jaw and searched for the right words. I felt pathetic because all I wanted to do was pull her into my arms and beg her to let this shit go. But fighting is what Charlotte and I did. We fought hard and loved harder. We always had. It was the dynamic of our relationship.

I loved this woman with every ounce of my being. And while things seemed to always get heated between us, I would rather freeze to death than lose that fiery passion that made me feel alive. Loving Charlotte was never boring and I wouldn't have it any other way.

"Can we meet for lunch today to talk?"

"I'm busy."

I pulled on the back of my neck. "Are you going to give me a chance to explain?"

She moved over to the coffee maker and filled up her to-go mug. Once she was done adding the cream and sugar, she popped the lid on and finally turned to face me. "Yesterday was an emotional day for both of us," she reminded me. "I have a lot to do today. So to answer your question, we're not going to talk about this right now."

I raised my eyebrow and grabbed her arm as she tried to pass by me. "Don't do this. Please."

She jerked her body out of my hold. "Maybe Bree can meet you for lunch."

That was a cheap shot, but I deserved it. "You have no reason to be jealous."

"Why? Because the kiss meant nothing?"

"What?"

"Those were your words last night. Before you passed out. You said you were sorry and that the kiss with Bree meant nothing."

I started to curse, but Emery came cruising into the kitchen, stuffing papers into her backpack. "I'm ready to go."

Charlotte reached over and grabbed her purse off the counter. My gut churned replaying the foggy scene in my head. She really was walking away without letting me explain. Now I had to spend the rest of my day worrying about how bad I fucked up.

I clenched my fists at my sides. "Charlotte, can I speak with you for a moment, please?"

It was a struggle to even talk, but I did my best to keep the edge out of my voice. I was so angry. Not at her but at the situation. Plus, Emery was standing right there which meant I needed to keep things calm.

"Sorry," she said, not sounding sorry one bit. "I'm running behind." She threw her purse over her shoulder and guided Emery out of the kitchen.

"Bye, Quinn," Emery said as her mother ushered her out the door so fast you would have thought the fire alarm was going off.

After taking a quick shower, I got dressed, grabbed a pack of muffins that Emery liked to pack in her lunch and stormed outside.

I walked out to my car, slammed the door, held my finger over the ignition button, and tried not to think about her giving me the cold shoulder. I pulled my phone out and shot a quick text to my brother, thanking him for dropping off my vehicle this morning. Instead of starting the car, I just sat there. My eyes slid shut and my forehead hit the steering wheel. It wasn't even eight thirty in the morning yet and my day was already turning to shit.

Somehow, I managed to make it through most of my day and kept busy in the field doing my job. I made a point to stay away from my desk because I didn't trust myself to not blow up Charlotte's phone with messages. Although, I did receive one from her telling me she was taking Emery shopping for school clothes and they would eat at the mall. I texted her back and asked if I could join them for dinner. She never responded, so I figured I was on my own.

Now here I was sitting quietly in the far corner of Lolita's, a little upscale Mexican restaurant on Thirteenth Street, with my brother.

"So, I'm a little curious," he said, popping a tortilla chip in his mouth. "How did it go this morning?"

I swallowed a sip of my Diet Coke. My stomach twisted uncomfortably as I slid the bowl of guacamole toward him. "Not good, bro."

"I'm not surprised." Brody glanced over my shoulder as the waitress set our plates down in front of us. "Things were pretty weird last night."

I leaned back in my chair as my hands fell in my lap. "Things have been weird since I've been back." I swirled my straw around in my glass. "But even so, I'm thankful for this second chance because I regret leaving her all those years ago."

He took a bite of his burrito and tilted his head sideways. "I know you do." He set his food down. "But that's in the past. You can't go back and rewrite history. It's obvious that you never stopped loving her. Which brings me to my next question. What the fuck were you doing with Bree last night?" he asked pointedly.

"I was so fucking angry," I admitted. "I wanted to hurt her. I know it's fucked up, but when she told me she wanted to slow things down, it set me off." I shook my head and sighed. "When Bree called and asked if we could meet up, I figured why the fuck not. I wasn't in a hurry to go back to Charlotte's house just to hear all the reasons why she didn't want to be with me."

"So, you thought meeting your ex at her hotel was a good idea? The same ex that's still crazy about you?" he asked, and I didn't say a word because he had me there. It was a dumb, stupid decision. I should have known better. In my defense, it wasn't like I planned on getting hammered, and I certainly didn't expect her to try to kiss me.

"I guess the one thing we know for sure is that I'm pretty good at fucking up a good thing."

"You need to stop this shit and figure out what it is you want. I know you want Charlotte back, but the fact is she is married with a kid, and things are complicated enough at the moment." He paused and I wanted to punch that smug look off his face. Even though he wasn't telling me something Charlotte didn't keep reminding of. "I can only imagine how frustrating this entire situation is. I'm not saying all this to bring you down, but you can't pretend that Grant doesn't exist or just wish him away."

"Are you fucking serious right now!" If anyone knew how to hit a nerve it was my brother. "Forget him? Did you forget why I'm even here? Why I'm staying at her house? Why I took a leave from my security job?"

When all this shit started brewing, I took a personal leave from the part-time job I had at the security firm so I could focus all my time on Charlotte and Emery. Something needed to give, and they were very accommodating.

"Then fight for her, you thickheaded bastard, but you're going to have to learn to be patient."

"What if that's not enough?" I didn't want to admit my biggest fear. That maybe things wouldn't play out like I had planned. That maybe the gap between us was too wide to bridge.

"Then let her go."

My heart cracked wide open at that possibility.

———

Charlotte and Emery were sitting at the kitchen table doing arts and crafts when I walked in. Her eyes were cast down, helping Emery stuff popcorn into clear shaped gloves.

"Hi, Quinn. Do you want to help us make popcorn hands?" Emery's eyes shifted back and forth between me and the project they were working on.

"Are those for your Halloween party at school tomorrow?" I asked, stepping closer and taking a peek at what they were working on over her shoulder.

"Yep. They're called popcorn hands. We're almost done, but you can help us finish if you want."

"I'd be happy to."

Emery giggled at my sloppy attempts to slide the candy corn into the tips of the gloves. Apparently, they were supposed to be the fingernails. Arts and crafts were not my strong suit. "Damn it," I said after my third failed try.

Emery poked her hand in my shoulder. "You said a bad word. You have to put a dollar in the swear jar."

"What?" I looked up confused. "That's not a swear word."

"Well, it's not a nice one either," she pointed out.

"Well, shit." I sighed, pulling my wallet out of my back pocket.

Emery held her hand out with a smirk. "That will be two dollars please."

I slapped the two singles into her waiting palm and watched her walk away to add my hard-earned cash into a stupid jar. Considering she rode a school bus everyday, I would bet my state pension that she's heard much worse than that before.

Charlotte still refused to look at me as she stayed focused on her task. It felt like I couldn't do anything right where she was concerned. Yet, I still tried.

"What time is the Halloween parade at school tomorrow again?" I asked like I didn't remember, when I knew exactly when it was. This was called making small talk and it sucked.

"Two o'clock."

"Do you need help with anything?"

"Nope."

I scrubbed my hand down my face and willed myself not to snap at her. "I planned on taking a half day. I can swing by and pick you up when I'm done so we can ride over to the school together."

"Thanks for the offer, but I'm going over early."

She was being distant and cold, like she was when I showed up at her door weeks ago. I knew I made a mistake, but I was a grown-ass man and she was treating me like a five-year-old child. Her point was made loud and clear.

I swallowed and braced my hands on the edge of the table. "I guess that makes sense, if that's the real reason."

"Excuse me?"

I've gone out of my way to accommodate her. To be sensitive to her situation, and to hold myself together. But I couldn't bear this passive-aggressive bullshit any longer.

"Are you sure you're not trying to punish me for yesterday?"

She sighed and walked over to the sink, placing her back to me. She turned the water on and started to rinse off the dishes. I wanted her to talk to me and open up about what she was feeling. Anything other than the attitude she was giving me. I wanted nothing more than to apologize for yesterday, but she wasn't giving me the chance.

Emery threw the last bag of candy on the table. "I'm done. Can I please watch a movie before I go to bed?"

"Make it a short one. Let me just finish up with the dishes and save me a space on the couch," Charlotte said without even looking at her.

Emery turned around in her chair and tilted her head back to meet my eyes. Her tiny little dimples were on full display. At least somebody liked me. "Quinn, do you want to watch a movie with us?"

My face softened, and I found myself running my fingers through her messy curls. "I'd love too. Go get it set up, I'll be right behind you."

"Yay." She clapped excitedly and ran out of the room.

I rubbed the back of my neck while Charlotte scrubbed the dishes so hard, I thought they might crack.

"You know," I said, "if you don't want me to watch the movie with you guys, I can keep myself busy."

She slapped the rag down into the sink. "It's fine."

I grabbed a bottle of beer out of the fridge, needing something to take the edge off. Every muscle in my body was wound tight. I set the bottle down on the table and braced my hands on the granite counter next to her. "I know you're pissed, and this situation is fucked up, and I hate the fact that there is nothing I can say to make things right."

I couldn't go back and change the events that happened yesterday. All I wanted was to go back to the way things were before Grant fucking Anderson decided to show his face at the law firm. I didn't want her to have doubts about us, and I sure as hell didn't want to question where her head was at.

"You're right. I am pissed. You were in a vulnerable position last night." She turned to face me. "I'll own up to my part. I said some things that I shouldn't have said. Yesterday was a very emotional day. But Quinn," her shoulders dropped and she squeezed her eyes shut, "you went and sought out the company of another woman. And not just any woman, but someone who you've been intimate with."

"Nothing fucking happened."

"You kissed her!"

"She texted me and told me she had some of my things. Here," I pulled my phone out and shoved it at her, "read the text messages. I've got nothing to hide from you." I plowed my hand through my hair wishing I could just apologize and be done with it. "She leaned in and kissed me. I stopped it. Do you honestly believe that I would fool around with her after everything that's happened between us?"

"You hurt me."

I lifted her chin, forcing her to look at me. "You hurt me too."

I felt helpless and would have done anything to put an end to this shit. Beg, grovel, whatever it took. She had no reason to be jealous of another woman. As far as I was concerned, she was the only one that existed, at least in my world.

When she blinked up at me, I saw a sliver of remorse in her green eyes. "I'm sorry, but I need you to be patient with me. I'm worried about Emery and how this will all affect her."

My arms dropped to her waist. "I understand that, but you can't shut me out the second things get complicated. And speaking of Emery, I want to tell her about us. I'm sick of sneaking around and acting like I'm just your friend."

"Quinn." She shook her head. "No."

"When?" I pressed. Anxiety started to grow in my gut.

"I don't know. Let's find Grant first and get my divorced finalized and then go from there."

"That could take forever," I whined like a fucking teenage girl. She couldn't be serious. She was really going to erect another wall for me to climb?

She eyed me carefully. "You told me you would be patient."

This was wrong on so many levels. There was so much to say and I was struggling. "I don't understand. It's not like I'm some new guy that you can't trust enough to be around your daughter. You've known me for years. You were planning on marrying me," I reminded her.

"That's part of the problem. I was planning on spending the rest of my life with you and look how that turned out." She might as well have taken a sledgehammer to my chest. "Emery practically lost her father. Clearly, she's already getting attached to you. What if things don't work out between us again?"

So that's what she was afraid of? Me leaving her again?

I dragged her into my arms and pulled her against my chest. "I can't undo the past, but we've been given a second chance. Let's focus on that."

Tears sprung from her eyes. We didn't get here overnight. If I was going to convince her that I was willing to stick this out with her, I had one choice. Find a way to make it happen. I've wanted this woman for almost half of my life and there was no way I would fuck this up again.

FIFTEEN
CHARLOTTE

THE THREE OF US WERE ON MY SECTIONAL, CUDDLED UNDER A blanket watching the movie credits roll across the screen. Quinn played with my hair while Emery slept next to us. My eyelids were growing heavy and it was a fight just to keep my eyes open.

He yawned and stood up. "I'm going to carry her upstairs." I scooted back, too tired to move from the couch.

I brought the blanket up to my chin and watched him lift my daughter with ease. Her long unruly hair fell over his arm, as he cradled her carefully against his chest. She looked like she fit perfectly in his arms. Like this was how it was always meant to be.

A few seconds later, heavy footsteps descended back down the stairs. He took a hesitant step forward. "She was dead to the world."

I moved my feet to make room for him to slide in next to me. "She's not the only one. I'm exhausted too."

He sat down and rubbed his eyes with the heels of his hands. It was obvious that we both needed the rest and maybe a little bit of space. I pushed the blanket off my legs and stood up, mentally kicking myself for getting so comfortable.

As much as I didn't want to go upstairs to my bed, I knew that's what I needed to do.

"I better go upstairs."

Quinn backed himself up against the couch, bent his knees and propped his arms along his legs. "Are we okay, Charlotte?"

A knot formed in my stomach, as he watched me closely. It was hard to pretend that everything was fine when there was still so much tension between us. Sometimes, I wondered if we were fooling ourselves into thinking we could make things work this time around. If our love for each other was enough.

"I want things to be okay." He stayed silent and watched me carefully while visions of Bree kissing him were still stuck in my head. Just the thought of her hands and mouth on him had me wanting to break every little bone in her body. "I just hate second-guessing everything."

He closed his eyes and sighed. "I wish there was something I could say to make things better between us, but I know I can't. All I can say is, I'm sorry."

"I know. I hate this just as much as you do," I said sadly. "I'm going to bed."

I stood up to walk away, but he grabbed my wrist. "I'm really sorry about everything that happened yesterday."

I peeked at him over my shoulder and met his gaze. "I know. Me too."

As soon as I completed my slow climb to the top of the stairs, I rested my hand on the banister and wondered if I should just turn back around. Sleeping on the couch didn't sound like such a bad idea. But if I did go back downstairs, he would probably want to have a conversation, and I'm not sure I would be up for that.

I forced that thought out of my mind and opened the door

to Emery's bedroom instead. I smiled at her sleeping under a big pile of blankets. I quietly padded over and smoothed her hair off her forehead, letting my fingers linger for a few seconds. Just watching her sleep calmed me. If I did anything right in this life, it was her. She never looked more peaceful than she did at that moment, and it made me both happy and sad.

Her father was either going to get caught or killed, and there was nothing I could do to stop either of those things from happening. She was old enough where she would remember Grant, and I wasn't sure if that would end up being a good thing or a bad thing. I kissed her cheek and forced myself to go to my own room.

I was unable to fall asleep and ended up tossing and turning for the next hour, wishing Quinn were lying next to me. I buried my face in my pillow and then threw it on the floor. There was no way I was going to be able to close my eyes. Not when I needed him close.

I fumbled my way through the darkened house and quietly made my way downstairs. Quinn was sound asleep on his side, his long legs stretched out on my couch that was way too small for him. He had to be uncomfortable. He must have sensed my presence because he slowly turned and blinked his eyes open.

"What are you doing?" he asked, the sleep evident in his voice. "Is everything okay?"

Without saying another word, I took a couple hesitant steps toward him. I nervously played with end of my T-shirt. "Everything is fine. I just didn't want to sleep alone."

He held his arm out, dragged me tight against his chest and kissed the side of my head. "I love you, Charlotte. Get some sleep."

———

Everything was a rush the next morning. I had packed Emery's costume in a tote bag, laid out the snacks that we had made for her class and somehow managed to find time for a quick shower.

When it was time to leave, I felt like I was winning. Quinn was just buttoning up his burgundy dress shirt while I laid Emery's shoes out for her to put on when the doorbell rang.

We both shared a look. "Expecting someone?" he asked, tucking his button-up inside his dress slacks.

"No."

We both glanced at the clock and Quinn stepped to the door and peeked out. "You've got company," he said, swinging the door open.

My stomach took a nosedive when I realized it was my mother-in-law. She mentioned last week that she might stop by to drop a gift off for Emery. With everything going on, it completely slipped my mind.

"Laura, what a surprise," I said, taking a deep swallow.

She couldn't look any more caught off guard if she tried. "Good morning."

There was an awkward silence as she watched Quinn fasten his belt. The scowl on her face had me wishing I had more time to prepare for this visit.

This was bad. Very fucking bad.

Laura's heels clicked on my hardwood floor, and the familiar scent of her Chanel perfume lingered in the air as she entered the room.

Quinn swung the door closed behind her and stuffed his hands in his pockets.

Her nose crinkled up making my living room seem small and cramped. "I'm sorry, but who are you?"

This was inevitable. But still....

"Laura, this is Quinn Walker..." My voice wavered, unsure of how this introduction was going to go. What did I introduce him as? My ex-fiancé? My new boyfriend? After gathering my wits, I finally settled on, "My friend."

The death stare Quinn gave me said it all. He wasn't happy with my choice. Saying those words felt like a lie, but it wasn't like we had a label, even though we were much, much more than that.

She extended her hand that was dripping in gold and diamonds. "Hello, Mr. Walker. I'm Laura Anderson. Charlotte's mother-in-law."

The practiced smile on her face was one I knew well. It was the smile she saved for the reporters when she was on the campaign trail. The one she used when she mingled with the Washington elite. She was even dressed for show in her navy-blue dress and three-inch heels. Over the years, I've learned that despite her formal appearance, she would much rather be in jeans and sneakers than the silk Prada dresses that she wore in public. "Are you visiting from out of town?" she asked.

Quinn reached over, grabbed his badge off the end table and clipped it on his belt. "No, I live here in the Philadelphia area. I'm staying here with Charlotte and Emery while the investigation on your son is still pending."

My eyes narrowed, as I reminded myself to breathe. The walls felt like they were caving in on me. I loved Quinn, I did, but sometimes his direct approach was too much to take.

"Really?" Her face grew heated as she squared her shoulders. "And why is that?" I could almost hear the silent judgment in her tone and feel the hostility oozing off of her. I didn't want her to feel betrayed by Quinn's presence. I had nothing but respect for this woman and the last thing I wanted was to alienate her from my family.

I tugged on my hands, trying to come up with a way to make her understand and offer her an explanation. I also fought the need to ridicule Quinn in front of her for putting us both in this awkward position.

I begged him with my eyes to not fuel her assumptions and make things worse than they already were. He shook his head and seemed to measure his words as he spoke. "I just want to make sure Charlotte and Emery are both safe."

Laura blanched, her voice dropped low. "Surely, you don't believe my son is a danger to his family, do you?"

His jaw ticked as he answered. "I would hope not, but Grant's actions have been highly unpredictable, wouldn't you agree? Truth is, I'm more concerned about the company he's been keeping than Grant himself."

His steely eyes dared me to contradict him.

Emery came rushing into the room. "Grandma!" she squealed, breaking the growing tension in the room.

Laura's eyes softened as she dipped her head and planted a kiss on Emery's cheek. "Good morning, sweetie."

"Did you bring me a present?" my daughter asked, spying the bag she was holding in her hand.

I tilted my head to the side. "Emery, remember your manners, please."

Laura laughed and ran a hand over Emery's hair. "Of course, I did."

She handed her the orange and black gift bag with pumpkin-colored tissue paper popping out of the top. "I was going to stop by later when you were done with school, but there is a dinner I have to go to with your grandpa tonight. I wanted to make sure I saw you. I was hoping you would have had your costume on."

Emery crinkled her nose in annoyance. "My teacher said we can't change into our costumes until the parade later. She's afraid they'll get ruined." She looked down at the bag and asked me with pleading eyes. "Can I open it, Mom?"

"Sure." I smiled while watching her tear into the package with excitement.

She pulled out a book and held it up. "It's the Junie B. Jones Halloween book I wanted!" She handed it to me and reached back into the bag and pulled out a bag of black and orange M&M's and a Halloween craft project. "This is so awesome. Thank you, Grandma. I love it."

Laura kneeled down and gave Emery a hug. There was so much about her physically that reminded me of Grant. But there was nothing about their personality traits that was even close to comparison. Laura was kind and compassionate and hadn't grown up entitled like her son.

She came from a modest upbringing and ended up marrying into money, but she didn't marry John for his wealth. She married for love and gave up her dream of owning a farm in Vermont, where she grew up to stand by her husband's side so he could serve his country. She was a doting wife and a loving mother. She was also loyal to a fault, especially to her family. I'd never understood how a woman like Laura Anderson could have given birth to a man like my husband.

She reached out to brush a piece of hair from Emery's face. "You're so welcome."

Quinn's phone rang. He picked it up off the table, pressed it to his ear and walked out of the room to take the call. Laura looked like she had a million questions spinning in her head. She remained quiet while Emery chimed in about the busy day she was about to have.

Laura's smile was sad when Emery confessed that she wished her dad were here to take her trick-or-treating later. I was thankful that she left out the part where Quinn would be filling in tonight. Regardless of my feelings for Grant, knowing how dejected my daughter felt had my heart in tatters.

Slowly, I turned my face so she wouldn't see how upset I was. I tried to appear strong even though I felt powerless. It was such a shitty feeling knowing the level of hurt that Grant's actions would continue to bring her.

Laura glanced over at Quinn as he walked back into the

room. "Do you want me to drop her off at school for you on my way to work?"

"Shit," I blurted out and looked at the time. She missed the school bus.

Emery put her hands on her hips and grinned at me. She loved it when I slipped up and cursed. Amusement danced in her eyes. She just couldn't wait to say it. "You need to put a dollar in the swear jar."

Everyone in the room snickered, including me.

"Go grab a dollar out of my purse and grab your backpack while you're at it. I'll bring your costume and party treats when I come to school later."

Emery scurried out of the room as I gathered her stuff and handed it off to Quinn. "Thank you." I chewed on my bottom lip with my eyes silently pleading with him not to cause a scene in front of my mother-in-law. There was nothing more that I wanted than to kiss him goodbye, but I couldn't do that to Laura. At least not until I talked to her. I owed her that much.

He gave my hand a tender squeeze as I passed him Emery's backpack. Relief flooded me, and I was thankful that he understood.

After he and Emery said their goodbyes, I picked up a few toys that were laying around the house and fixed Laura a cup of coffee.

"Do you want to sit outside?"

She grabbed her cup and patted my arm. "I would love to, dear."

We sat on the two wooden rocking chairs and sipped our coffee, while the orange and red leaves swirled around the yard. Even though the sun was shining bright, the autumn air was nippy.

"I talked to Detective Rubin yesterday." Laura sighed, tightening the sweater around her shoulders. "He said there was no new information, but they were working on a few leads. I'm not sure if I should be relieved or upset."

I set my coffee down on the railing, trying to give her encouraging words. I was at a loss of what I could say to ease the hurt over the son that she still loved very much. "I completely understand. Although, as his wife, I'm at the point where I'm ready for a little bit of closure. I'm sure as a parent it's much different."

"I feel like I've failed him." She looked off into the distance. "I think he was so blinded by power and struggled so hard with his insecurities that something inside him broke. I'm not making excuses for him, but Grant was always meant to do great things, and now that's all gone. As his mother, I'll always love him, but I'll never be able to forgive him for what he has done."

Laura and I had become desperately close over these past few weeks. Relying on each other and making sure the other was okay. She needed me which meant I had to brush my own personal feelings about Grant aside. Bashing him to his mother wasn't going to help anyone.

"You are a wonderful mother, Laura. The blame is on Grant and no one else. I guess we all failed him in our own way. There are many times when I've thought, if I was a better wife, if I could have shown him more love, then maybe he wouldn't have turned to such a dark place."

She ran her hands through her hair. "I don't think any of us saw this coming." A faraway look crossed her face as she watched the UPS truck pull up to the curb across the street. The neighbor's dog started barking like crazy. We both winced at the endless high-pitched yelping coming from across the street.

"How are you doing? Honestly."

I pushed back against the rocking chair and brought my knees up to my chest. "I'm doing okay. My focus right now is on moving on and providing a safe and stable home for Emery."

"Does the gentleman from earlier have anything to do with you moving on?"

I wasn't going to lie to her, but I didn't want to rub it in her face either. I brought my cup up to my lips and blew into my hot coffee. "Do you remember when I told you that I was engaged once?"

She nodded as I dragged her through the events of the last few weeks. I told her how Quinn showed up on my doorstep unexpectedly and gave her the CliffsNotes of our past. She cringed when I told her about the note that Grant left on his windshield, and we both shook our heads in disgust at the mention of the dangerous people he was involved with. She covered her mouth and cried when I told her that I was going ahead with the divorce. Even though she knew it was coming, it still hit her hard.

She took a tissue from her purse and dabbed her eyes. She looked sad and it broke my heart to see her that way. "You have every right to be angry with my son. And you are entitled to move on. It's just hard to see someone else stepping into the role that Grant left behind. A role that should have been his, but I understand."

I wanted to contradict her and tell her that this role always felt like it belonged to Quinn. That Grant had stolen seven years from us. Even though Quinn was more to blame for our years apart than anyone. But this moment was about picking up the pieces and moving on. Starting fresh, even with the dark cloud hanging over our heads.

"Thank you." I reached for her hand, grateful that she was being so understanding. I didn't want her to think that I was rushing into things. "I loved your son, and I could never really hate him because he gave me Emery. But Quinn has always been the one for me," I admitted honestly.

"I believe everything happens for a reason. I don't know

what caused my son to sink into that downward spiral, I just hope someday he'll be able to find redemption and peace."

I averted my gaze and hoped that she was right. Though this wasn't an easy conversation, I was glad that we finally had it.

It's been roughly two months and Grant still hasn't been found. Eventually, he would get caught. When that time came, my only wish was that he would finally be able to own up to what he had done.

I gave her a smile filled with sympathy. "I'm so sorry, Laura. I hope so too."

SIXTEEN

QUINN

"This is bullshit. These cards blow worse than a hooker with braces," Enzo grumbled, slamming his cards down on the wooden poker table.

I could feel the bass of the music vibrating the hardwood floors underneath my feet. We were in the private room that I rented out over the dance floor at the Infusion Lounge. It was a hotspot in downtown Philadelphia that everyone wanted to go to. I got damn lucky that I had a personal connection who came through for me with a reservation on such short notice. The waitlist for this joint was over a year long.

"I think you should double up your bets, moneybags." I looked over to Chip Phillips, Brody's supervisor, as he scooped up his winnings into a mason jar, all while keeping his eye on the scantily clad hostess that just passed by. We had a group of girls that were assigned to our party. The ladies were dressed in tight black skirts that were short enough to cure the blind and keep the bar bill flowing. No doubt they were attractive and probably to most men enticing, but they did nothing for me.

"That's easy for you to say," Enzo shot back, keeping an

eye on his chips or what was left of them. "You're the fucker over there winning every hand."

"Easy, girls." I squinted over the bright neon lights flashing across the room. "Let's calm down and finish this game up. Stop acting like a bunch of pussies and start dealing."

"Fuck off, Quinn." Enzo chuckled, and they all started ribbing each other relentlessly. Their little comedy hour had been going on all night. Normally, I would be laughing along with everyone else, but I was grumpy as hell with everything going on and the lack of sleep I'd been getting.

"You okay over there, little brother?" Brody asked over the rim of his glass. This was his special night and every time he'd ask me that I'd feel guilty.

I rolled my shoulders back and took a sip of my drink, trying to hide how tired I was. I was happy for my brother and the last thing I wanted to do was mess this night up for him. "I'm good. Just tired."

He eyed me skeptically. "You sure?"

"I saw a couple of empty couches in the other room if you guys need to have a shrink session." Chip snickered along with the rest of the table.

I closed my eyes and wondered why the hell I willingly arranged to hang out with a bunch of assholes when I could be home with Charlotte. I looked across the table, feeling sorry for their wives, and understanding why the other ones were still single.

This next move was going to bring me great pleasure. I hid my smirk as I laid my cards flat down in dramatic fashion.

"Fuck!" they all shouted at the same time. "A full house."

"Sorry, ladies," I gloated as I moved the pot in front of me. Winning that hand felt good and served those fuckers right for getting on my nerves.

We played a couple more hands of Texas Hold'Em before

moving back out to the bar area. Although I didn't win big, I won enough to take Charlotte out for a nice meal.

Chip slid into the barstool next to me while the other guys sat at the table I had reserved with a full bottle package. We were waiting on the rest of our group.

His hands gripped the edge of his crystal tumbler as he leaned in. "I talked to Marco the other day. That's some fucked-up shit he found out this week."

My head moved to face him, ignoring the raucous laughter booming from the table of suites next to us. "What are you talking about?"

My brother walked up, catching the tail end of the conversation and drew his fingers across his throat, signaling for Chip to shut the hell up.

The manager came over to have me sign the bill. I grabbed the leather binder, signed my name and stuffed my credit card back in my wallet. I turned to Brody who was giving his boss the evil eye.

I glanced at my brother and then back to Chip. "Somebody wanna fill me in?"

Chip took a look around and then dropped his gaze to his leather loafers. My brother's forehead was creased in worry. He looked guilty, and I didn't like it. Not one bit. I stood and waited for one of them to speak.

Finally, my brother seemed to find his voice. "Come on. Let's go have a chat." He put his hand on my shoulder and tried to usher me away to a more private spot. "We have a couple of bottles of rum to finish off."

"Hold up." I pointed my finger over to Chip. "I'm not going anywhere until you tell me what he's talking about."

Brody sighed, and it was clear that he was keeping something from me and wasn't in a hurry to get into the details. "Can we discuss this later?"

"That depends." I tilted my head to the side and tested

him to see if my instincts were right. "Does this have anything to do with the Grant Anderson case?"

At that moment, Chip slipped away to the john. I probably would have done the same thing if I were him.

Brody swallowed, keeping his gaze steady on mine. "I'd rather not have this conversation here. Why don't we wait until we're someplace a little quieter where we don't have to shout over the top of each other to be heard?"

I was losing patience with my brother. If he had information on Grant and thought I would wait to discuss it, he was drunker than I thought.

"We are talking now."

He looked at me with tension in his jaw. His eyes shifted around the room. "Fine. Let's see if we can find a place to talk that's more private."

I didn't like the way this was going, but I remained calm and followed his lead.

He turned on his foot as we moved through the club. His tall height pushed through the room, making people clear a path so he and I could pass with ease. His steps were filled with purpose. He was in protective mode. Ever since we were kids, he always looked out for me, even though I was big enough to handle my own battles.

I caught a couple curious stares from our friends as we passed by. I felt like shit that I was taking him away from his bachelor party. He should be throwing back shots and getting lap dances, instead of worrying about setting me off. Still, I couldn't shake the feeling in my gut that this was something big.

We scouted out two seats at the other bar set up by the back room. He crossed his arms and I did the same. Brody would never lie to me, but I wasn't convinced that he would tell me everything either.

He uncrossed his arms and slid his hands into his back

pocket. A moment passed and then another. I arched my eyebrow waiting…

"Spill it, bro."

He cleared his throat. "Marco and the US Marshals followed up on a lead this week," he said, inching closer to me.

The seriousness in his voice sent chills up my spine.

"Yeah, I'm aware." I ran my palm across my jaw. "Marco has been dodging my calls all week." I assumed the reason he was ghosting me was because the lead ended up in a dead end. Now I wasn't so sure.

My brother was silent before he continued. "This is serious, Quinn. I want you to listen to what I have to say and promise not to lose your shit. I need you calm and focused."

His warning was clear, but I wasn't guaranteeing anything. "Tell me. Please."

"They met with one of Grant's law school buddies who was very chatty." My eyebrows rose, signaling for him to continue. "Grant reached out to him recently, looking for some help. The guy's got a family and isn't looking to be dragged into his friend's drama, so he refused to help Grant when he called."

I leveled him with a hard stare. "Care to elaborate on why he didn't report that to the police?"

Brody pulled a cigar out of his pocket and lit it up. "I'll get to that in a minute." He dragged his cigar to his lips and let out a huge puff of smoke. "Thompson is good with getting people to talk, as you know. They interviewed him for hours, no break, nothing. The guy's a lawyer, so he knew the deal. Once they started talking about filing charges for not reporting the phone call, he started singing like a bird."

I was on the edge of my seat while he casually rotated the cigar along his lips. He swirled the smoke around in his mouth before letting it out.

"Can we move this story along, please?" I moved my hands around, gesturing for him to get the hell on with it.

"Brace yourself." He turned around and flicked the ashes from his cigar into an ashtray.

"Brody, I swear to fucking God. Get to the goddamned point." The frustration in my voice was clear. I plucked the damned cigar out of his hand and stabbed the hand-rolled Cuban into an empty glass filled with ice.

He watched the flame go out and let out a long heavy sigh. "When you broke up with Charlotte, Grant knew she'd never be with him willingly. Not when she was still hung up on you. But he was starting his job at the District Attorney's office and moving out of the apartment he rented across the hall from her, so he knew he didn't have much time."

"Much time for what?" I asked, running through everything he had just told me.

He stared past me with a solemn look on his face. "To make her his."

My conversation with Charlotte that night at the diner came rushing back to me. "Are you talking about the night that she got drunk and slept with him?"

He nodded while dragging his thumb along his bottom lip. "He spiked her drink."

A chill swept into my bones. "I'm sorry. Repeat that, please."

"His friend was there that night. He saw Grant score a roofie from a known dealer. When his friend confronted him about it, Grant blackmailed him. Apparently, the friend was cheating on his girlfriend at the time and didn't want any trouble."

His words churned in my stomach. Visions of him violating her flashed in front of my eyes. It took me a minute to compose myself. "Are you telling me he raped her?"

The muscle in his jaw pulsed. I could see the veins in his

neck expanding. He knew what Charlotte meant to me. How this news would impact me. "I'm so sorry, man."

"No." I shook my head. I wanted to kill him. Make him pay. Have him on his knees begging for mercy. Charlotte would be devastated.

He leaned in and gripped my shoulder. "You can't let your anger get the better of you. I know you already have killed him in your head at least a thousand times." Oh, he had no fucking idea. Grant Anderson would die a slow and painful death when I was done with him. "Listen to me," he said sternly. "Letting your personal feelings control your thinking will get you nowhere."

My gaze whipped to his. "You don't understand." My words were barely heard over the music and the noise. "He violated her. He will pay for that."

"Yes, he will." My brother's attempt to calm my anger was unsuccessful. I didn't have the patience to wait for him to be captured. I wasn't willing to spend another second of my time knowing he was out there. He should be dead already. "He will be brought to justice, but having you in a cell next to him won't do Charlotte and her daughter an ounce of good."

Oh my God, Emery. A sick feeling crept up in my stomach. Charlotte only married Grant because she was pregnant. He orchestrated the entire thing, every goddamned step was calculated and planned out. He took advantage of her trust and her friendship without a second thought. He knew his only chance was because I was out of the picture.

Fuck!

I forced a swallow. A part of me knew it wasn't my fault. But it didn't change the facts. If I hadn't left her behind, none of this would have happened.

Rationally, I knew connecting the two events was ridiculous, but my fucking heart was shattered by the truth. Thoughts ran wild in my head as a glass of amber liquid was placed in front of me. There wasn't enough alcohol in this bar to save my soul from dying.

The ice clinked against the glass as my unsteady hands brought it to my lips. I took a heavy gulp and then another until there was nothing left.

The crinkle in my brother's forehead told me he knew exactly what I was thinking. He knew I would blame myself. He knew I would want to hurt that fucker in the most inhumane way possible.

"Tell your boss, Chip, to keep his mouth shut. I don't want Charlotte to find out about any of this," I told him and wondered how I was supposed to pretend everything was okay the next time I saw her.

He took a minute to consider my words. "This isn't something you can keep quiet. It's documented in the investigation. She can fucking sue the police department if she finds out."

"It won't come to that."

Every ounce of me was consumed with dread. My mind went to a dark, dark place thinking about what she went through without even knowing about it.

She would never be the same when she learned what that monster had done to her. The damage. The horror. The reality. It would destroy her.

Brody let out a sigh. "I know you want to protect her, but she won't see it that way."

"You let me worry about Charlotte."

She was going to be pissed if she ever found out that I knew and didn't tell her. But I was going to have to take my chances and convince Marco to keep quiet. I was determined to keep the truth buried because no good could come from her finding out.

Grant, on the other hand, would soon learn what I knew and he would pay dearly.

SEVENTEEN

CHARLOTTE

THE RIDE DOWNTOWN WAS TAKING FOREVER. I HAD TO WAIT until Emery was asleep, so I could sneak out of the house. Erica promised me that she would call me if she woke up. If Emery knew that I was surprising Quinn, she would guilt me into letting her come along.

It was only a little after ten o'clock, and I knew the guys would still be out horsing around. I was hoping to get to the hotel before they got back. I could barely contain my grin knowing how surprised Quinn would be to find me waiting for him in his hotel room.

I took advantage of the break in traffic and sped my way through the open lanes. I was so distracted and hell-bent on getting there that I didn't see the cop car off to the shoulder of the road tagging cars.

"Shit." The lights on the top of his patrol car spun as he came right up behind me. Great, just what I needed...a speeding ticket.

I pulled off to the shoulder and resisted the urge to flip off all the other motorists as they slowed down to get a better view.

I placed my car in park and rubbed my hands up and

down the steering wheel nervously, wondering if I should call Quinn for help. No. I couldn't do that knowing he would probably ask what I was doing on Interstate 76 heading toward the city.

I grabbed my registration and insurance card out of the glove box while it seemed like the officer was taking his sweet-ass time getting out of his car.

He finally approached my window. "Evening, ma'am. Do you know why I pulled you over?"

I glanced up and had to concentrate on not swallowing my tongue. Tall, dark, and hot as hell. Damn.

He smirked when he caught me staring. "Yes, I was speeding. I'm sorry. I don't have a good enough explanation. I wasn't paying attention."

He licked his bottom lip and flashed me a pair of dark black eyes. "You were going fifteen miles over the speed limit."

"Wow!" I acted shocked. "I didn't realize I was going that fast. I'm so sorry." I handed him the envelope on my lap containing all my information. "Here is my registration and insurance."

He took the envelope and smirked at how flustered I was. He probably got this type of reaction all the time. "Thanks. I need your license too."

"Of course, you do. Duh." I reached in and took my identification out of my wallet and handed it over. I was nervous even though I had no reason to be. It was just a ticket, nothing illegal.

"Thanks." He winked and swaggered back to his car.

I blew out a deep breath and glanced at the clock on the dash. I really wanted to get to the hotel before Quinn and the guys got back to their rooms. Now I had to worry about how many points this would be on my license and how much of a fine this would cost me. I really couldn't afford to have my insurance go up.

About five minutes later the officer reappeared at my driver's side window. "Here you go, Mrs. Anderson." He handed me back the white envelope with all my information. "Seeing that you've been very cooperative and have no prior tickets, I'm going to cut you some slack tonight. I'm just going to give you a warning. Please slow down."

"Really? That's it? Thank you, Officer. I really appreciate that."

He cleared his throat, looking uncomfortable. "I recognized your last name." His eyes flickered across the inside of my car. "I figured you've had enough bad luck lately and could use the break."

My heart pounded in my chest when I saw the pity in his eyes. "Thanks. For what it's worth, I want my estranged husband off the streets just as bad as you guys do."

His eyes widened and I watched a grin tug at the corners of his mouth. "Is that right?"

"Yes, and I appreciate your kindness. I promise to obey the speed limit from here on out."

Jesus. I sounded like a dork. I wasn't trying to be such a brownnoser. I just wanted to get the hell on with my night, but the gleam in his eye told me he liked that little piece of information I just shared about my relationship status with the runaway DA.

Why the hell did I have to open my big mouth?

"Where are you headed in such a hurry?"

My smile was automatic just thinking about Quinn. "Downtown, to meet a friend."

He blatantly stared at me. He was definitely checking me out. That made me even more nervous for some reason. Not that I was interested, just uncomfortable.

"Lucky friend." He moved a little closer inside my car. I held my breath, unsure of what to do. "My name is Caleb." He held his hand out to me.

I grabbed his offered hand and gave it a firm shake. This

encounter was awkward and completely unprofessional, but he did just do me a favor.

"It's nice to meet you, Caleb." I smiled, trying to find the right balance between being polite and not leading him on.

He reached inside his front pocket and produced a county-issued business card. "Got a pen?" he asked.

His question took me by surprise. "Sure."

He scribbled something on the back and handed it to me. "My personal cell is on the back. If you ever find yourself in trouble, use the number on the front. If you're looking for a fun kind of trouble and just want to have a good time, use the one on the back." He winked.

"Thanks." I smiled, feeling uncomfortable and knowing that I'd never use either number.

He flashed me a flirtatious smile. "I look forward to hearing from you soon."

I internally rolled my eyes at him and purposely didn't respond. While there was no denying that he was attractive, there was zero interest on my end.

He gave me a curt nod before swaggering back to his car. I let out a sigh of relief and watched him pull away. I looked at the GPS on my phone and prayed that I would get to the hotel in time.

———

I pulled up to the valet stand, grabbed the stub, and gave them my keys to park my car. My little law-breaking pit stop put me behind fifteen minutes. I fetched my overnight bag out of the back seat and strolled into the lobby.

I walked up to the front desk and gave them my identification. Quinn had added my name to the reservation when he booked the room, hoping that I would use it. I told him to go have fun with the guys and I'd see him when the weekend was over. Surprising him was a last-minute decision.

Once I was in the room, I wasted no time with getting ready. Now, I just had to wait. Hopefully, I wouldn't have to wait too long. I was anxious to get my hands on him. To finally be alone without any interruptions, even if it was only for a few hours.

I heard the click of the door and watched Quinn's shadow step into the darkened room. He flicked the light switch on and froze. His eyes widened when he saw me splayed out on the king-size bed. I had to catch my breath at the sight of him. He had on a black button-down with a pair of dark jeans that I couldn't wait to peel off his legs. My stomach tightened with jealousy just thinking about all the women who got to look at him tonight.

"What are you doing here?" he asked, staring at me as if he couldn't believe I was really there. I just texted him a couple hours ago telling him I was home in bed.

I shrugged my shoulders, giving him a playful smile. "I couldn't sleep."

He moved toward the bed; the sexual tension in the air began to spark.

"Really?" His eyes did a slow crawl along my bare legs before they trailed slowly up to my face. My hair was loose and wild, just the way he liked it. I was wearing a sheer, black, lace baby doll, that crisscrossed along my breast, leaving little to the imagination. There was a tie right beneath it that looked like he couldn't wait to tear open. I fiddled with the ends of the fabric, revealing the thin matching G-string.

He released a sharp breath. "So you drove all the way down here just so you could sleep?"

I spread my legs open, letting him know my intentions. "I never said I wanted to sleep. Just that I couldn't."

Without wasting time, he started to unbutton his dress shirt. "Is that so?"

I nodded my head, unable to speak. I wasn't sure what kind of exercise routine they had taught their cadets in the academy, but it was clear that Quinn had maintained his physical frame over the years. I was glad to see my tax dollars well spent.

I cleared my throat and dragged my eyes over every inch of him. "I was in such a hurry, I almost got a speeding ticket on the way here."

He unzipped his jeans and started to slide them down his legs. "A speeding ticket, huh?" He lifted his eyebrow and chucked his shoes off, so he could easily kick his jeans away. He stood before me in nothing more than a tight pair of black boxer briefs. "Should I be concerned that you endangered the other motorists on the road and risked your own safety, just to come here and get fucked?"

I gave him a half smile, feeling part sheepish and part brave. "The officer was feeling generous, so he let me go." I decided to tease him a little. "All it took was a bat of my eyelashes for that ticket to turn into a phone number."

His smile turned into a frown as his eyes ran over me. "It better not have been your number."

He seemed on edge like something was bothering him. I pushed that thought aside and focused on making the most of the time we had. "Are we going to sit here and talk about this all night, or are you going to come join me on this bed?"

Quinn wasted no time closing the gap between us. His one knee landed on the mattress, while his hand reached out and cupped my cheek. "We'll talk about that later, but right now," his lips ghosted over mine, "I think it's time I give you what you came here for."

His lips were soft, but this kiss was branding. It was a promise and a threat, and it stirred something inside me that I couldn't quite understand. I shivered when he positioned his body over mine and covered my breast with his palm.

His tongue pushed against mine, as if he owned it. He

tasted like cigars and whiskey, like sex and hunger. There was no hesitation on his part as his skilled fingers ran across my skin.

I wanted to cry and weep for all the time we've lost. To kick myself for ever thinking he could be replaced.

My hands moved up his shoulders, to the back of his neck where I urged him closer. I didn't just want him; I needed him, and I was desperate to connect with him. I tried to match each stroke of his tongue, each thrust of his hips, but he was moving at such a slow torturous pace, that it wasn't enough.

I brought my hand down to the waistband of his boxers, slipping my fingers inside. He let out a loud growl as I wrapped my palm around his thickness that seemed to grow as I stroked him at a relentless pace.

"Charlotte," he rasped as I ran my thumb over the tip, letting my fingers play with the precum. "You need to have patience baby, or I'm going to come all over your hand."

"Do it," I taunted him.

"No. That's not what you came here for." He breathed against my mouth, moving his hands down to my panties and pressing his thumb to my clit. My head flew back when his mouth landed on my neck. He began to nip and suck at the same rhythm that his fingers were now moving in and out of me.

"Quinn." I started to talk, but he smothered my mouth with his. He was done letting me lead. He was taking control, and I couldn't even be mad, because he was so damn good. I wanted nothing more than to rip his boxers off and end this little tease, but I doubted he would let me. No, Quinn was now in the driver's seat, and I couldn't even bring myself to care.

I moved my hands up his chest and dug my nails into his shoulders. I wanted to mark him like he was marking me. So, I brought my mouth down to his neck and sucked hard, practically biting through the skin and releasing my lips with a pop.

He hissed against my mouth. "You little minx. You want to play dirty?" His eyes challenged me. Hell yes, I silently agreed. There was nothing sexier than seeing Quinn come undone. I wanted to unleash the beast. The last time we were together we had to be quiet. This time, there were no rules or fear of getting caught. We were free to do whatever the hell we damn well pleased and I was taking advantage of that. I wanted to feel wanted and desired, like a woman should.

"I want you to fuck me, Quinn."

His hand stopped moving. I've never been vocal during sex, other than your typical groan and moan here and there. But tonight, I didn't want to be a mom. I didn't want to be careful or quiet. I just wanted to let go, with a man who made me feel safe and loved and wanted.

His lips crashed to mine in urgency. I rubbed my throbbing clit against his swollen cock, begging him to hurry up. I wanted him inside me. I needed him to soothe the ache and put out that fire that he started. I was slowly burning from the inside out. Every touch, nip, and thrust only heightened my arousal.

I wanted to cry with relief when he finally removed his boxers. I copied his movements, sliding my barely there panties down my legs.

He reached over and undid the tie that was holding the scrappy piece of material together and lifted the top over my head, exposing all that I had to offer.

He darted his tongue out to wet his lips, a hint of appreciation played on his mouth. "You're like a fine wine that just gets better with age."

My eyes were smiling as I splayed my fingers through his hair. "That was pretty cheesy, but I'll take it."

Having a "mom body" has never bothered me. I made peace with the fact that giving birth changed me in more ways than one. It's sad, but I never cared what Grant thought. If he found me attractive or not. With Quinn, I wanted him to look at me with lust. I wanted to please him.

Just like with most young couples, our relationship was very physical. They say that after a while, the fire dies out and the longing fades away. But I never wanted to lose that connection with him. Not when he was the only one who could make me feel this way.

"It's the truth," he said, holding my eyes with his. "You're the only woman for me, Charlotte. Walking away from you was the biggest mistake of my life, but I'm ready to correct that now." He brought his tip to my entrance and ran it along my folds. His eyes were focused on mine. "I'm going to fuck you now. Hard and fast. Then when I'm done, I'm going to spend the entire night making love to you."

Without another word, he thrust inside. My muscles tensed as I drew in a ragged breath. He began to move, grinding against my pelvis, delivering exactly what he promised.

He drove in and out with a force that triggered every sensation possible. It was like an explosion, erupting out of control, consuming me with pleasure. Every single part of me felt like it was being ripped apart and put back together at the same time.

The feeling was too much. I wanted to look away, but I couldn't take my eyes off of him. The muscles in his neck were straining while his fingers dug into my hip bone. It was such a beautiful fucking site, watching him lose control as he moved his body over the top of mine. The mingling of our breaths, the smell of sex, and the sound of skin slapping skin took over the room.

He slammed into me, harder and faster, testing my restraint. We pushed against each other, our mouths and hands laying claim. My pants became heavy as he stretched me and filled me with a force that had me arching off the bed. "I'm coming," I shouted, tightening my muscles around him.

He held me in place and rotated his hips and drove into me like he couldn't get deep enough. I'd missed the feeling of being with someone who knew my body so well. Quinn spent years learning how and where to touch me and how to please me, and it felt like he hadn't forgotten a single thing. I wanted to cry when he trailed his mouth over my exposed throat.

No one loved me the way he did. I knew that now, and he was making sure I never forgot it again. His thrusts became faster, and I dug my nails into his shoulders, feeling them stiffen under my fingertips. He buried himself to the hilt, threw his head back, and finally let go. I felt his pleasure pulse and jerk through me.

It took a few minutes for his body to relax before he dropped his head to my shoulder. I threaded my fingers through his hair, enjoying the silence, wondering how I ever let this man get away from me.

"I love you, Quinn."

He lifted his head, bringing his thumb up to my bottom lip. He traced a pattern along my mouth. "It's always been different with you," he said, holding my gaze. "I've slept around, had my fun, but it never meant anything. Even with the few relationships I had, it was never like this."

God, I loved this man. I spent so many years hating him and feeling lost, now I couldn't imagine my life without him. Everything finally seemed right. I pulled his face up to mine, needing him to hear what I had to say. "Even when we were apart," I said, measuring my words carefully, "my soul still sought you out. My heart was always searching for that missing piece. You are the only man who has had all of me. Every single bit that I had to give, has always been yours." I inched my mouth to his. "Every tear, every laugh, and every breath belong to you."

Moisture flooded his eyes. "Baby," he choked out. Quinn

rarely got emotional. On the few occasions that he did, you felt it. I wasn't sure if something happened tonight or if his emotions were getting the best of him. "I want you divorced tomorrow. I want my ring back on your finger where it belongs. I want the whole world to know that you're mine." He swallowed and cupped my jaw. "I want us to have that life we always talked about. I want to buy a house and fill it up with little boys who are strong like me and little girls that look just like you. I promise to love Emery as much as I would my own flesh and blood."

My heart burst with emotion. "I want that too, but it's going to take time."

"I know that, but I want to tell Emery about us. I want to help you both through this. Not as some friend, but as the man that will show her and teach her all the things her father won't be able to. I want her to know that she's loved, and I want her to feel protected. I'll take on whatever role she'll let me. Hell, I'd adopt her right now if I could."

A hiccupped sob poured out of me. I wanted to feel guilty for never loving Grant the way I should have. But how could I when I had this? What Grant and I had was short lasting, but with Quinn, he was my beginning, my end, and my forever. Our love wasn't perfect, but when he pressed a kiss to my forehead and wrapped me up in his arms, it felt like everything I had to go through led me straight to this moment.

EIGHTEEN

QUINN

"Good Morning." Charlotte's sweet morning voice feathered against my chest while I ran my fingers through her hair. I wanted to chuckle because there was nothing sweet about the way she looked when I took her from behind last night on all fours.

I have officially been upgraded from the couch to the bedroom, and I couldn't be happier about it.

After cleaning out Grant's bedroom and ridding the house of his shit, we finally sat down and had "the talk" with Emery. At first she was quiet, but I think she understood more than she let on. I assured her that I wasn't trying to replace her father. Even though I would in a heartbeat if she would let me.

"I'm headed into work early. I'm going to be working late this week, so I can take Friday off for Brody's wedding," I told her, while tucking a piece of her unruly hair behind her ear.

She slipped her hands under my shirt. The feeling of her soft fingertips caressing my skin had my dick swelling through my sleep pants.

"That's a shame. I was hoping we'd have enough time to shower together before you left."

It was cute watching her trying to persuade me. "I'm all for preserving water and saving the planet, but you wore me out last night, and the night before, so my dick is the one that needs saving right now. How about we give him a little rest."

She smacked me in the chest. "Your dick will get a permanent rest with that attitude."

I raised an eyebrow. She was feisty this morning. Over the past two weeks, I was starting to see parts of the old Charlotte reappear. Sure, she still called me out on my bullshit and put me in my place. But I liked how her eyes lit up whenever I walked into a room. The way she would laugh at my stupid jokes and turned my heart into a puddle just from a simple smile. And I loved how she made me feel.

Happy. Content. Peaceful.

"We're official now, right?" I asked, staring at her mouth. For some reason I needed to hear her say the words. Maybe it was because the thought that this could all be pulled away from me weighed heavily on my mind.

"Define official, please," she answered, stretching her bare legs out under the sheets and then wrapping them around mine.

I folded my arms around her, pulling her close. "Meaning you're mine and I'm yours."

God, I sounded like an insecure teenage girl. Normally, I wasn't such a sap, but she still had no clue about what Grant did to her. My only hope was that she wouldn't kick my ass to the curb when she found out I kept it from her.

She wet her bottom lip and dragged her fingers up to my neck. "I've always been yours, Quinn."

I rolled her on her back, loving how easy things were between us. "I think I need to dirty you up a bit before we take that shower."

She grinned. "Well, what are you waiting for? We don't have all day, remember? You've got a job to get to. Ticktock."

I laughed, crashing my mouth down to hers. She wrapped her ankles around my back and drew me closer. There was no rush, no urgency as I slowly made love to her like we had all the time in the world.

By the time I finally pulled out of her, I took the quickest shower of my life. Alone. Promising her a rain check because I really had to get to work.

When I got to the precinct, I spotted a few guys that I knew and gave them a brief hello. I hopped on the elevator and headed downstairs where the patrol cops were getting ready for roll call.

I was surprised to see my target already standing by the door. "Officer Garcia," I greeted him and slipped my hands inside my pockets. I took quick stock of his appearance and liked the fact that I had to look down at him in order to talk to him.

He looked like Mr. Smooth, standing there all confident like he was some top-notch cop that thought he was better than everyone else. I had a sixth sense about people. We were taught that we were all equals no matter what our titles said. We were brothers. But Caleb Garcia hit on my woman and I needed to address that.

"Yes." He took me in from top to bottom, sizing me up. "Can I help you?"

In smaller departments, where everyone knew each other this would have been a bit awkward. With a city the size of Philadelphia, we had over seven thousand officers expanding over one hundred forty square miles with fifty-five different locations, so not everyone was on a first name basis. Officer Garcia was going to learn who I was really quick.

"Detective Walker." I held my hand out for a shake.

He must have sensed something was up because he squared his shoulders and met my gaze.

"What can I do for you, Detective?" His grip was equally as firm.

I pulled the card that he gave Charlotte out of my pocket and handed it to him. "I wanted to return this to you."

He flipped it over and eyed it with confusion. "Did you find this somewhere?"

The briefing sergeant, Anthony Sardino, passed us by and patted me on the shoulder. "Walker, good to see you." Then he looked at Garcia. "Two minutes, Officer."

Sergeant Sardino expected everyone in their place, pens in hands on the dot. You toed the line or else. There was no bullshit during his briefing. You got your assignments, had your questions answered, grabbed your stuff and started your shift. In order words, I needed to be quick.

"As a matter-of-fact, I found that in my girlfriend's purse. You pulled her over a couple nights ago for speeding and gave her a break, which I appreciate. However, I do not appreciate you hitting on my woman when you're on the clock."

"Woah." He put his hand out in front of him. "I have no idea who you're talking about."

"Charlotte Anderson," I reminded him, watching pieces of the puzzle fall together. If I didn't have his attention before, I had it now.

He stared at me for a minute and crossed his arms over his chest. "Grant Anderson's wife?" He cocked an arrogant eyebrow as if he had it all figured out. "I remember her."

I knew the second I laid eyes on the little punk that I didn't like him. A few of his buddies stood off to the side waiting to walk in with him. He tried to play it cool, like we were just standing around shooting the shit. His pride and his ego looked way too big for his small frame.

"Her estranged husband. And she's not going to be his wife for much longer." My eyes narrowed, warning him that he needed to proceed with caution. "And it would be in your best interest to forget about her."

His back went straight and he stood taller. "I wasn't trying to steal your girl. I wouldn't have even given her my number if she hadn't offered up the fact that she was in the process of a divorce."

"Well, I guess now you know."

He cleared his throat as his eyes flickered over to the briefing room. His friends were still watching. "So, she's already got herself a new man before the ink is even dry." He whistled for show, trying to save face. "Damn, she moves on pretty quick."

My eyes narrowed, and I felt my calm exterior fading. I wanted to break his fucking neck for antagonizing me. "Officer, you're making a fool of yourself trying to impress your buddies over there." I nodded, my tone was hard and emotionless. It only flustered him. "I've been out of high school a lot longer than you, so let me give you a piece of advice. Grow the fuck up and act like a man. When you're wrong, admit it! I approached you directly and with respect. And if you ever see Charlotte Anderson again, you better turn in the other direction and walk away."

He hissed through his teeth. I looked down at my watch. "Oh, would you look at that. The second hand just hit the number twelve." I gave him a smug smile. "You know Sargent Sardino…Chop-chop, buddy."

With that, I turned on my heels and strolled over to one of the break rooms to get my caffeine fix. Just as I was checking my messages and sipping my watered-down coffee, a hand slapped me on the shoulder, causing the liquid to spill over the edge of my cup.

"You got a few minutes?" Marco asked over the voices out in the hallway, bits and pieces of conversations spilling into the room.

"For you, I've got plenty of time. I came in early this morning."

He smirked. "I caught the tail end of the conversation out there." He laughed. "I didn't want to interrupt the teacher."

"Little fucker needed some lessons in common courtesy."

Marco helped himself to an empty seat at one of the round tables. He wiped his hand down his face, scraping his jaw. "We should have the room to ourselves for a few minutes."

I leaned back in the small plastic chair and crossed my ankles. "What's up?"

He cleared his throat and sipped his coffee. "We've made great progress in the investigation. We got a lead. A very good lead."

I blinked, afraid to get my hopes up. "Tell me."

"The friend from college," he stated, waiting for my reaction. "The one who informed us about the night that Grant took advantage of Charlotte," he said gently. "We did a little more digging. You're never going to believe who his daddy is."

"Who?" I asked through a clenched jaw, urging him to hurry the fuck up and tell me.

"Vinny Valentino."

I nearly choked on my coffee. "The mob boss who owns a good chunk of the Eastern Seaboard?"

"The one and only."

"Jesus." I pinched the bridge of my nose. "How did you guys not know this?" I snapped.

"The son goes by a different last name. Romano, after his mother. He went to a lot of trouble to bury his connection to his father, as you might expect."

I tilted my neck to the side, willing the tension to leave my shoulders. "What's the word on the street?"

"We got our informants looking into a couple strip clubs that Vinny owns, as well as his restaurants and real estate properties."

My jaw was locked tight. "It's starting to make sense. How Grant's been able to stay hidden for so long. Not to mention, Vinny Valentino is a lot higher up on the food chain than a drug trafficker like Scarantino."

"Exactly. There is no way this is just a coincidence." He smacked his hands on his knees and leaned in whispering, "I'm telling you this as a friend. The Feds are all in this shit now. You cannot breathe a word."

"I would never do anything to jeopardize this case. If Grant is messed up in this shady shit, Charlotte's safety comes first."

"Agreed. So, watch your back." He stood up and threw his coffee out in the trash can. "I'll keep you posted."

NINETEEN

CHARLOTTE

I turned my attention to the DJ announcing the bride and groom while the sound of applause echoed through the white and gold decorated ballroom.

I smiled when Brody walked into the middle of the dance floor and pulled his wife into his arms. He looked dangerously handsome in his tux and his eyes sparkled with happiness as he spun his bride around to the lyrics of "Marry Me" by Train.

I never thought I would see the day where Brody Walker would find someone who was worth giving up his playboy ways for. There was no doubt a trail of broken hearts left along the state of Pennsylvania.

I was thankful that I was sitting down when I noticed Quinn's mom, making her way toward my table.

"Hello, Charlotte."

I stood up, wiped my sweaty palms on my dress and gave her a light kiss on each of her cheeks, just the way she preferred. Ever since Quinn and I dated, this woman has hated me. At least that's what it felt like. She was against us from the beginning and I'd never understood why. I'd tried to get her to accept me, but for whatever reason, it seemed like I could never quite win her over. She always made me feel like I had something to prove.

"Ann Marie." I smiled, feeling my heart beat faster than normal in my chest. "It's so good to see you," I lied.

She set her silver clutch that matched her dress down on the table.

"I didn't get a chance to talk to you at the church earlier. How have you been?" She gave me a kind smile that slightly eased the knot growing in my chest.

"I've been well." I watched as Quinn and the bridal party circled the room. Seeing my boyfriend in a tux was doing things to my insides that even I didn't anticipate. I'd known this man for almost half my life and he still had the ability to steal the breath right from my lungs.

Ann Marie watched me carefully, making me squirm in my seat. "It was nice of you to attend on such short notice."

I wasn't sure if that was a snub or not. So, I took a sip of my drink and smiled, hoping it would calm the nerves in my stomach.

"It was a beautiful ceremony. I'm glad I came."

I glanced around the room and my eyes connected with Thomas Walker. He raised his glass of scotch when he saw me. "There she is."

I stood to greet him as he got closer. He reached for me and slung his arm around my shoulder, pulling me into his warmth. "You're just as pretty as I remember," he said, pressing a kiss to my forehead.

He relaxed his hold, and I took a step back and patted his shoulder. "And you're just as charming as ever."

A genuine smile took over his face. "I can't tell you how happy I am that you are here. I've missed you."

Thomas was always like a second father to me. From day one, he welcomed me with open arms. Where Ann Marie always treated me like a threat, Thomas treated me like an ally.

"I've missed you too," I said, overcome with emotion. "I'm so glad you're doing well. Quinn told me you had quite a scare a while back."

He let go of my arms and snatched a glass of champagne from a passing waiter and handed it to his wife. "My son was being a drama queen as usual. I'm as healthy as a horse." He winked.

"And I'd like to keep it that way," Ann Marie said, taking a sip from her champagne glass. "Now please, Thomas, come sit down so they can start the toast."

He pressed his lips into a grin before taking a seat next to Ann Marie. He reached his hand out to me. "I'm glad you and Quinn found your way back together," he said, giving me a squeeze in support.

I swallowed the lump in the back of my throat. "Thank you. Me too."

After Quinn and another one of Brody's best friends made an embarrassing toast, we were finally able to sit down and eat.

I took a few bites of my salad when I spotted Quinn's sister Nora. She did a double take when she saw me. She let go of her daughter's hand and I watched the little girl run over to her father who had a plate of food waiting for her.

"I heard you were going to be here. How the hell have you been?" she asked enthusiastically while pulling out the chair next to mine.

"I've been okay. You look like you haven't aged a bit," I said, admiring her floor-length burgundy gown that hugged her curves perfectly. "You look amazing. That dress looks stunning on you."

She raised her eyebrows conspicuously. "You won't be saying that in another month or so." My eyes followed hers to her stomach.

"You're pregnant?" She nodded her head. "That's wonderful! Congratulations."

She nervously played with her hoop earrings that were dangling. "Thanks. We just found out a couple of weeks ago." She looked at the waiters who were carrying the food out on silver platters. "I am going to miss not being able to eat fish for the next few months though."

I patted her knee. "Don't worry, you'll be able to go back to eating all the food groups in no time. My biggest hang up when I was pregnant was no caffeine, and wine, of course."

She stuck her tongue out. "Blah. This conversation is getting depressing. So, tell me all about you and this little girl of yours."

We spent the next ten minutes catching up and exchanging parenting stories. Nora and I had always got along, and it was nice knowing that we could just pick up where we left off like two old friends.

"Listen, I gotta get back to my bridesmaid duties, but I wanted to get your number. I was hoping we could do lunch sometime."

"I would love that," I said, pulling out my phone and handing it to her so she could add herself to my contacts.

Once she was done, she handed it back to me. "Don't forget to call me," she warned.

"I won't. I promise."

"Great. We'll catch up later." She winked and strolled over to kiss her daughter on the head as she shoveled a fried mac-n-cheese bite into her mouth. Her husband, Dylan, was sneaking looks at his cell phone and looked like he would rather be anywhere else but here.

Our server placed the teriyaki salmon I'd selected down in front of me. For some reason the smell wasn't sitting right with me. I put my fork down and lifted my water glass. My stomach felt a bit off. At first, I blamed it on my nerves. Now, after talking to Nora, I was starting to think it could be something else. I pulled out my phone, not paying any attention to the conversation around me, and checked my calendar.

I was only a couple days late. Nothing to be anxious about.

"So, Charlotte." Thomas's voice broke through my thoughts while he sliced his knife into his steak. "Quinn tells us that you're teaching now."

I pushed my plate away and broke off a piece of bread. "Yes, it's just a temporary position until something more permanent pops up, which is fine, because I need the flexibility with everything going on in my life right now."

I dipped the crust in the oil and wished I had kept my mouth shut. Why the hell did I have to go bring that up? They hadn't seen me in years. This wasn't the time to remind them of my fucked-up life with an estranged husband on the run.

"That's understandable," Ann Marie said. "Quinn mentioned that your daughter, Emery, just started second grade. He talks about her all the time."

Her sincerity caught me off guard, but I went with it. "He's been great with her. I don't know how I would have made it through these past few weeks without him."

"Well, hopefully we'll get to meet her someday." Thomas winked while Ann Marie nodded in agreement.

I swallowed. This reunion was going a lot better than I had planned on. "I would love that."

Everybody polished off their plates while I sat and barely touched my fish. I was doing my best to stay occupied, but my hands kept finding their way to my stomach.

After posing for about a thousand pictures, Quinn finally made his way over to my table. He leaned down and kissed my cheek. "You look like you could use this." He extended a glass of wine to me. I eyed the red liquid like it was poison as he held it high out of my reach. "You have to agree to dance with me first."

Everyone paused their conversation. "Only if you promise not to step on my toes."

He laughed while pulling me up from my seat. "I promise." He kissed my cheek. "My dancing skills have improved over the years."

If that comment was supposed to make me feel better, he needed to work on his lines. The last thing I wanted to think about was him dancing with other women.

"I'm warning you," I said playfully as we found an open spot on the dance floor.

He spun me around before bringing me to his chest. It was hard and warm and it smelled like him. "You look beautiful tonight," he said, placing his hand on my lower back and leading me across the dance floor with ease.

I reached up and threaded my hands around his neck as we swayed to Adele's, "Make you Feel My Love."

I relaxed into his arms, wishing we could stay just like this forever. There was no lingering tension, no hurt feelings or misunderstandings. Just two people in love, dancing to soft music in the background, enjoying each other's company.

"I've always loved this song," I said, pressing my cheek against his shoulder.

His face split into a knowing smile. "Why do you think I requested it?"

My steps slowed and I leaned my head back to look at him. Really look at him. "I know I shouldn't be surprised that you remembered, but I am."

"We had a lot of good times to remember." He grinned, looking down at me. Even in my heels, I was no match for his tall frame. "And I'm never letting you go again."

I rested my head against his chest right over his beating heart. "Good, because I won't let you."

He kissed my forehead, letting his mouth linger for a moment. "Has my mother been on her best behavior tonight?"

"Did you say something to her?"

His lips twitched. Of course, he did. Quinn has always been attuned to me and my feelings. He knew I was nervous about seeing his mom. He understood how much I wanted her to accept me. Especially now. After all these years, and after everything we've been through.

He hooked his arms tighter around my waist. "She means well. She said she wanted to talk to you. She feels bad for how she treated you in the past."

I had a hard time believing that. The reality was, I could do no right in Ann Marie Walker's eyes. But for her son and the sake of our relationship, I would give her the benefit of the doubt.

"I would like that."

His hand raked up and down my back. "Have you thought about what kind of wedding you want?"

"Quinn." I sighed. "We've been over this. I told you we would revisit the conversation once the ink was dry on my divorce papers."

"I know we can't get married yet, but it's going to happen. It was always supposed to happen. Nothing is going to stand in our way this time. So, tell me, Charlotte, what's your dream wedding. Because after everything we've been through, I'm giving you at least that."

My eyes misted over and I told him the truth. "I don't care."

He looked like he didn't believe me. "Every woman cares."

"I don't care if it's a backyard barbeque, on the beach, or at the county courthouse. As long as you're at the end of the aisle waiting for me, that's all I need."

His eyes hooded over and he grabbed my wrist, practically dragging me off the dance floor.

"What are you doing?"

"I've fulfilled my best man duties. Now it's time to get out of here. We have a room upstairs and a night to ourselves and I don't want to waste a single second of it."

"But they haven't even cut the cake yet," I reminded him.

"I don't give a shit. Plus, you're not a dessert eater anyway."

Well, he had me there. I just didn't want him to get in trouble for bailing too early. We said our quick goodbyes as he pushed us through the crowd like a man on a mission. Thankfully, everyone was too hung up on the bride and groom to think too much about us leaving before the dinner plates were even cleared from the tables.

Within minutes we were sliding the key card through the door. Quinn didn't even bother turning the lights on. The glow from outside was the only light that lit the room.

"Take off your dress," he ordered.

At his words I turned around, giving him my back. "I need your help," I said, showing him the zipper.

With deft fingers, he slowly guided the fabric apart leaving a heaping pool of wetness between my thighs.

He sucked in a breath when I turned around to unhook my black lace bra. My nipples hardened into peaks as he stared down at me with so much intensity, I had to force myself to look away.

His mouth sealed over mine as he guided me toward the bed. His hands gripped my hair like a starving man and he was demanding his last meal.

My back hit the mattress and I lifted myself on my elbows as he very skillfully pulled the thong down my legs. I threw my head back when his hands began to explore every curve I had to offer. He knew exactly where to touch and how to bring me pleasure. Hell, he knew my body better than I did.

My hips bucked forward, and whatever battle I was trying to fight was lost. Watching his thick corded muscles as he moved above me triggered every single nerve ending to spark to life.

"I could never get enough of you," he breathed into my neck as he trailed his tongue along the shell of my ear. I wanted to beg him to keep going, but my voice was lost. "You drive me fucking crazy." He rolled his hips into me causing a groan to fly from my throat. "It's insane how much I want you."

His words were too much. I couldn't talk. I couldn't breathe. All I could do was feel every touch, every lick, and every caress. I grabbed his hard length and started to stroke him through his dress pants. I didn't think it would be possible for him to get any harder, but he did, and I swear to God, every part of my body ached with need.

"Fuck," he growled and stood up. "On your hands and knees," he commanded and started to unbutton his dress shirt. I peered up at him through my heavy lashes and got on all fours.

I peeked a glance at him over my shoulder and watched him slide his pants down his muscular thighs. A small whimper left my throat at the sight of him.

He slowly stalked toward the bed and ran his hand through my hair. He pulled back and bent his head to kiss me on the mouth. "You good?" he asked, raking his eyes over my face.

"I'll be better once you're inside me."

"That's my girl." He smiled and placed his hands on my ass and brushed his thumb along the seam of my crack. A place he hadn't been in years. We had only done it back there a couple of times and he was the only man to ever go there. The only one I trusted.

"Not tonight," he said, moving his mouth painstakingly slow down my spine, "but soon I'm going to get reacquainted with every part of you."

My mouth dropped open as he slid his hands between my legs. He dipped two fingers inside at once, gliding them in and out, pleasuring me in a way that only he knew how.

My head fell forward in a moan. I gripped my hands on the comforter when I felt his teeth bite down on my shoulder. He was taking his time and it was driving me insane.

"Quinn, please," I begged as his fingers continued to move in and out. His other hand reached over and covered my breast. I felt my release climbing higher and higher, ready to tear through me. His fingers continued to thrust and stretch me wider, making sure I was good and ready for him. My mouth parted, and I arched my hips, nothing had ever felt so incredible. I felt my orgasm building, but I still wasn't prepared. This was intensity on a whole other level, and it just continued to build and build. I was so damn close I wanted to cry. My walls tightened and piece by piece I came apart around his hand.

He gave my racing heart a minute to calm down before he positioned himself at my opening. He slid his erection between my wet folds and ran the tip along my opening. His free hand locked tightly around my hip while his mouth trailed over my shoulder, peppering tender kisses along my exposed flesh.

"I love you," he said, before sliding in and filling me up completely. His hand slid up my back and he fisted his hand in my hair. The sharp pinch of pain had my mouth dropping open. He rolled his hips with greed and slammed into me with a punishing force, hitting that sensitive spot over and over again.

My legs grew weak and my body began to tremble. I could tell he was getting close when his speed increased. I closed my eyes, unsure of how much longer I could last. I knew my battle was lost when he withdrew and slammed into me with a force so hard, I saw stars.

His hands held onto my waist to keep me from collapsing on the bed as he pushed into me harder. Every thought left my mind when I heard a strangled growl come from his throat. His hips drove in deep one last time before he exploded inside me.

My body was spent as I sunk into the mattress. Quinn collapsed down on the bed next to me. He gathered me in his arms and brushed a tender kiss to my temple. His kiss was soft, yet packed with so much emotion, that I didn't want this night to end.

After taking a few minutes to get our breathing back to normal, he leaned over and stood up to go to the bathroom. He came back with a warm wet washcloth and gently cleaned me up. This was his thing, and I hated wondering if he did this with his other partners. I shook those thoughts from my head and decided that I didn't want to know.

I nuzzled my nose under his neck and tried not to think about anything else. Things had been too quiet lately, too uneventful. Almost too good to be true. I kept waiting for the other shoe to drop. And I couldn't seem to get rid of that nagging suspicion in my gut that he was keeping something from me.

"Hey, everything okay in here?" he asked, gently stroking my hair and tapping on my temple.

I curled into his warm chest feeling the most content I'd ever felt in my life. I decided to focus on that and not let my mind wander too far off track. "I've never been better."

TWENTY

QUINN

My phone started buzzing on the nightstand. The drapes were still drawn and the room was pitch-black. I leaned over on my elbow and peeked at the time on the alarm clock next to the bed.

I picked up my phone and squinted my eyes, giving them a second to adjust to the bright screen. Marco wouldn't call unless it was urgent.

I shot straight up in bed and swiped to answer. "This better be good for you to call me at the ass crack of dawn," I whispered as quietly as possible, trying not to wake up Charlotte, who was sprawled out naked on her stomach next to me.

"We got him."

The hairs on the back of my neck stood at attention. "You're shitting me!"

"He's being booked as we speak."

I rubbed my hand down my face and kicked the comforter off my legs. "I'm literally at the Marriott right around the corner. I can be there in fifteen minutes."

"You know the drill."

Yeah, I did and it sucked for me in that moment. There

was a strict legal process that had to be followed and all I wanted was five minutes alone with that fucker.

Soft fingers rested along my back. I slanted my head and looked down. "I have to see him. Please..." Charlotte stared at me with pleading eyes. "I need you to be understanding and not fight me on this."

The thought of the two of them in the same room together had every single muscle in my body pulling tight. There was no way I would be able to hide my discomfort.

I searched her face trying to figure out what was going on in her head. God knew I was conflicted as hell right now. I hated this, but it wasn't like I had much of a choice.

I brushed my thumb along her cheek. "I'm not going to fight you on this. I understand. I'm not happy about it, but I won't stop you."

Her eyes filled with relief. "Thank you."

She tried to move around me on the bed, but I grabbed her wrist. "Everything is going to be fine. I promise."

She stared into my eyes, her voice pained. "I just want this to be over."

I leaned down, putting my lips over the top of hers. "Me too."

I gave her a quick kiss and watched her scramble out of the bed and run into the bathroom to get ready.

I quickly got dressed and clasped my watch over my wrist. I glanced around the room making sure everything was ready to go. My head was spinning, and I was caught in a weird state of shock.

I'd wished for this moment, prayed that he would be caught, and now that they finally got him, I wasn't feeling the relief that I'd thought I would. The worst part was, that I wasn't sure why. Maybe I'd feel better once I could see with my own eyes that he really was finished. Perhaps, I just needed to see him behind those metal bars before I'd feel any peace.

I walked over and grabbed my phone and keys off the nightstand. Charlotte stepped out of the bathroom, zipped up our overnight bags and then followed me out of the room.

The air was stiff and stale as we walked through the police station. Once we made it through the metal detectors, I reached for her hand as we headed toward the elevators that would take us up to the floor where we would, hopefully, get a few answers.

"Are you going to be okay?" I asked as the elevator doors closed behind us.

She tilted her head to the side; the distress was written all over her face. "I'm nervous, but I'll be okay."

Her response wasn't very convincing, and all I wanted to do was help her.

I wrapped my arm around her shoulders and drew her body to mine. I kissed the top of her head. "It's okay to be nervous, but this is his mess, not yours."

Moisture built up in her eyes. "I'm really worried about Emery." While I shared her concern, there was no way in hell that little girl was going to suffer any more pain because of that jackass.

"I promise you that I will do whatever it takes to spare her of any more pain."

Emerald green eyes stared up at me. "I don't know what I would do without you."

I brushed a tear off her cheek with my thumb, feeling my heart stretch across my chest. I wanted her to understand that she wasn't alone. That I would always be there for her. "Luckily for you, you'll never have to find out."

Nerves knotted in my stomach with each step closer we got to the interrogation room. Charlotte's palm was sweating as she clung to me with everything she had. There were a few familiar faces that passed me by and a lot of black suits that I recognized as Feds. This was bad. Very fucking bad.

"What's up, John?" I said, leaning my arms on the desk

and glancing at the monitors. John was the desk sergeant on duty tonight. His round belly built from way too many beers after work and sagging skin was a telltale sign that he was way past his prime. He was also a hard-ass who constantly reminded everyone that life hadn't been too kind to him. The extra weight around his middle and the two heart attacks he'd had should have pushed him into retirement. Instead, he settled for desk duty. A position he hated, but I guess it was better than the alternative.

John's eyes shifted to Charlotte. Judging by the frown on his face he looked to be in a shit mood. What a surprise. "We got a full house," he said, caution in his voice. "She can't go any farther, and you're not allowed either."

"I'm aware," I said, trying to ignore the agitation that stirred in the pit of my stomach. I knew I wasn't allowed in that little soundproof box adorned with nothing more than a desk and a couple uncomfortable chairs. That didn't stop me from hoping to sneak a view through the glass.

I ran my fingers through my hair and then pulled on Charlotte's hand. "I'm going to bring you to a waiting room."

"Where are you going?" she asked in a lowered voice, as I steered her down the hall. She kept looking over her shoulder, probably making sure Big John didn't try to stop us.

"I'm going to the observation room," I said as calmly as I could, even though I felt anything but calm.

She sighed in frustration. "I want to see him."

Hatred spun in my gut. I had to clench down on my jaw to keep the words trapped inside my throat. I didn't want her anywhere near him. I wanted Grant Anderson behind bars and out of our lives for good.

I scrubbed a hand over my face. "I fucking hate this."

"Quinn, we can't avoid this. I need to talk to him."

"You're not going to be able to talk to him yet," I said, helping her sit down on the cold metal chair along the wall. It was right under the vent where the cold air would blast through. I took my jacket off and wrapped it around her shoulders. "This interview could take hours. Let me see what I can find out."

She sagged forward and wrapped my jacket tightly around her arms. "Okay."

I kissed the crown of her head before walking away.

The outside was buzzing with voices of people coming and going. My gaze searched out a friendly face, one that could fill me in on what was going down behind those closed doors.

"Scott." I held out my hand for a greeting as I approached the man standing vigilant outside the door. Scott Kerr was a retired cop who now worked in the District Attorney's office in the investigations bureau. He's an old friend of my father's who was well connected. If anyone knew anything, it was Scott.

"What's the word?" I asked, planting my feet firmly on the linoleum floor. I'd spent many hours in that interrogation room over the course of my career. Yet, as I stood there, I had no idea what to expect or how to prepare myself.

He nodded his head to the side, and I followed him to the far end of the hall so we were out of earshot. "They found him in a studio apartment upstairs from The Pleasure Room." He paused. "I guess he wasn't the straight shooter everyone thought he was. From what I gather, he was doing some questionable shit and dealing some dirty deals on the side. He was in deep with these bad dudes."

I roughed a hand down my face. The Pleasure Room was a well-known strip club owned by none other than Vinny Valentino. Marco's predictions were right. All that time he was hanging out with the kind of people that he once made a career of putting behind bars. It was ironic how the tables had turned. Grant Anderson went from white-collar wunderkind to back-alley bullshitter.

I cleared my throat and shifted my gaze away. "I don't

want any of his shady shit to touch my girls. I don't care what he landed himself in. He needs to understand that his family's money and influence isn't going to make any of his problems go away. He's not going to be able to buy his way out of this."

The guys that he was mixed up with would put him in an unmarked grave before he even had a chance to blink. They killed for laughs and wouldn't think twice about harming anyone associated with him.

Scott straightened his tie and stood straight. "Speaking of money. His daddy and his team of lawyers are on their way. We have a special counsel coming in and he has his first arraignment tomorrow at noon. We are doing this by the book. He's not leaving. So, for right now your girls are safe. The evidence against him is solid. You might want to convince Charlotte to cut all ties with him as soon as possible though. It will make things a lot easier for her and her little girl."

I shook his hand and went to go find Charlotte. I pushed past the doors to the waiting room, noticing she wasn't alone. The Anderson family had arrived and they all looked very fucking cozy. Grant's mother and Charlotte were sitting next to each other holding hands, while his father and brother sat across from her. All four of them looked to be in a deep family discussion. I hadn't even stepped a foot into the room yet and I could already feel the frosty air.

Grant's father looked up at the sound of my dress shoes squeaking against the floor. I've been in a lot of awkward situations over the years, but this was a whole new level of awkward.

"Quinn, right?" Mrs. Anderson asked, eyeing me carefully.

Charlotte swallowed and nervously crossed her legs. She pulled my jacket tight across her shoulders. I wanted to lift her from that chair and pull her into my arms, but I didn't think that would go over very well. So I nodded and stood off to the side, feeling unsure of where my place was.

John Anderson lifted his eyebrow, his eyes shifted from Charlotte to me. "Grant's attorney is on his way." He sneered, trying to rile me up.

There was no reason to address his comment, so I positioned myself against the wall and crossed my arms over my chest. His eyebrows shot up higher at my lack of response. I didn't owe him anything. I especially wasn't going to argue with him. So, I met his stare with the same level of discontent that he gave me. If he thought he could intimidate me, he could try his best. I wouldn't go down easy.

I cracked my neck from side to side, gearing myself up for a long fucking night. This was going to take hours.

I cleared my throat and lifted my chin to Charlotte. "They're going to be awhile. What do you want to do?"

It felt like there was an invisible line drawn in the middle of the room that separated us. Me on one side, her on the other.

She lifted her eyes, looking directly at me. "I'm going to hang out here for a while," she said, folding her hands in her lap, seeming anxious.

It felt like she didn't want me here.

Grant's brother leaned forward in his chair. He rested his elbows on his knees and studied us with interest.

I inhaled deeply, not sure what the hell to do with myself. "Okay. Then we'll wait."

"Actually, I was going to ask you for a favor." She gave me a tight smile that did nothing to calm my nerves. "Grant's parents had to leave Emery with a family friend. Would you mind picking her up and staying with her until I get home?"

An awkward silence took over the room. I could practically see the wall between us being built brick by brick. I searched her expression, trying to figure out what the hell she was thinking. It felt like some kind of sick joke. She needed me by her side. Not to serve as a fucking babysitter.

I wanted to question her, but my head was screaming at me to give her the time she needed. The realization that I didn't know how to handle the situation only made the tension spread through my jaw faster.

Fuck this shit!

With a quick jerk of my head and with my fist clenched to my side, I finally snapped. "Charlotte, I'd like a word in private, please."

I did my best to school my features and keep the edge out of my voice. I told myself not to get worked up, but the longer I stood in this room staring her other life in the face, the more agitated I became. I felt like an outsider.

She excused herself as I held my hand out for her to walk with me down the hall. She glanced back at the Andersons before reluctantly following me out. She fell into step beside me, but she might as well have been on another continent. She was so close yet felt so far away.

The more distant she seemed, the angrier I became. The elevator ride was silent. I knew there were cameras and I was crawling out of my skin trying to keep my mouth shut. The last thing I wanted was to air my dirty laundry at my place of work. I was a private person and people already knew more about my personal life than I wanted them to.

Once we reached the main lobby and walked through the revolving door, I spun around and glared at her. A burst of anger flew out of my mouth. "What are you doing, Charlotte?"

She was slow to look at me. Her entire demeanor had changed since we left that hotel room just hours ago. She was a completely different person, one that concerned me.

"I can't just abandon his parents. They have been a part of my life for the last seven years. Regardless of how you feel about the situation, I care about them." She shook her head.

"They're still my family, and whether I like it or not, Grant is still my husband. I feel like this is where I'm supposed to be right now. Why can't you understand that I'm just trying to do the right thing?"

She was slipping away from me. And all I could do was watch it happen. The stress of everything around us was getting to her. She was already questioning and second-guessing everything I was to her. I could feel it. See it with my own eyes.

She loved me. I knew that much. Yet, that didn't stop the feeling of helplessness from taking over my thoughts.

Time passed and all I wanted to do was pull her into my arms and take her as far away from here as I could. She belonged with me. Not them. Not him.

Life was so fucking unfair sometimes.

I cautiously stepped closer, cupping the back of my neck, and feeling more insecure than I ever had in my life. "You know that I've loved you for as long as I can remember and that will never change. A life with you and Emery is all I want." Trying to come up with the right words without shredding my heart in the process was impossible. I swallowed, knowing there was no way to keep the pain from my voice, and I refused to hide it from her. "But I can't stand by for much longer. You're going to have to choose whose life you want to be a part of. Mine or theirs."

All the color drained from her face, breaking my heart in the process. Instead of fighting for me, she stood there and said nothing. The unspoken words between us were causing more damage than she realized. I was losing her right before my very eyes.

"I'm going to stay at my place tonight." She stared back at me in shock. "I'll watch Emery until you get home. With Grant behind bars, you are no longer in immediate danger."

With those parting words I did something I promised I'd never do again. I turned my back to her and walked away.

TWENTY-ONE

CHARLOTTE

"Mom, everything is fine. You and Dad don't need to fly up here," I reassured her with the phone pressed to my ear while I attempted to shove a peanut butter and jelly sandwich into Emery's lunch box.

"It's been a rough couple of months for you and now that your father is feeling better, our main priority is supporting you."

I shook my head and grabbed the carrot sticks out of the fridge. "Mom, we are fine."

"No, you're not."

"Okay, you're right, but we are slowly getting there. I promise. Dad is not ready to travel yet. Seriously, please stay down in Florida and enjoy that sunshine."

My father had back surgery a few months ago and has had complication after complication. The last thing I needed was to worry about him not being comfortable here without all of his equipment. He still had physical therapy sessions a couple times a week and needed special accommodations. Flying up here would be a disaster for everyone.

"Maybe you should reconsider our offer and move down here. A fresh start is just what you need."

"You know I can't that do that, Mom."

"Why, because of Quinn?" The disdain in her voice was clear.

There was a time when my parents thought of Quinn as a son. My family loved and adored him. The day we got engaged, my mother gathered all our friends and neighbors over to our house for a celebration. There was champagne and enough food to feed our small neighborhood.

My parents believed in us. We may have been young and foolish, but our love was real, and it was big. The kind that only comes around once in a lifetime. Everyone could see it, even my parents. That's why they felt so betrayed and disappointed when he broke things off. I swear their hearts broke almost as much as mine when he dumped me.

When I told my family that I was pregnant and marrying Grant, it took them a while to accept it. Eventually, they had no choice but to come around. Grant never quite measured up in their eyes. And believe me, he tried.

Emery trudged down the stairs with her unkempt hair flying along her shoulders. She was trying to balance her overflowing backpack on her shoulder. Her class was working on a huge holiday project and we had spent the better part of last night searching for supplies.

"I gotta go. Love you." I hung up before she could get another word in. I glanced down at Emery who wore a troubled frown on her face.

"Do you want some toast and cereal?"

She set her backpack down with a loud thump and climbed into the chair. "I'm not hungry."

"Is everything okay?"

She sniffed and stared at the floor. "I hate school. I wish I didn't have to go."

I closed my eyes and took a deep breath. "You have to go to school. Besides, you would miss all your friends."

Her bottom lip trembled. "I don't have any friends."

I rested my hand on her arm. "Are kids being mean to you?"

A rush of tears poured out of her eyes. "No one wants to be my friend because they said my dad is a bad man and I must be bad like him."

I pulled in a deep breath and forced myself to calm down. I didn't want to lose my cool, because I knew they were just kids being kids. Yet, seeing my daughter so upset had me wanting to storm into her classroom and give those little shitheads a piece of my mind. I was an adult and I knew I had to act like one, but kids today could be so cruel.

I reached for her and pulled her into a hug. "Who said that to you?"

"I don't want to talk about it." She pulled back and twisted her hands in her lap. "I wish he wasn't my dad. Why can't Quinn be my dad?"

"Emery." My heart ached so badly I wanted to tear it out of my chest. I pushed a few strands of hair off her forehead. "I know you love Quinn, but he's just a friend," I explained, gently trying to soften the blow.

There has been so much unbalance in her life, and Quinn staying at his place the past couple of nights wasn't helping. I felt partly responsible for the pain she was going through. I let her get attached to him. I allowed myself to need him. Now here we both were, missing him and wishing he were here.

This was all my fault, and I was in a no-win situation. Not only was she losing her father, but she was upset that Quinn was absent from her life too.

She crossed her arms over her chest and pouted. "Well, I hate my dad. I don't want to be his daughter anymore!"

She was lashing out, and I felt completely helpless. "Listen to me. I know this has been hard for you and I know you're hurting inside, but I promise things will get better."

There was no way I could hide the sadness in my voice.

Emery didn't hate her father. I could see it in her eyes and hear it in her voice. She loved him, but he hurt her beyond measure, and I wasn't sure she would ever be able to forgive him for it.

"The bus is here," she grumbled and started down the hall.

I folded my arms across my chest and leaned against the front door while watching Emery step onto the school bus. It was my job to make sure she was happy and secure. I was failing miserably. If I couldn't provide those simple necessities for her, what good was I?

I was in the middle of picking up the kitchen when those damn stomach cramps came back. I sprinted toward the bathroom.

I'd spent the last couple of days with my head buried in a toilet bowl. And when I wasn't puking my brains out, I was nauseous and feeling lightheaded. Not only did the smell of fish bother me, but you couldn't even say the word hamburger without me running out of the room in search of the nearest trash can. There was no way this was just a stomach bug.

After brushing my teeth and washing my hands, I checked my appearance in the mirror. My skin was puffy, and I was so damned tired. All I wanted to do was sleep.

I knew I'd need to stop by the pharmacy. But what the hell was I going to do if I was actually pregnant?

———

Mackenzie and I were having lunch in my classroom. It was my first week on the job, and instead of eating in the teachers' lounge like the rest of the faculty, I chose to hide out in my classroom.

I was filling in for a teacher that was out on maternity leave, which was kind of ironic. Even though it was only temporary, I was thankful for small miracles because I really needed this job.

"Do you want me to watch Emery later so you can visit Grant tonight?" Mackenzie asked, sitting in a chair opposite of my desk.

"I suppose I'm going to have to face him at some point." I sighed, opening the lid to my hot tea from Starbucks and blowing into the cup. "Thanks for this, by the way."

She shook her head and unwrapped her sandwich. "Don't mention it." She eyed the untouched salad on my desk. "Have you talked to the Andersons since his arraignment?"

I looked up from the papers I had to take home with me tonight and grade. I was exhausted, and trying to get caught up to speed on 7th grade US history wasn't helping my fatigue.

"We've exchanged a few text messages. I think they're disappointed that I haven't visited him yet."

I never got to see him the morning that he was arrested. I waited as long as I could, but he was detained for hours. He called the house on Monday morning before his arraignment with the judge, but I had already left for work. Now, it's been three days since he's been in custody, and I still haven't talked him.

"Well, it's not like you can abandon your responsibilities." She leaned back in her seat. "You have a job right now and a life you're trying to get back on track. I know they love their son, but it's not like he didn't do what he was accused of doing. They also have to understand that you and Grant are separated and your marriage is basically over."

"I think they are finally starting to understand that, and even if they don't, they won't have much of a choice," I said, moving a tomato around in my bowl while she watched me carefully. "I know that I can't keep putting my conversation off with Grant, no matter how difficult it may be. I'm worried that he hasn't accepted his fate or come to terms with the end of our marriage. I'm nervous that he won't just fight his sentence, but that he will also drag this divorce out for as long as possible."

I looked up to see her watching me with sympathy.

It really wasn't my intention to spend our lunch hour unloading my troubles on her, but I needed her advice. I needed her words to make me feel better. I needed her to tell me what to do. Basically, I wanted her to make this decision for me.

"He's going to have plenty of time while rotting away in that jail cell to figure out that shit just got real. Grant may be an arrogant son of a bitch, but he's not stupid. He'll have no other choice than to accept that his marriage is over and his freedom is gone."

"Let's hope you're right," I said and took a sip of my tea.

We both looked up when we heard a commotion outside my door. It was just a couple kids horsing around in the hallway.

"How is Emery holding up? I'm worried about the little princess."

I glanced at my phone to check the time and to see if I had any missed calls or messages. Nothing from Quinn. What a surprise.

"I'm not going to lie. She has her moments. She's upset and lashing out. It's been so bad that I've resorted to paying her off with these..." I held up a bag of Reese's Peanut Butter Cups. "And this." I pulled out the Target bag from under my desk and showed her the plastic pony I bought for her doll.

Her lips lifted into a smile. "While I don't normally condone bribery, I do encourage parents to provide incentives for good behaviors with children. Plus, those are the Christmas trees, which are way better than the original peanut butter cups."

"Exactly." I smirked, sliding a piece of candy her way.

"What she's experiencing is completely normal. You're

going to have to let her go through the emotions. You're doing a good job, Charlotte. My only advice is try not to say anything negative about Grant in front of her. Not that I think that you would," she clarified, and unwrapped her chocolate.

I sighed and stared down at my outfit. We may not have had the perfect marriage, but Grant was a good father up until this point.

"I know, but believe me, I've had to bite my tongue more times than I can count."

"How are things with you and Quinn? Have you talked to him?"

"Can we talk about something else?"

She shook her head at me. "Charlotte, you're human. As stubborn as he is, he knows that you have a mess to sort out. This whole situation is unique and confusing, and unfortunately, there is no instruction book to follow. You'll just have to give it time for everything to work itself out."

"I just want to close my eyes, snap my fingers and wake up from this nightmare."

"A little sleep could probably do you some good. You look like hell."

"Thanks for the compliment."

She shrugged. "That's what friends are for. Just keeping it real." She stood and stared at her shoes, looking like she wanted to say more. We've been friends long enough for me to know that she wasn't finished.

"I know you have something to say, so just spit it out." I waved my hands around for her to get on with it.

She adjusted her bag along her shoulders. "Things are tricky right now, but Quinn loves you. At the end of the day, I think you guys will be fine. The sooner you get those papers signed, the closer you'll be to getting your life back. Stop avoiding Grant and get it over with."

I reached for the box of tissues sitting on the corner of my desk. I wiped the edge of my eye, trying not to smear my makeup. "I want all that. Believe me, I do. More than you know."

"I'll help you with whatever you need."

I watched my friend walk away, knowing what I had to do. She was right; I needed to get the visit with Grant out of the way. But first I needed to talk to Quinn. I was a fucking mess and I really needed to hear his voice. I was falling apart and his strength was the only thing that kept me together.

I pulled out my phone and dialed his number.

"Detective Walker speaking." His tone was cool and impersonal.

"I miss you," I said, walking over to the window that overlooked the parking lot.

He sighed heavily into the phone. "I miss you too."

I let out a breath that I didn't even know I was holding. Obviously, things were strained between us, but it was comforting knowing that he was just as miserable as I was. That I wasn't alone with my misery.

"When can I see you?"

"I'm trying to give you space, remember? This is what space feels like."

"I know. I appreciate that but, God…" I sighed. "This is so damned hard."

"Well, it hasn't been a whole lot of fun for me either, but you can't have it both ways."

Jesus. He was so frustrating. "You're acting like I don't want to be with you and that couldn't be further from the truth."

"I refuse to be treated like the other man. You made it perfectly clear that Grant was your husband and that your place was with his family."

I might still be legally married to Grant, but my heart belonged to Quinn. It always had. I might not have handled things the right way, but there was no way I could allow him to think that I wouldn't choose him in the end.

"I'm not having doubts about us, I'm just trying to…"

"Do the right thing. Yes, you've mentioned that."

"Quinn." My palms were shaking. "I don't want to fight with you, but you can't possibly believe that I don't want you."

"I'm going to be honest here. I've done a lot of thinking." His voice sounded so tired and defeated. Nothing like the man I knew. "Maybe you were right."

I swallowed, almost afraid to ask. "About what?"

"Maybe I should back away and give you the time you need to get your life figured out."

I rested my head along the wall, feeling the tears spring to my eyes. "It sounds like you're giving up on me."

"Never." His voice was quiet. "I'm just trying to give you what you need."

"You know that I love you, right?"

"I don't doubt that you love me. You just need a minute to focus on Emery and to process what this new reality means for you both."

My body felt numb. I didn't blame him for feeling the way he did. It's what I'd been asking for. I just wished there was something I could do to take his worry away.

Up until this point, I'd been so focused on myself and my situation, that I hadn't allowed myself to see things from his point of view. He knew how difficult this was for me and he was putting my needs before his own.

My throat all of a sudden became thick with emotion. "Just because I need a minute, doesn't mean that I don't want a life with you." The line went quiet. "I know I sound selfish, but I can't lose you."

"You can't get rid of me that easily," he teased and it felt good. "You and I will be fine. I know we will. Just focus on you and Emery. I'm not going anywhere."

I clutched my throat feeling slightly relieved. "Do you still want us to spend Thanksgiving with you and your family?"

"Of course, I do."

"Okay then. We will be there."

He let out a deep sigh. I heard voices in the background. "I gotta go. I'll see you soon. Give Emery a kiss for me."

"I love you."

"I love you, too."

He disconnected the call. I closed my eyes and rubbed my stomach. I needed to buy a damn pregnancy test sooner rather than later.

TWENTY-TWO

QUINN

HE STEPPED INTO THE ROOM WEARING AN ORANGE JUMPSUIT WITH his state issued slip-on sneakers squeaking against the floor. I took a moment to really look at him. Gone was the clean-cut, golden boy in a perfectly pressed business suit.

He looked like shit and I couldn't be happier about that. I wished this man the most miserable existence, because that is exactly what he deserved.

Looking back, it was clear to me that we were all a sick little game to him. He toyed with us in a way that would change the lives of everyone involved. I blamed him for all that's gone wrong in my life. Hating that he got to hold her, love her, give her the child that was supposed to be mine. He was the man who gave her the life that I had once promised to her.

Then again, maybe I shouldn't give him so much credit. I should've seen the warning signs. Maybe if I wasn't so young and foolish, I could have stopped him from putting a ring on her finger.

He looked smug as he pressed his hands along the metal table and leaned forward. "It didn't take you long." His angry eyes shifted over my shoulder to the door.

I widened my feet and folded my hands across my chest. "If you were expecting to see Charlotte, you're out of luck."

"You mean my fucking WIFE!" He sneered, trying to act cocky and show arrogance when he had no right to. He may have been powerful and in control at one point, but those days were over.

I walked over to the table and squared my shoulders. He was trying to act tough, but I could smell fear from a mile away.

And he was trembling like a little bitch.

I pushed the envelope across the table. "Sign the fucking papers."

He looked down at the manila envelope and narrowed his eyes. "I'm not signing shit. If you think I'm just going to hand over my wife and daughter without a fight, you've clearly underestimated me."

"I don't need you to hand her over. She's already mine. If you inch a little bit closer, you'll be able to smell her on me."

Just as I expected, he reacted. He tried to lunge toward me, but the guard was already on him. "You son of a bitch. She's my fucking wife!" he boomed, while being pulled back by his shoulders. "Show me some goddamned respect."

I nodded my head to the guard and held up my hand. "Mr. Anderson isn't going to lay a finger on me." I cocked my head to the side. "Isn't that right?"

The muscle in his jaw ticked so hard it looked ready to break through the skin. "I want to tear your fucking eyeballs out."

I looked at my watch pretending to be bored with this conversation. I just wanted to say what I had to say, force him to sign the damn papers, and get the hell out of here. If I got him a little riled up, well that was just a bonus.

"I have a proposition for you."

His eyebrows dropped low. "You can take your proposition and go fuck yourself. I'm not interested."

I scrubbed my chin and pointed to the empty chair. I wanted to wait him out and watch him squirm in his seat, but unfortunately, I didn't have all day. I promised Marco that I wouldn't do anything stupid.

I folded my hands into a tent and placed my fingers under my chin. "Sit, we have a few things to discuss."

He let out a sarcastic laugh. "No, we don't. I'd rather eat a bowl of dog shit with a hair in it than discuss anything with you."

I found that hard to believe. Unlike me, he was trapped in a six-by-eight-foot padded cell with nowhere to go and no way out. He had all the time in the world, and by the way he looked, he hadn't slept in days. Exhaustion was etched across his face. He was probably desperate for a change in scenery. Even if I was the last person he wanted to see.

I stared at him for a minute and imagined all the years he stole from me and the fucked-up shit he did to Charlotte that night when he slipped her that roofie.

My muscles clenched, and I took in a deep breath. I needed to keep a cool head and focus on what I came here to do. "Grant, let's play a game. It's called Guess Who. I'll start." His beady little eyes turned into slits. "I had an interesting chat with an old buddy of yours. Would you like to *guess who*?"

His jaw clenched, and I paused, trying to keep my tone flat. "You can't think of anyone? Okay, I'll give you the answer. Michael Romano. Ring a bell?"

I watched his Adam's apple move in his throat as he swallowed hard. I stood taller, all six foot two of me, and watched as the realization settled in. The tension burned across my chest, ready to explode.

I slammed my hands down on the table. "You're a worthless piece of shit." My words were seething with rage. "Charlotte trusted you as a friend and you took advantage of her. You knew exactly what you were doing when you drugged her." My voice dropped to a whisper so only he could hear me. *"When you raped her…"*

He ran his thumb along his bottom lip. Sweat was already forming along his hairline. "I don't know what he told you, but I didn't rape her. I gave her a sleeping pill, that's it." He was visibly shaking. "She asked me for one. She probably doesn't remember. She was so shitfaced that night."

"You're right, she doesn't remember. In fact, she doesn't remember a damn thing from that night with you."

He looked to the hidden cameras that were capturing every word spoken in this room. He knew the drill almost as well as I did, having spent most of his time on the other side of this table. What he didn't know was that I wasn't here to get him to spill his guts, that was Marco's job. The only thing I wanted was his fucking signature on the divorce papers.

His shoulders rose and fell with heavy breaths. The tension in the room was suffocating. Every second that ticked by hung heavily in the air. "I love her." He dragged his handcuffed hands down his face. "I've always loved her. I would never hurt her."

"You've got no idea what it's like to love someone so much that you would do anything to protect them. All you ever did was lie to her right from the beginning." His regret-filled eyes turned sideways. It was obvious that he cared for Charlotte. And I would bet my last dollar that he spent the better part of their time together hoping she would return his feelings. Maybe, if he wasn't so obsessed with claiming her, he could have seen that she was never his to have. She was always mine.

"I know how privileged men like you work. It's all about your big egos and small dicks. You're all about control." He clenched his jaw, looking like he wanted to take me out from across the table. God, I wish he would fucking try.

He leaned forward, contempt spilling from his mouth.

"You think you love Charlotte?" he said offhandedly. "But you don't. You never would have left her if you did."

I wanted to rip him apart, limb by limb. It took me a minute to compose myself. Who the hell was he to judge my love for her? He had no idea what we had. Or maybe he just wasn't capable of understanding it. "And you think you do? Exactly when during your marriage did that pretty little DA catch your eye again?"

He turned away, trying to keep his cool. "That's none of your damned business. Charlotte and Emery are all that matter to me. You don't deserve Charlotte. You never did."

"You're right, I never did. But that doesn't change the fact that she chose me. That it's me she loves. It's always been fucking me!" I shouted as heat spread up his neck and onto his cheeks at my words. "But you knew that, right? You eventually figured out that you would always be second choice. The only reason why she married your sorry ass was because she was pregnant. She thinks she slept with you willingly. She thinks she just had too much to drink that night, but we both know better, don't we?"

His intense brown eyes narrowed on mine. "She doesn't know? You didn't tell her?"

"No, she doesn't. It would destroy her." I paused. "But you know, Grant, if you're willing to cooperate with me, I'll do my best to make sure she never finds out what you did to her. All you would have to do is sign your name along the dotted line."

"You think I'm dumb enough to fall for that? Like you'd do me any favors."

"I'd do it for Charlotte. There isn't anything I wouldn't do for her."

His lips twisted in disgust. "Of course, you would, because you two share this bond that no one else could ever compete with." He rolled his eyes. "It didn't matter what I did or how much I gave her." He paused for a moment, seeming to catch himself on his words. "I thought once she had Emery, that things would change, but it didn't exactly turn out that way. I never understood why she could never return my feelings after I gave her everything."

I dropped into the chair across from him, not knowing what else to say, because honestly, everything he said was true. It didn't matter what he did for her, or how much money he threw her way on things that didn't matter. Even if I wasn't in the picture, it wouldn't change the end result. She would never love him back the way he wanted. Especially now.

"Is that why you were sleeping around on her?"

"My marriage was falling apart. I didn't know what to do," he confessed as I hung on to every word. "So, I started drinking to numb the pain, but after a while it wasn't enough. I was a drowning man. I had a reputation to protect, a family to support. But the blow and the drinking helped me forget about it all just for a little while. When Pamela came to me and told me she was pregnant with my child, I—"

"Wait," I cut him off, "back up. She's pregnant?"

"She was. She lost it."

That was interesting, because she never mentioned that. He also didn't look too upset about it either.

"Look, as wonderful as this little heart-to-heart chat is, I'm not your fucking therapist. Although I did take a few psychology courses in college, I'm no expert. Let me use a few technical terms a lawyer like yourself can understand. You're in deep shit. So deep you'd need a ten-story ladder just to get yourself halfway out. Your family name isn't going to do you an ounce of good. The buddies that you worked with in the DA's office want nothing to do with you. And that law degree that you worked so hard for…Gone, once the State Bar strips it away. So, as you can see, you're screwed."

Angry eyes slid to mine. "You sure about all that?"

A laugh burst out of me. He really was an entitled ass. He

had zero chance of getting off. All I could do was shake my head at his stupidity and look up at the ceiling. "And here I thought you were a smart man."

"I am a smart man, which is why this isn't as cut and dry as you think it is. I can tie this up in the courts for years, dragging this divorce out longer than my sentence. I can make sure that Charlotte is never free from me."

He fucking smirked, but all I saw was red.

I didn't even realize what I was doing until my fists grabbed ahold of his shirt and I was lifting him up from his chair. I was ready to escalate this to a level that was going to put his physical health and my job in jeopardy.

The guard at the door was watching my every move. He shot me a look that said make your point and wrap this up quick, and then he turned his back to play on his phone. It took Grant half a second to realize that he was royally fucked.

"Let me spell this out for you, nice and slow, so I don't need to repeat myself. I'm only going to say this once, so you better fucking listen. I've spent half of my life loving that woman. If you think for one hot minute that I'm going to let you stand in my way for another fucking second, then you clearly don't know who the fuck I am."

I wanted to strangle him. I should have trusted my gut all those years ago when I first laid eyes on his pretty boy face.

Unfortunately, Charlotte only saw what she wanted to see. She saw good where there was none. She saw loyalty only to find out it was manipulated. Because Grant Anderson didn't give a shit about anyone but himself.

I let my eyes run over him. He was playing a big game. One he wasn't going to win.

His face was full of rage. "Your threats change nothing."

I inched closer. "You better be careful, Grant. You're not in a position to be going up against me."

The skin on his knuckles was turning white as he squeezed his fist tighter with each passing second. "You paint a pretty bold picture there, Detective. I'm very well aware of how our justice system works. I've spent many years on the other side of the courtroom, and I have no doubt my experience will be very helpful when it comes to putting together my defense."

Anger and annoyance sliced through me. "Do you honestly think your dumb ass isn't going to prison?" I asked, feeling the cords in my neck tighten. "You left five people for dead and fled because you panicked. And for what? Because you had enough nose candy in the back seat of your car to bring down you and your drug dealing network. You were so fucking afraid of getting caught that you ran to one of the most violent crime bosses in Philly for protection. All because you were a scared little bitch." I stood up and walked to the corner of the room. I needed to put some distance between us before I did something stupid. "You can't have blood on your hands and expect to walk out of here with a clean conscience."

The thought of what those monsters might have done to Charlotte and Emery sent me into a blind rage. Those men had no morals. They didn't care about women and children. They only cared about protecting their ass.

"Vinny didn't know I was hiding out in one of his apartments. He never saw me." My head tilted to the side as my eyes followed his gaze to the red blinking light in the corner. There were cameras everywhere. "He never saw me. I only went there because I knew that apartment was empty."

I folded my arms and leaned back. "I didn't know that you and Vinny Valentino were so close."

"We're not. I only know him because of Michael."

I should have known that there was no way he would implicate a mob boss. Not unless he had a death wish.

"Here's the thing. You're guilty as fuck. I don't give a flying shit what happens to you. I just want you out of Charlotte's life. So think about my offer, and sign the fucking papers." I threw the pen across the table hoping he would catch it. Of course, the shithead let it land on the floor.

"You don't call the shots here, Quinn. I'm not doing a damn thing until I talk to my wife."

The asshole leaned back in his chair like he was in control, even though he wasn't in a position to bargain. At this point, he was a man with nothing left to lose.

"So, tell me." I slipped my hands in my front pockets. I needed to do something with them. "Where does that pretty little DA you were screwing play into all this?"

His jaw was set. "She isn't anyone important. Not that it's any of your business."

"Apparently, she was important enough for you to call her that night."

"I'm not saying anything else regarding the case without my attorney present. But what I can say is that it was a horrible accident. I lost control when I went around the curve. It all happened so fast. I knew it was bad, but I panicked. I couldn't call Charlotte, so I called the one person I knew would help me."

"Right, a woman that you knocked up that wasn't your wife," I reminded him.

"Again, I'm done discussing this with you." He stood up to leave.

"Grant, you've always been an asshole." He raised an eyebrow in my direction. "I know what you're hoping for. If you think you have a shot in hell of somehow keeping Charlotte, you're not just an asshole. You're fucking delusional."

He slammed his fist down on the table. "You're really starting to piss me off. So, let's cut the shit. Charlotte is my wife, whether you want to acknowledge that or not. Emery is my daughter, not yours." He twisted his lips looking seconds away from going nuclear. "They are my fucking family, and if you think I'm going to sign away the only thing I have left in this world, you're the one who is fucking delusional."

I never hated anyone as much as I hated Grant Anderson. Why he wanted to drag the people he claimed to love through his bullshit made no sense. I expected him to blow up at me. I knew he wouldn't sign the papers without a fight. I expected him to challenge my offer. But it was his boldness and conviction to hold on to something he would never have again that spoke the loudest.

I scrubbed my hand over my face; my gaze flickered across the room. I was seconds away from exploding and breaking every bone in his body. "You know, Grant, making sure Charlotte and Emery are free from your bullshit is at the very top of my list. But there is something you don't seem to understand."

"No, there is something you don't seem to understand, Dick-tective. I still have rights." His glare was murderous. "You think that just because you wear that badge in here that you're holding all the cards?" He gestured around the room. "Well, I have one more ace up my sleeve, so you might as well end this little 'tough cop' show of yours."

The muscles in my neck strained against my collared shirt. "Don't fuck with me."

I took a step back and started toward the door.

"We agree one thing, dickhead. This isn't over. Far from it."

TWENTY-THREE

CHARLOTTE

I stood in the driveway of Quinn's parents' house. The wet snow covered our feet as Quinn helped Emery out of her booster seat. There was a Christmas tree standing in the big bay window just like there always was on Thanksgiving Day. It was a tradition at the Walker house. After dinner, the whole family gathered around and helped decorate the tree because Ann Marie lived for the holidays.

There were already lights strung along the roofline of the house, and the singing Santa that drove all the neighbors crazy was placed on the front porch, greeting everyone who came into the house. I wasn't expecting to be hit with a feeling of nostalgia, but the snow, lights, and Santa had taken me there. The three of us walked along the shoveled path that led to the decorated door adorned with a huge wreath.

I took a deep breath and held onto the casserole I was carrying in a firm grip, as Quinn took Emery's hand and led her through the front door.

This was the first time I'd seen him since he packed his bags and left. Things were still tense between us, but I was thankful that he was honoring his promise to include us in his family gathering.

I had to remind myself that Rome wasn't built in a day.

"Hello," Quinn called out as we entered the foyer. The smell of the turkey roasting in the oven hit my nose and I prayed that it wouldn't make me sick.

I curled my toes in my boots to keep my feet from running out the door. I'd had anxiety all week about this dinner, especially since Quinn and I were on such shaky ground.

Ann Marie's face brightened when she saw us. She held her arms out for Quinn, while I set the casserole dish on the table so Emery and I could take our coats off and hang them on the hooks in the hallway. I removed my gloves, noticing that my palms were sweating with nerves.

Quinn bent and gave his mom a quick kiss. "Mom, you look tired," he said, pulling away.

"That's because I've been up since four a.m. trying to get everything ready." She looked over her shoulder with a smile. "Charlotte, I'm glad you came." She walked over to my daughter and placed both her hands on her tiny shoulders. "You must be Emery. I've heard so much about you. I've been looking forward to meeting you all week." She looked up at me with her brown eyes softening. "She's beautiful, Charlotte, and she looks just like you."

"Thank you. And thanks again for having us," I said, handing her the green bean casserole that I had made. I shifted on my feet and tucked my long curly hair behind my ear, not knowing what to do with my hands.

"Hey, Peanut," Quinn said as he gently ran his palm over the top of Emery's head. "This is my mom, Ann Marie. Can you say hello?"

"Hi." She waved and tucked her body into Quinn's side.

The connection between Quinn and my daughter was not lost on Ann Marie. Emery was acting shy and timid, but I hoped once she got a little more comfortable with the Walkers, she would come out of her shell.

"Come on." He grabbed onto Emery's hand and led her

down the hallway. "I've got a few more people I want you to meet."

I glanced around the house as we made our way into the kitchen, noticing that it looked exactly the same as I remembered it. The last time I was here felt like another lifetime ago.

Thomas and his broad shoulders stepped into my line of sight. "I'm so glad you're here," he said, throwing one arm around my shoulder while safely holding onto his beer with the other hand.

"I'm happy to be here." I smiled, just as Emery sidled up next to me. She looked from me to Thomas with hesitation. "Emery, this is Quinn's dad, Mr. Walker."

"Well, hello there, young lady." He kneeled in front of her so they were at eye level. "It's nice to meet you. You are just as pretty as your mama." He playfully tapped her on the nose. "How about you come over and give this old man a hug?"

She looked up at me for permission. When I nodded my head to let her know it was okay, I watched as Thomas drew her into his chest.

Quinn chuckled from behind us. "Careful, old man. You don't want to squat too low, because you might not be able to get back up without some help."

Thomas cocked an eyebrow. "I'll show you old."

"I'd like to see you try, old man."

"Okay, Emery," Nora said, trying to hold her laugh in as she walked into the kitchen. "I'm this guy's sister." She smacked Quinn on the stomach. "My daughter, Taitlyn, is in the other room and is dying to meet you. Would you like to help us set the table and hang out with us?"

Emery's eyes lit up, and I gave her a wink. Quinn talked about his niece all the time and Emery was craving for some companionship from someone her own age. She'd been struggling with her friendships at school since the scandal. Spending time with Taitlyn would do her some good.

"Maybe after dinner we can play a game of Candy Land," Nora said, steering her out of the kitchen toward the dining room, where Taitlyn was gently laying out all the silverware and dishes.

"Can I help you with anything?" I asked Ann Marie as she added a little milk and butter to the potatoes.

She pointed to the pot next to her. "Would you mind stirring the gravy?"

Quinn eyed me from across the kitchen. His mouth lifted into a knowing grin. This was always my job. It was the only thing she let me touch. Probably because there really wasn't much I could do to screw it up.

Thomas patted Quinn on the shoulder. "Why don't we make sure those newlyweds are behaving themselves?"

Ann Marie grabbed a towel from under the sink and wiped her hands. "You don't need to make up excuses. We all know you just want to park your butt in front of the TV and watch football."

Thomas walked over and kissed his wife on the lips. I always envied their relationship. Where my parents were always bickering about everything and anything, these two were always stealing touches and glances whenever they could, even after thirty-five years of marriage.

Once the men were in the living room talking about sports and Nora and the girls were setting the table, Ann Marie and I were left all alone.

"Did Brody and Gretchen have a nice getaway?" I asked, attempting to make small talk. They decided to postpone their honeymoon until next year and just went away for a long weekend away after the wedding.

She shook her head. "Like that boy would tell me anything. I just found out today that they have been living together for the past three months. Here I thought they were going to wait until after the wedding. I don't know why he lied to me."

Oh, I knew why, I thought as I looked around noticing the familiar red and gold Tuscan-style themed kitchen with the big framed picture of Jesus and The Last Supper on one wall and a crucifix on the other. Ann Marie was a strict catholic girl with old-fashioned values. It was one of the reasons why she didn't approve of me. She made it very clear that she didn't like the idea of Quinn and I living in sin before we were married.

"I'm sure they probably didn't want to upset you."

She pointed her long, white painted acrylic fingernails at me. They looked like they needed a trim. "Honesty is always the best policy."

"I agree. At least that's what I always tell Emery."

"How are you girls holding up?" she asked, tightening the strings along the back of her apron.

I sighed while trying to work the lumps out of the gravy. "It's been a rough week for both of us."

I didn't expect to see the sympathy in her eyes. "I'm so sorry, dear." There was something different about Ann Marie. She seemed softer. More down-to-earth. I couldn't quite put my finger on it, but this whole exchange felt different than what I was used to.

"I want to apologize to you," she said, causing me to stop whisking the gravy.

"What for?" I asked with my hands frozen on the whisk.

"For how I treated you in the past."

I swallowed thickly, overcome with emotion. "Ann Marie, you don't owe me an apology."

Actually, I was being polite, because she totally did. She treated me like the anti-Christ.

She stopped what she was doing and walked over to the fridge and pulled out a bottle of red wine. By the looks of the bottle it was homemade, something her family was known for. "Yes, I do." She gestured to the kitchen table. "Please?"

Nerves danced in my stomach as I sat down on the wooden chair at the familiar oak table. Ann Marie poured two generous glasses and took a hefty gulp from hers. I just stared at mine and wondered if she would notice if I didn't take a sip.

She set her glass down and leaned across the table. "Regardless of what you think, I've always cared about you, Charlotte. I know I didn't always act that way, but I did. I just didn't like how serious you and Quinn were. You both were so young and moving too fast." Her confession surprised me, and there was so much I wanted to say, but I kept my mouth shut and let her continue.

"I used to tell all my friends that I wished you two met later in life, because you're only young once. I got married at nineteen and had Brody at age twenty. I wanted my kids to know that there was a whole world out there to explore, and that they had the rest of their lives to settle down."

My knees shook under the table. "Ann Marie, as a mother now, I can appreciate that. I know that you only wanted what was best for your son."

She pressed her lips together and took another generous sip of her wine. "That boy went through hell when you broke up. He may have been on the other side of the country, but I know my son. Just like I know that you are it for him."

Tears fell from the corner of my eyes. I always wanted Ann Marie to like me, but I never wanted to force it. Knowing that we finally had her acceptance meant more to me than anything.

Gretchen walked into the kitchen and cleared her throat. "I hope I'm not interrupting; just thought I would make myself useful."

The three of us spent the next half hour cutting up vegetables, while Nora and the two girls shuttled the food from the kitchen to the dining room. Emery and Taitlyn seemed to be getting along really well. They kept whispering in each other's ear and snickering over God knows what, and it was adorable. It was nice to see her smiling after the lousy week she just had.

I stared across the table, holding onto my untouched glass of wine as everyone polished off their plates. Quinn and the guys were arguing over trading picks in their fantasy football league while Gretchen passed around wedding pictures that she had just gotten back from her photographer. I sat up taller and played with the napkin in my lap while Nora and Ann Marie chimed in with stories of their own weddings.

I had no fond memories to share of my own marriage, and not just because it would be awkward and inappropriate. No, there were no happy stories to be told, because I married the wrong man for the wrong reasons.

The only man I ever wanted to marry was sitting next to me. And now after everything, I wasn't sure if we would ever get our happily ever after.

Quinn met my eyes, his brows dipped as if he could read my mind. He placed his hand on my leg in calming support. I glanced around the table and wondered how I could excuse myself without being incredibly obvious.

Once they changed topics and started talking about the upcoming holiday, my shoulders rose in relief. I pushed myself away from the table and wandered down the hall, needing a minute to myself.

Heavy footsteps sounded behind me. Quinn wrapped a hand around my bicep and pulled me into the tiny bathroom.

He shut the door and looked me over with concern. "Talk to me. What's going on?"

I'd been so emotional lately. It was taking every ounce of self-control not to burst into tears. How was it I could feel so many conflicting emotions at once? I was pissed at him for leaving me and upset that he's been avoiding me. Yet, here I was, happy and relieved that I was even here to begin with.

I squeezed my eyes shut and looked away. "I'm sorry. I'm just emotional lately. It's been a long week."

His dark eyes peered down at me like he didn't believe me. "Are you sure that's all?" He lifted my chin up, seeing right through my lie. Because, of course, it was so much more than that, but I didn't have the emotional strength to get into it with him, especially with his family right down the hall.

I ran my hands up his chest and around the base of his neck. "I wasn't sure if you still wanted me here today."

His hand skimmed along my sides until his palm was resting along my back. "I'll always want you. Even when I'm pissed at you." I tried to look away again, but he wasn't having it. "What happened in that dining room? What made you so upset?"

There was no use trying to tiptoe around the truth. Not when he could read me so easily. "Sitting in that dining room made me want something I was afraid I'll never have. It feels like all the work we've put into rebuilding our relationship is slowly slipping away."

He brushed the hair off my shoulder. "What is it you want, that you think you'll never have?"

"I want to someday be able to sit around that dining room table as a Walker and not as an Anderson. I want the wedding that you promised me and the future that we planned on."

"I want those things too. You already know this." He pressed a tender kiss to my forehead. "I hate seeing you like this. What can I say to make you feel better, because even though things are strained between us, you should never doubt my feelings for you?"

"Don't leave me."

He drew back and looked me. "Why would you think I would leave you?"

"Because this is so unfair to you, and I'm afraid that you'll get sick of all this back and forth and decide that it's not worth it." A knot formed in my throat, wondering how much further he could go without reaching his limit. "I don't know what's going to happen with this divorce or if Grant will drag it out. I don't know how Emery will adjust to a life without her father. But I do know that I need you, Quinn, more than I ever have."

I laid my head into the crook of his arm and tried to fight the tears that were threatening to fall. I was sick of pretending that everything was okay. Tired of putting up a brave front for everyone.

He used his free hand and wiped the tears off my cheeks. "You are ridiculous, you know that. You are the love of my life, Charlotte. I could never get sick of you." His voice was strong and unwavering. "As for your divorce, I will wait forever if that's what it takes."

He pulled me against his chest, and I looped my arms around his waist and held on tight. My life had been so weighed down lately, that the tears that spilled from my eyes felt freeing.

I dropped my head to his shoulder and rested it there. "Will you come home with me tonight?"

His fingers flexed along my back. "I think it's best for now that I stay at my place. Emery needs you, and if I'm being completely honest, I hate fucking sleeping in his house."

"So where does that leave us?"

He sighed and tilted his head toward the ceiling. "I'm not breaking up with you if that's what you're asking me. I'm just giving you the time you need." He pressed a kiss to my lips, letting his mouth linger a bit. "I want you to come to me when you're ready to give me one hundred percent. Until then, I'm just going to steal little moments like this whenever I can."

I gripped his strong shoulders and forced him to look into

my eyes. "You don't need to steal something that already belongs to you."

Before I could even blink, his mouth was on mine. I wanted to keep it light and gentle, a promise of what was to come, because hello, we were in his parents' bathroom. But Quinn had other plans. He pushed me up against the bathroom sink, our tongues grew urgent with need.

I pressed myself against him, and he wrapped his arms along my ass. He hitched me up and set me down on the bathroom vanity. His hands were strong and demanding as they ravished my swollen breasts. My head fell back when he skated his fingers over the peaks of my nipples. I sank further into the kiss, my need for him was unbearable. The ache between my thighs had me rubbing up against him like a dog in heat.

I slid the zipper to his dress pants open and pulled him out. Time was ticking away and I didn't know how much longer we would have. I gripped him hard, carefully flicking my hands over his swollen crown.

I closed my eyes and was ready to drop down to my knees when I heard the knock on the door. "Mom, how long are you going to be in there for? I have to go potty."

We both paused. I pulled away and rested my hands on his arms. For a split second, I wasn't sure what to do first. Fix my appearance, zip him back up, or get to the door.

"Fuck," he muttered, and shifted on his feet, trying to tuck himself back in his pants. *Cross one item off my list*, I thought and tried not to laugh. It was a good thing he was quick even though he looked uncomfortable and downright miserable. I managed to pry myself away from him and address the little interloper.

"I'm going to be a couple more minutes, honey. Why don't you use the other bathroom?" I said, running my fingers through my hair and smoothing the wrinkles from my shirt. It was a miracle I could even talk.

It wasn't until I heard her retreating footsteps make their way down the hall that I was finally able to breathe again.

Quinn ran his hands through his thick black hair. "You want to make sure the coast is clear?"

I quietly opened the door and peeked outside. Once I was satisfied that she was gone, I gave him a nod. He kissed my forehead. "I'll go out first." He gave me a sly smile that had my pulse kicking up a notch. "Maybe we can finish what we started later."

I nodded in agreement. Hell yes, we could. I shut the door and turned around, staring at myself in the bathroom mirror. There was a smile on my face and a warmness in my chest that I didn't want to lose.

I stepped out into the hall. Quinn and Brody looked to be having a heated discussion. I tried to be quiet because it looked like whatever it was, was serious and I didn't want to interrupt. It wasn't until I heard my name that I paused. Curiosity got the better of me, so I inched closer.

"You have to tell Charlotte. It's going to come out. It will be better if she hears it from you." Brody's voice was stern.

"How the fuck do I tell her? How the hell do I tell her that her piece of shit husband slipped her a fucking roofie the night her daughter was conceived?"

A gasp flew out of my mouth causing both men to turn around.

TWENTY-FOUR

QUINN

She looked shocked to the core and way beyond confused, while I stood there unable to form a single word.

"Is it true?" She stared at me, and I felt the weight of that question like there was a bag of cement resting on my chest. There was no good way to answer that without hurting her. There was no defending or justifying why I kept that information to myself. My brother shared a knowing look with me that said *I fucking told you so.*

"Answer me!" she demanded, folding her arms across her chest. I advanced toward her, wanting to comfort her. She took a step back, obviously it was the last thing she wanted from me. She wanted answers not my compassion.

I dreaded this conversation. The last thing I wanted to do was cause her any more pain.

"Um…" Brody coughed into his hand. His cautious eyes met mine. "I'm going to help clean up." I flashed my brother a pleading look that said, *please don't leave me.* He gave me one back that said, *you're on your own, asshole.*

He gave Charlotte a chin jerk as he rounded the corner, leaving me alone and feeling completely helpless.

"How much did you hear?"

She pinched her eyes shut. "Oh my God." Tears streamed down her cheeks that were still flushed from our moment in the bathroom. "It's true, isn't it? How did I not know?"

"Sweetheart." I softened my tone. I was trained to deal with situations like this. I had delivered and listened to much worse than this, but seeing the look of pain and betrayal on her face felt like a swift kick in the fucking stomach. "It was not your fault. You were drinking, you had no idea that he slipped you something."

She gripped the strands of her long hair like she wanted to yank it from her scalp. She started pacing a small path along the narrow foyer. I looked to my right to make sure everyone was out of earshot.

"I remember being at the bar with him. I remember him flirting with me. I was so hurt and so confused thinking that you didn't want me anymore. He was saying all the right things. I knew." She shook her head. "Deep down I knew that he had feelings for me, but I just wanted one night to forget. To feel numb."

The emotions and the guilt I felt in my throat as I listened to her run through the events of that night in her head were so strong, I practically choked on them.

"I remember we danced and we drank. I started feeling dizzy and had trouble walking. That's when he offered to take me home. We kissed in the back of the cab. He carried me upstairs and laid me down in bed and that's when my memory gets fuzzy. The last thing I remembered was his hands on me and that's when I realized that I was in over my head. But I kept kissing him. I never told him no. I never told him to stop."

"You were incoherent," I growled. "He fucking knew exactly what he was doing."

"When I woke up the next morning in his bed, I just assumed we had sex and that I blacked out."

I grabbed her shaking hands and stood there in my

parents' hallway, hoping that they couldn't hear what the fuck was going on. We had been gone long enough that they were probably wondering where we were.

"Charlotte." I swallowed, brushing my thumb along her wrist. "He gave you a sleeping pill. You were passed out. You had no way of knowing."

She blinked at me for a beat, and then two, before a frown took over her face. "How long have you known?"

I tore my gaze away from her, not wanting to have this conversation. My hesitation had her pulling her hand away and taking a step back.

I could feel my blood pressure rising. There wasn't a chance in hell that she wasn't going to get pissed at me. No matter how much I would try to reason with her, I knew my girl, and I could already see the fight brewing in her eyes.

A heavy exhale slowly left my lungs. "Since Brody's bachelor party."

"You've known for weeks?" The tone of her voice was mixed with shock and anger.

Her chest was rising and falling. I've seen Charlotte pissed, angry, and hurt. Yet, I wasn't prepared to see her so furious. My training had me observing her and trying to prepare myself for whatever the hell happened next.

"Why didn't you tell me?" Her voice was calm and controlled, giving nothing away. "Why am I just finding out about this now?"

I put my hands in my pockets and shifted on my feet. "Because I didn't want you to know. I knew it would devastate you."

Her mouth dropped open in disbelief. "Who the hell do you think you are keeping something like that from me?"

I tried to come up with a reason good enough. Struggled with how to explain myself. Somehow, I only made this situation worse and I hated myself for it. "Someone who loves you and wants to protect you."

She tried to move around me, but I wasn't having it. Before I could process what was happening, she shoved at my chest. She looked like she wanted to run away from me. And for the first time in as long as I could remember, I felt a sense of panic that I could actually lose her forever.

I grabbed her wrist, halting her movements. I looked down at the woman who I loved more than anything. Tears leaked from both corners of her eyes. I hated seeing her cry. And the worst part was that I wasn't sure if she was crying because of me or because of him.

"Talk to me," I pleaded.

"Let me go."

"You know me well enough to know that won't happen."

"Fine." She wiped the tears from her cheeks and looked back at me with a pained expression. I wanted nothing more than to pull her close, but I was afraid she would only shove me away. "Then take me home. I need time to process this. I need to wrap my head around everything."

The desperation in her voice had my heart sinking into the pit of my stomach. I could do that. I could give her that. I would do anything for her.

Things were awkward when we told my family that we were leaving early. Obviously, they knew something had happened. Emery threw a little fit when we told her it was time to go home. It only made things more difficult when my parents offered to let Emery stay and Charlotte said no.

The tension in the car on the way back to her place was so thick; I had to roll the driver's side window down just to breathe. I snuck a glance in the mirror and gave Emery a calm and gentle smile. Even she was quiet, which was a dead giveaway that she knew something was wrong.

Feeling out of control was not something that I was familiar with. I was used to being strong and put together. It was foolish of me to think that keeping this from her was the best way to handle it. She was silently crying in my car, trying her best to hold it in, when what she really needed to do was let it all out.

I'd been worried about how she would react. How this would affect her. It turned out that I had every right to be.

"Quinn, you've got to understand that I'm doing my best to hold it together, but it seems fucking impossible," she whispered while staring out the window, unable to look me in the eye. "I just need to be alone tonight."

I shifted my hands along the steering wheel. I was tempted to turn the damn car around. To where, I had no fucking clue. I just didn't want to bring her and Emery home and just leave them both. Not like this.

It didn't feel right, but what the hell did I know? Clearly, the only thing I knew was how to fuck everything up.

TWENTY-FIVE

CHARLOTTE

THE DOOR TO THE SIDE OPENED AND IN WALKED MY HUSBAND. His hair was longer and slicked back as opposed to the short-gelled hairstyle that he preferred. Gone were his Brooks Brothers suits and, instead, he now wore an orange jumpsuit. I didn't think I could ever get used to seeing him this way.

He tried to smile at me and it only pissed me off.

Every emotion I could think of pushed through me. Anger for marrying him in the first place. Disgust for what he's turned into. Embarrassment for what he has put his family through. Fear for what will happen to him once he reaches prison. But most of all, sadness for the only truly innocent person in all of this, Emery.

"I'm glad you came."

I frowned at him. "The only thing I came here for was to talk to you about signing the divorce papers."

"Well, today is your lucky day." He looked over his shoulder to the guard standing by the door. "I seem to have all the time in the world."

His attempt at humor only annoyed me further. "You think this situation is funny?" I asked, glaring at him from across the table. "You know what? Don't answer that." I sat down with a million questions burning on the tip of my tongue. Yet, I still didn't know where to even begin.

I shifted in my seat and scooted forward. My mind was still trying to process what I learned, and every time I thought about it, it made me sick to my stomach.

When I got dressed this morning and practiced my speech, I swore that I wasn't going to lead with this. But the mere sight of him had red hot fury racing through me.

"I know you tricked me into marrying you."

His head tilted to the side, looking clueless. "Pardon me."

I ground my teeth together and stood up. "You pretended to be my friend and you struck when I was at my weakest moment. You lied to me, played me for a fool, and controlled me for years. You tricked me into believing you were somebody that you weren't. Was it fun for you, by the way? Did you get some sick satisfaction when you finally gained my trust?"

"What exactly am I admitting to here?"

"Oh, please, don't pull this lawyer bullshit on me. It's not going to work this time." I placed my hands on the table and leaned forward. "I wasn't just drunk when I slept with you that first night, was I Grant?"

He opened his mouth and closed it. Searched the room, probably forgetting the only exit was to his jail cell. His shoulders dropped, and I watched him pinch his eyes shut in discomfort.

It seemed like it took him forever to respond. I waited on bated breath for him to answer me. But when he finally did, I wanted to reach across the table and throttle him.

There was no apology. No remorse. And certainly no guilt. Just his typical bullshit.

"Charlotte. It was an Ambien. It was a just a sleeping pill."

"Which was crushed up and put in my drink. You have a fucking law degree, don't you dare act stupid." I felt like I was staring at a complete stranger. "It was rape." A sob broke free and I felt ashamed and disgusted. Everything inside of me cracked wide open, the truth of my words ripping apart everything I was led to believe about our life together.

He averted his eyes to the guard and nervously moved his gaze back over to me. "I never wanted you to find out. I was afraid you would see it that way. I didn't want you to jump to the wrong conclusion. I know it sounds bad, but that wasn't my intention."

"Well, Grant, you know what they say, the road to hell is paved with good intentions...And you seem to be in the express lane right now."

Denial. Lies. Deceit. Here we went around and around. God forbid Grant Anderson own up to anything.

"How could you do that to me?" I swallowed down my anger, not even sure how I was supposed to feel anymore.

"Do what to you? Want something real with you? Want that genuine smile and affection that you gave him?" he spat. Clearly, my relationship with Quinn was a trigger for him.

"So, let me get this straight. You thought the best way to build something real between us would be to trap me into a relationship by drugging me?"

He drew his eyebrows together and brought his thumb up to his chin, toying with the little dimple in the center. Emery had that same dimple. She may have been my mini me, but her skin coloring and the curve of her chin, along with the tiny cleft in the middle were all Grant. She also had his smile and that reminder hurt like hell.

"You only saw me as a friend and I wanted more. I wanted a chance with you so that you could see how good we were together. I won't apologize for loving you. I'm not sorry for that." He shook his head. "I do regret spiking your drink, but I don't regret my daughter."

My eyes narrowed on him. "Do you hear yourself? Are you listening to yourself? It's all about you, Grant." I threw my hands up in frustration, wishing I had the balls to punch him in the face. "You wanted what Quinn and I had, but you were too arrogant to understand that it could never be yours. I wasn't some trophy to be won."

His eyes fell forward to the floor. Maybe my words had finally pierced his thick skull.

"You are always saying how much you love me." I said the words as calmly as I could, trying to push past the hurt and the betrayal. "Well, actions speak louder than words. Prove it. I'm done, Grant. I want a divorce. I want your signature on the papers. Today. I want to move on with my life. I don't want to be tied to you a second longer than I have to be. In fact, I want nothing more to do with you."

He jerked back like he'd been struck by lightning. Something dark, resembling a storm, passed across his features.

"I see." His voice was so cold it sent a chill across my skin. Humble Grant was gone and the calculating narcissist was back.

"I was arrested six days ago, and this is the first time my wife found the time to see me." He cocked his arrogant head to the side. "What's the matter, Charlotte? Have you been too busy playing house with your boyfriend, spreading your legs and fucking him in every room that I busted my ass to pay for?"

My mouth dropped open as he continued his rant.

"I can't even remember the last time you let me touch you. Do you think pretending to be the perfect husband was easy? The pressure of my job and trying to maintain a good public image was exhausting. I couldn't catch a fucking break."

"Don't you dare blame everybody else for your fuckups. You are a grown-ass man." I glared at him. "Do you even feel an ounce of guilt for the five lives that you took? Can you even comprehend what you have done to your own family?"

"Of course, I do." I watched him swallow hard. "What

happened was a horrible accident. You know me. I'm not a monster, Charlotte."

I shook my head. "I don't even know what you are anymore. I don't think I ever truly did."

"I'm not sure you really cared to know the real me. You never loved me."

"That's not true. Maybe not the way you needed me to, but I did. Now," I swiped my eyes, "knowing what you did to me, all I feel is hate."

"Fine. Hate me all you want, but that doesn't change the fact that we have a child together. A child that I love more than anything on this earth. A child that I won't allow you to keep from me."

"A child you love more than anything, huh? Do you have the slightest clue how devastating this has been for her? She's lost her friends, her confidence, her security. She's lost the only father she's ever known."

Grant exploded. "That's fucking bullshit! I may have fucked up with many things, but she is the one thing I've done right. I was the best goddamned father I could be to her and you know it. And if you think I won't fight for her, you have drastically underestimated your opponent."

His arrogance was astounding. Here was a man who was going to spend the rest of his life in prison and he had the gall to threaten me. "Sign the papers or not, Grant. At this point, I don't give a shit. As your opponent, let me tell you this. As the only person in this marriage who can actually come and go as they please, I am in control of whether or not you will ever see Emery again. Not you. Me. I'm in control."

His hands rested along the table as he rolled his thumbs back and forth. He glanced at the clock on the wall and then back to me. "I'll sign the papers, because I owe you that much. But I'm not letting you take my daughter away from me. I want to see her."

I couldn't help but notice that it was still all about his wants and his needs.

"Emery is having a very rough time. She has her first appointment with her counselor next week. Give me a chance to talk to her therapist first."

"I'm her father. She needs me."

"That's rich. Where the hell have you been since the night you crashed your car and left everyone for dead? You basically abandoned her."

"I didn't abandon her. I panicked. I've thought about Emery every single day."

"You're going to prison, Grant. I'm still not sure what that means for your relationship with her. I'm doing the best I can here. I'm trying to keep things as normal as possible for her. I'm trying to make sure she doesn't end up hating you, but other than that, I can't guarantee anything else. And if I'm honest, I think I'm being very fucking generous. So I wouldn't push it."

"Wow." He leaned back, keeping his cuffed hands firmly planted on the table. "You really do hate me, don't you?"

I reached into my bag and pulled out the envelope. I slid the pen and the paperwork across the table where he could reach it.

"Finding out that the person that I trusted took advantage of me and violated me when I couldn't defend myself, doesn't really bring out warm and fuzzy feelings."

A part of me didn't want to feel anything for him. He lied to me and made promises to me, knowing that he hurt me. As much as I didn't want to feel an ounce of pain over what he did, I still felt betrayed.

My husband raped me. That word alone made me cringe, but isn't that exactly what it was?

I always assumed that rape was when someone beat you and forced themselves on you. That they were monsters lurking in bushes and breaking in through bedroom windows. Yet, if you look up the definition on Wikipedia like I did, it boiled down to one sentence. It's a sexual act carried out without a person's consent. Grant was my friend. A person I trusted. He touched me, knowing that I was unaware of what was happening. He was inside of me without me even remembering. Because he gave me a fucking pill to put me to sleep and took advantage of me when I was most vulnerable.

All these years I always thought I was too drunk to remember. Yes, I let him kiss me. Yes, I let him into my apartment and into my bedroom. Would I have gone through with it? I don't know and I guess I never will because he took that choice away from me.

I lifted my head to the piece of shit in front of me. Tears rolled down his cheeks, remorse filled his eyes. "I don't know what else to say other than I'm sorry."

"There is nothing you can say or do that can take away the damage you've done." God, this was so difficult. "All you've done since the moment I met you is lie and deceive me. You stole seven years of my life. But hear me when I say this. We are done."

He nodded his head and looked away. His face was carved with pain and regret. I took a minute to study him. There was no denying that Grant Anderson was a handsome man, but he was also damaged and broken too. Much more than I ever knew. My eyes traced along his strong jaw up to his lips that were pinched tight from my words. Lips that I've kissed many times, lips that whispered endearments and assurances. He brought his hand to the bridge of his nose and squeezed his eyes shut like he was begging the universe to make this all go away.

The agony from the sob that broke free caught me off guard. "Please," he begged. "Tell me what I can do. I'll do anything to make this right."

And there was my opening. My Hail Mary that I'd been

praying for. "You can start by signing the divorce papers." My tone was even and unwavering. "And then you can sign away your parental rights to our daughter."

His eyes shot open. "No."

"Grant, you cannot physically care for her. Do you really want her to spend the next twenty to thirty years visiting you in prison? Is that what you want for her? Think about what is in her best interest. Think about someone other than yourself."

"I love my daughter more than anything. I know I fucked up. But Charlotte," he pleaded. "I've been a part of her life since the day she was born. I raised her. Rocked her to sleep when she was sick. Built her swing set in the backyard. Taught her how to ride a bike." His frustration was rising. He slammed his palms down on the table. "I'm her father!"

I jumped. "Really?" I knew I shouldn't poke the bear, but there was no stopping. I had enough. "You want to play that card? If you love her you will put her first. She has been through enough. I will promise you this though. If she wants to see you, I won't tell her no. I won't keep her from your family. I just want her to live a normal life. Free of all this. Do you really want to shackle her to weekly visits? Expose her to this kind of environment?"

He was quiet, finally understanding the consequences of his actions. He closed his eyes, trying to keep the tears back. There was a crazy battle going on inside my own heart. I had the freedom to get up and walk out of this room after our visit. Live my own life. Where he will be confined to cement walls for the next twenty years at least.

The air was heavy, leaving us with nothing else to say. He reached for the manila envelope and pulled out the documents. I expected the lawyer in him to read them over at least twenty times. Go through them with a fine-tooth comb.

I held my breath and tried to steady my heartbeat. Instead

of stalling and drawing this out any further, he picked up the pen and did the last thing I expected.

He signed every last one.

Seeing him sign his name across the legal documents destroyed something inside of me. Don't get me wrong, it was what I wanted, but it seemed so final.

"You know." He sighed, throwing the pen across the table. "I always knew that I was on borrowed time with you. Yet, I still tried to give you everything you needed and hoped that it would be enough to work through our issues. But I failed you and Emery. You both deserved better."

My eyes snapped up and locked onto his, searching for any sign that he was playing me and found none. "You know the sad thing about all this, Grant. I believe you. I know you're sincere. I know you love us, and believe it or not, I really tried to make it work with you, but the end of our marriage was inevitable."

Grant cleared his throat. "Now that I've done everything you've asked me to do, can you do one little thing for me?" His bottom lip trembled as he struggled to control his emotions. "Let me see my daughter one last time."

I fought against every belief I had to promise him the one thing he wanted. The thought of exposing her to any more pain made me want to rip my heart out from my chest.

I knew that there came a time to fight and a time to give in. Sitting across from my soon to be ex-husband, it was clear which one I needed to do. We could go back and forth for days, but it wouldn't do an ounce of good.

I stood up and wiped my eyes. "I will do my best."

"If I write her letters, will you give them to her?"

"I'll hold on to them until she's ready to read them."

He nodded while staring at the ground. "Thank you."

I needed to leave before I really broke down, so I scooped up the papers and turned to the guard and signaled that I was ready to leave.

I thought his hurt would bring me pleasure. But as I walked away without looking back, I felt sad instead of gratified.

Ending it this way hurt more than I ever could have imagined. I just stripped away his entire world to ensure my freedom and my daughter's well-being. Having him sign away his rights to Emery was to ensure that I was in complete control of her safety and basic needs. I didn't do it to be vindictive and I was relieved that he saw it that way. But again, it hurt like a bitch. My life would be a lot easier if I didn't have a fucking conscience.

I walked through the revolving doors, letting the taste of freedom take over me. I tightened my scarf around my neck and focused on putting one foot in front of the other. It wasn't until I was alone in my car that I let the sobs break free. I owed him and my previous life one big ugly cry. A few minutes to mourn. A past that I was done with. It was time to move on once and for all.

TWENTY-SIX

QUINN

I BOUNCED ON THE RUBBER MAT BENEATH MY FEET, MY GLOVE covered fist landing punch after punch to the heavy bag in front of me. I clenched my jaw and ignored the pain of my burning knuckles as I pounded away. I was covered in sweat and so fucking irritated I couldn't stop.

"Woah," Marco said, coming up to my side but keeping a safe distance. "I think I know whose face you're picturing right now."

I wrapped my arms around the bag to get it to stop moving. I shook out my body and tore out my AirPods. "What's up?" I asked, grabbing my water bottle off the floor. I tried to breathe through the rage and focus on anything other than smashing Grant Anderson's face in.

"I wanted to see how you're doing." He eyed my red, swollen hands as I yanked my gloves off.

"Slow day at the office."

He rolled his eyes. "I figured having public enemy number one locked up where he belongs would have you in a better mood."

He had a point. I should have been elated, but I was far from it. Was I relieved? Hell, yes. Did it change my current situation with Charlotte? No. Therefore, I was in a shitty mood.

"You really need to get laid and stop focusing on my personal life."

He chuckled. "Trust me, I have no issues getting laid."

Oh, didn't I know. Marco loved to bang and brag. If he got laid, the story got more coverage than Donald Trump's daily tweets.

"I'm really not in the mood for a heart-to-heart right now."

"You're obviously pissed off and I'm going to go out on a limb here. Maybe you're not the one getting laid?" I gritted my teeth and glared at him. "If this shit with Grant is causing problems between you and Charlotte, do something about it instead of being a fucking asshole to everyone."

The thing with being friends with Marco was that he was brutally honest. He didn't mince his words and he sure as hell didn't sugarcoat his thoughts. He had no trouble laying it all on the line for me and calling me out on my shit.

"She asked for space," I snapped and threw my hands out at my side. "I'm doing what she asked me to do."

He angled his head and stepped closer. "Yeah, I see that, but since when does Quinn Walker back down from a challenge?"

"I'm not backing down from anything. She made her wishes crystal fucking clear. I'm just trying to respect them."

He shook his head. "Then you're an idiot. If I were you, I would move heaven and earth to make my intentions known to that woman."

"What the hell do you think I've been doing?"

Was Marco stoned or just stupid? I've done everything I could think of to show her how important she was to me. I faced the mistakes of my past head-on. I've denied her nothing. I've opened my heart up to her daughter. I've stood by and watched her grieve over a marriage that never should have happened to begin with. I've comforted her when she was scared and took a step back when she needed space. What more on this God given earth could I do to make her see that I was here to stay? That the future we always wanted was still waiting for us and all we had to do was take it.

A few boisterous laughs echoed in the room interrupting my thoughts. A group of guys walked in, ready to start their workout.

Marco pulled his phone out of his pocket and checked the time. "I gotta run. Let me know if you want to grab a beer later." As he walked past me, his hand landed on my sweaty shoulder. "And to answer your question on what I think you should do? Well, my mama always said that actions speak louder than words."

I narrowed my eyes at his retreating back. Marco and his fucking riddles. No wonder the idiot was still single.

After I got dressed, I slammed my locker door shut, spun the combo lock and powered my way out to the parking lot. I had one destination in mind, shitfaced island.

As I exited the off-ramp, I spotted a familiar bar that I passed by every night on my way home. I'd never been inside before, but the red neon sign in the window advertised "Warm Beer and Lousy Food." Judging from the three shitty cars parked out front, it looked like the perfect place to drink away my troubles.

I walked up toward the bar as AC/DC's "You Shook Me All Night Long" blared through the jukebox in the back of the room. I ordered a Jameson neat and asked the bartender to leave the bottle. I enjoyed the burn from my first sip of whiskey as I waited for the effects to numb my body and erase all the shit going on in my head.

"You got a name, boy?" My head popped up and my eyebrows pulled together. The old Italian man behind the bar kept his eyes trained on me as he wiped the beer glasses off with a white towel.

When the hell was the last time someone called me "boy"? I wanted to correct him and tell him that I was in fact a man, not a boy, but there was something about his approach that had me sitting back in my stool.

"Name is Quinn."

He tilted his body to the side, resting his hips against the bar so he could watch the old married couple in the back bickering over a game of pool. He shook his head and threw his white dish towel over his shoulder. "All right, Quinn. You look like you have something on your mind. I'm a good listener. So, if you're ready to get it off your chest, I'm listening."

A laugh rumbled out of me. "I'm sorry, your name is?"

He held out his hand. "Name's Claude, I own this place." I took notice of his tattooed arms, which I'm sure probably told his life story. There were faces, names, dates, and shit I couldn't even make out. I squinted my eyes at the old man, trying to figure out what was so fascinating about him.

"What makes you think I'm looking to bare my soul tonight?"

He leaned his arms along the bar and studied me. "I can tell what you are looking for, you ain't going to find in a bottle of whiskey."

"Is that so?" I smirked at his obvious assumption.

"Take a look around you. Most of these people in here are my regulars. They come here every night, sit at the same barstool, order the same drink and tell the same stories. Some have families, and some don't. The one thing they all have in common is that they are all here trying to forget their problems."

"I take it your words of wisdom come from years of experience," I said, letting my gaze trail across the worn-down bar that had seen better days. The wood was chipped, and the legs on my stool felt like they could give out at any second. Good thing I wasn't here for the atmosphere.

"I opened this place over forty years ago."

"Damn." I squinted my eyes and tried to do the math in my head to figure out how old my parents were when he started the business. I gave up trying since I was already on my second drink.

He laughed as if he could read my mind. "Me and my Lottie, we bought this building back in the seventies when I was done with my tour of Vietnam."

I raised my glass in the air. "Thank you for your service. What branch?"

He lifted up the sleeve of his navy-blue T-shirt to display a bald eagle with the words Semper Fidelis on the top and the USMC logo on the bottom.

"A Marine. Not surprised." I finished off the rest of my drink. "You look like you were a badass back in the day."

He lifted a challenging eyebrow. "Back in the day, huh?"

I raised my hands in mock surrender. "Hey, no offense. I'm sure you could kick my ass if you wanted to."

He laughed again and reached behind the bar to the stock of liquor bottles that were lined neatly in rows. A black-and-white picture caught my stare. The lady was pretty with black puffed-out hair curling at her shoulders. She had on a white lace dress that reminded me of the doilies that my grandma used to put on her end tables. The woman had a set of pearls resting along her neckline. The photo looked to be as old as this bar.

"Is that your Lottie?" I asked as he poured the whiskey in my glass.

He pushed the amber liquid toward me. "That's her. It was taken about a year after we got married."

"Nice. How long have you been married?"

He paused, his silver eyes met mine. A sadness took over his features. "She passed away about five years ago."

"Shit. I'm sorry, Claude."

"Don't be," he said, surprising me. "There's nothing to be

sorry about. I got to spend forty-two years with that wonderful woman. I wouldn't trade a single second spent with her. Even the years we were apart and with other people." The wrinkled skin around his eyes deepened like he was getting lost in his thoughts. "You see, son, I almost didn't get a second chance with her."

"What happened?"

"I was young and stupid. I cheated on her when I was in the service. I thank the good Lord every day that she forgave my dumb ass."

"Sounds like she was a good woman," I said, curling my hands around my glass.

"She was the best." His eyes went soft and he gave me a knowing smile. "Speaking of women, I'm assuming the reason you ended up here tonight is because of a woman."

I nodded my head. "It's complicated."

"It always is," he replied with a distant look on his face.

"I don't even know how we ended up here." I chucked softly.

"Why don't you start from the beginning then?"

And so, I did. We sat and talked for over an hour, and before I knew it, the bar had filled in. We continued to talk and he still listened in between taking orders and pouring drinks for his customers. When I finished telling him about Charlotte and me, he grew silent. It was clear I had nothing left to say.

He leaned forward, talking over the loud music and the chatter of customers. "Very rarely does a first love end up being your last. You and I were lucky enough to have that big love. The one and only. It sounds like you've learned from your mistakes, but there's only one way to learn and grow. Just be patient."

"That's your big advice?" I questioned. "Be patient?"

He chuckled. "I'm not done." He cocked a bushy gray eyebrow. "What I want you to do is to look back on your life.

All your accomplishments and your failures. All that you've built for yourself so far. Then I want you to fast forward about forty years. Could you imagine wasting all those years and not spending them with the woman you love?"

I couldn't even imagine it. The only thing I wanted to do with the next forty years was spend it with Charlotte and Emery. Even the years when we were apart, she always lived inside of me. There hasn't been a day since we met that I didn't love her. After all this time, I couldn't see that changing anytime soon.

"Are those your kids?" I jerked my thumb to the family photo next to Lottie's.

"Stepkids." When he saw my reaction, he smirked. "Lottie married someone else during our years apart. He was a fireman. He died when Allyn was three months old and Addy was two."

"Wow."

"Yup. I came home from serving my country, found out the love of my life was not only a widow, but a mother of two. I knew that God was sending me a sign. I fought like hell to get her back, adopted those kids and never looked back. Best thing I ever did."

He turned and walked away to pour a draft beer for the customer who just sat down, leaving me alone in my thoughts. I replayed our conversation in my head while staring down at the worn wood flooring.

I had so much running through my mind and Claude's story hit too close home. While I never cheated on Charlotte, I still fucked up and broke her heart. She ended up marrying another man and had a kid with someone who wasn't me. Yet none of that mattered, because I had a second chance to be with her. And like Claude, I would make her see that we belonged together and that everything happened for a reason.

Maybe Marco wasn't as dumb as I thought. I actually think he had a point. Whether it took me a day, a week, or a year. I would show her in every way I could that we were meant to be together.

If all I had in my life was her and Emery, then that would be enough. They would be more than enough. End of story.

I pulled out my wallet and threw a hundred-dollar bill down on the bar. Next I dialed up an Uber to drag my drunk ass back to my apartment. I had a lot of planning to do tomorrow.

My phone lit up with a text message from Charlotte.

Are you home?

I paused before I typed out my reply. *No, I'm out.*

The bubbles jumped and stopped across my phone screen, letting me know that she was typing while I finished off my drink. I looked at the visitors log today while I was at work, so I knew she had finally paid a visit to her husband.

Can you can come over so we can talk?

I stared down at my phone and prayed that she had finally come to her senses. If she wanted more space, I wasn't sure I could give her that. Patience wasn't my strong suit, and I was already running out.

Claude grabbed my money and rang me up. He slid my change across the bar. "Keep the change," I told him. I figured my therapy session tonight was more than worth it.

"Good luck to you, kid."

"Thanks. Maybe I'll see you again soon."

"I hope not." He smirked and picked up my empty glass and placed it in the sink.

My eyebrows pinched together as I climbed off the stool. He laughed at my expression. "Don't waste your time here. Life is too short. Spend it with the people you love." He looked behind the bar at the black-and-white picture. "Everything can be gone in the blink of an eye. Never forget that."

Damn. This old man and his words struck something inside of me. I nodded my head, too choked up to talk and walked out.

I pulled my phone out and tipped the Uber driver that just dropped me off and climbed the three steps to her front porch. She opened the front door before I even had a chance to ring the bell.

We stood with a heavy, awkward silence stretching between us. Just the sight of her made my chest tighten. My gaze trailed down her body. She had on a low-cut top that exposed the swell of her breast. Her plump lip was practically begging me to take it in between my teeth. Then like a bucket of cold water, I remembered that she was with him today. A deep possessiveness took over me.

"How was your visit with Grant today?"

She swallowed and took a step back. I hated that there was an invisible line between us. One that she felt she had to draw to keep me away. "It was harder than I expected."

I scratched the back of my head. "I'm sure it was tough."

Her smile was soft and tentative. "It's over. He signed both documents."

"Damn. I wasn't expecting that."

Never in a million years did I think that Grant would give up his parental rights. The divorce papers were inevitable. But giving up Emery, I never saw that one coming.

She held my gaze and leaned against the door. "I'm just glad it's over."

I stepped up to her and slid my fingers between the soft strands of her hair. "Me too because I hate sleeping without you."

She leaned into my touch. "Then don't," she whispered, and I blinked, making sure I heard her right.

I swallowed, glancing at her lips. "The only way that I'm climbing into that bed with you tonight is if I know that you are completely mine."

"The second I walked out of that room, all I could think about was how much I wanted the comfort of your arms around me. But I needed to talk to him on my own. To handle it on my own. I needed him to see that I was done with his lies and his games. I'm sorry it's taken me so long to admit this to you, but I finally realized that nothing matters more than what's in my heart. And it's yours, Quinn. It always has been."

I pulled her mouth to mine, loving the way her soft lips tasted. She leaned in and opened her mouth so I could sweep my tongue against hers. Charlotte relaxed into me as I brought her even closer. Kissing her was as natural as breathing to me and I never wanted to stop.

I let my hands drift from her head down to her shoulders. I'd missed her. I'd spent our nights apart lying awake in bed, wishing she were next to me. Wishing everything could be different. Now that I had her back in my arms, I was never letting her go.

She placed her hand up against my chest. "Let's go upstairs."

She turned to walk away, but I grabbed her wrist. "Charlotte, we need to talk."

"We'll talk after. I need you now, Quinn."

Fuck! Like any man could deny that request.

TWENTY-SEVEN

CHARLOTTE

MY EYES POPPED OPEN AT THE SOUND OF SOFT FOOTSTEPS padding across the hardwood floor. I threw the covers back and grabbed my robe hanging along the chair in the corner of my bedroom. Quinn was snoring with an arm resting over his face. His chest rose and fell with each breath.

We had both given into sleep sometime right before the sun came up. We spent the entire night talking about the future and making love like two crazy teenagers who couldn't get enough of each other. There was no other perfect feeling than being back in his arms.

I quietly made my way across the room, hoping not to wake him. I needed my coffee, even though it was only decaf, and a few minutes to myself. Unfortunately, my daughter had other plans for me.

"Mom, why is the door locked?" Emery asked from outside my bedroom door, jingling the handle back and forth.

I ran a hand through my tangled hair and swung the door open. Emery stood there in her long monkey nightgown with matching slippers.

I looked down at her, wishing I had prepared myself

270

better for this conversation. "What are you doing up so early?"

She looked at me funny while rubbing the sleep from her eyes. "I don't know. I waited for you to come wake me up, but you never came."

I glanced over my shoulder to see if we had woken up Quinn. Emery tracked my line of sight and gasped. "Mommy, Quinn's sleeping in your bed."

I was about to haul her downstairs and tell her that he needed to rest when his deep morning voice spoke up. "Morning, Peanut."

I turned to see him sitting up against the headboard. He shot me a hopeful smile. One that said, I got this. Having him back in her life would be the one positive outcome from all this. She had been upset lately and did absolutely nothing to hide her true feelings. Any chance she got, she told me in as many ways as she could that she missed having him around.

Her frustration was just too big for her little body. Her attachment to him kind of freaked me out, because I knew better than anyone what it was like to all of a sudden have Quinn Walker disappear from your life. It worried me that someday I might have to endure that again, only this time it would be my daughter's feelings on the line if we crashed and burned like before. It almost felt reckless and people probably thought we were crazy, but I didn't care. No one knew our love like we did.

She looked more than pleased to see him and rushed at rapid speed toward his grinning face. Her tiny body skidded to a halt at the end of the bed. God, I wish I had her energy first thing in the morning. "You're back."

He gave her a warm smile, while scrubbing his jaw with his left hand. His morning scruff was sexy as hell. My thighs clenched, remembering how good it felt between my legs last night. "I missed your mom's banana cinnamon pancakes." He winked at me, causing a flush to hit my face. The man was lethal when it came to women, regardless of their age, and he knew it too. "Do you think we can convince her to make some for breakfast?"

She nodded her head enthusiastically. "I know she will, but she won't eat any because she gets sick in the toilet every morning, so she doesn't eat breakfast anymore."

Quinn's eyes flew to mine. "You didn't tell me you haven't been feeling well."

My heart dropped. This was not how I wanted him to find out. I still wasn't sure if I was pregnant, but I had a sinking feeling that I was.

Unease crawled up my spine. Maybe I was being paranoid, but at that moment I started to feel queasy and nauseous. I brought my hands to my temple and that dizzy feeling had me rushing into the bathroom.

Quinn was right behind me, holding my hair back as I emptied the contents of my stomach. After a couple minutes of hovering over the toilet bowl, Quinn helped me up and walked me over to the sink so I could brush my teeth.

"Emery." I wiped my mouth off with a towel and looked to my daughter who was standing in the doorway watching this all unfold. "Can you get the ingredients out for the pancakes and we'll be down in a couple minutes?"

"Okay." She started to walk away but stopped. "Do you want me to make some tea, so that your tummy will feel better?"

"Yes, thank you," I said, and watched her run out of the room.

Quinn leaned against the bathroom vanity. He crossed his bare feet at the ankles and folded his hands against his chest. "What's going? How long have you been getting sick?"

I hung my head and averted my gaze. "A couple of weeks."

"Have you called a doctor?"

I shook my head. "Not yet."

"Have you had a fever, sore throat, cough? Any other symptoms?"

I snaked a hand through my hair and tried to untangle my thoughts. "Just dizzy, lightheaded, and nauseous. Other than that, I've been extremely tired lately."

He had that detective stare. The one that unnerved me. The one that had me all figured out. "When's the last time you had your period?"

Jesus Christ! He didn't beat around the bush. No wonder he was so good at his job. "I'm a little late. I've been meaning to buy a test. I haven't had the time. Plus, whenever I'm at the store, Emery is with me. And that's the last thing I want to explain to her."

He flew out of the room and started to throw his clothes on. He ran over to the dresser and pocketed his phone and wallet. My heart felt like it was going to fly out of my chest. My mind started to run with all crazy thoughts. Was he really going to leave me?

"What are you doing?" I asked, surprised I could even locate my voice.

His lips pinched tight and his eyes darted frantically across the room. He came over, placed his hands on my shoulders and stared into my eyes. His face grew soft as he spoke. "I'm going to the closest fucking store I can find. You are taking a test today. Within the next hour we will know for sure if we are having a baby."

His words made my insides go liquid. Having a child with him was something I never thought would happen. Tears slipped from my eyes as I buried my face in the crook of his neck.

"I love you so damn much," I said, pressing myself against his chest.

"I love you too. No matter what the outcome of that test."

The conviction in his voice was strong, and I knew he

meant every word. I also knew he wanted a baby with me more than anything.

I followed him downstairs and we rounded the kitchen where Emery was getting a coffee mug out of the microwave.

She dunked the tea bag in the cup and added a little sugar before handing it to me. "I made the lemon flavor that you like."

I bent down, took the tea out of her hand and planted a kiss on her cheek. "That was very thoughtful. Thank you, sweetie."

"Hey, Peanut. I'm running to the store really quick." He looked to me and back to Emery. "To get your mom some medicine for her tummy ache. I'll bring back a can of that root beer soda that you like."

She giggled, the sound was sweet and infectious. "You're not supposed to say that in front of her. Remember, I'm only allowed to have soda on special occasions."

A sly smile pulled at the corner of his mouth. "Whoops."

They didn't think I knew that he snuck her things that she wasn't supposed to eat and drink when I wasn't around. Considering she was being helped by a cop, neither one of them did a very good job at hiding the evidence. I was always finding chocolate wrappers, empty bags of candy, and bottles of soda laying in the garbage bin. You would think Quinn would have taught her to push the garbage down farther into the bag, but I knew he was doing those things to make her happy, so I never said anything. I wasn't a food Nazi, it just wasn't a whole lot of fun dealing with a strung-out child coming down from a sugar high.

"Come on." I tickled her side and pretended I didn't hear Quinn. "Let's get those pancakes started."

Her sweet sounds filled the air as Quinn closed the door and walked out.

Somehow, I managed to make it through breakfast while Quinn ran to the store. Emery was downstairs watching cartoons and Quinn was now pacing my small bathroom. My knees bounced, waiting for the timer to go off on my phone. Our three minutes were up, and I couldn't take it anymore. Quinn's eyes were wide as he stared down at the three sticks that we had placed on the bathroom counter. He insisted that one wasn't enough. We needed three for one hundred percent accuracy.

I peered up at him as he held the three tests in the palm of his hand. Each one had two pink lines. I was definitely pregnant.

Tears filled his eyes. "We're having a baby!"

I nodded.

He tossed the tests on the counter and lifted me up by the waist and twirled me around. "I'm going to be a father!"

I held his face in my hands with an abundance of joy blooming inside of me. "I love you, Quinn."

His eyes were filled with emotion as he carried me across the room. "I'm going to be the best father to this baby," he promised as I wrapped my legs around his waist. "And I swear to you that Emery will know no different. I promise that both kids will get equal amounts of love. She will never feel like second place."

I captured his mouth with mine, feeling at a loss for words. The kiss centered me in a way that I didn't even know I needed. Fear and happiness ran equally through my brain. While the timing might not have been perfect, I wouldn't trade this moment for anything.

TWENTY-EIGHT

QUINN

Charlotte's parents lived in a gated retirement community just north of West Palm Beach, Florida. As we pulled into the pale brick, circular driveway, my confidence took a slight hit. It had been years since I'd seen the Donavons. Their house in suburban Philly was always a place where I'd felt at home. Yet, staring at the unfamiliar yellow house with pale blue shutters had me feeling out of place.

The front door opened, and Emery rushed up the driveway to greet her grandparents. It was my idea to come here and get away, so why was I so damn nervous? I grabbed Charlotte's hand; she gave mine a gentle squeeze fully aware of how on edge I felt.

Charlotte's mother pulled her into her arms while her dad stood off to the side with a bouncing Emery in front of him. The flight was only two and a half hours, but the little girl had so much energy she didn't know what to do with herself.

"Quinn." He extended his hand. "It's been a while." His tone was polite, but there was no escaping his scrutinizing stare. I felt more nervous than a long-tailed cat in a room full of rocking chairs. No matter what happened between

Charlotte and I, it never changed how I felt about her parents. I'd always cared about them and considered the Donavons my second family.

"This visit is long overdue," I said, knowing that I had a lot to make up for. "Thank you for having me. It means a lot."

Susan pulled me into her arms. She was always a hugger. "It's so good to see you."

Susan Donavon looked nothing like her daughter. She dyed her hair a yellowish blond and kept it cropped short. Her skin was golden tan, and she wore more makeup in one day than Charlotte did in a month.

Charlotte was more like her dad, minus his receding dark hairline. She had the same green eyes, and the exact olive skin coloring.

"Let's go inside so we can catch up," her father said, walking through the front door. I glanced at the car and determined that I would grab our luggage out of the trunk later.

This house was nothing like the traditional colonial home that Charlotte grew up in. The walls were coral white instead of covered in colorful wallpaper. The home had an open floor plan, decorated in soft blues and greens. I looked over to a white shelf, noticing it was covered with pictures of Charlotte and Emery. Charlotte was an only child. Her parents had a hard time conceiving, so she arrived later in life. She was always the sole focus of their attention.

"Emery." Susan reached for her hand. "Why don't you and your mom take a ride on the golf cart with me? I want to introduce you to a few friends of mine up at the clubhouse."

Emery eyes lit up like fireworks. "Will there be lizards running around the pool like last time?"

Everyone laughed. "I think I saw a few earlier." Susan smiled. "Why don't we let your grandpa give Quinn a tour of the house?"

Charlotte's eyes met mine. I gave her a subtle nod letting her know it was fine. After the girls took off, her father gave me a quick tour. We kept the conversation light as we walked from room to room.

He patted my shoulder as he finished showing me around. "I'm going to fetch us a drink. Make yourself at home," he said and disappeared into the dining room.

The oversized ranch style house was located on the 9th hole of a beautiful golf course. Ryan Donavon always had a love for golf, just like Susan Donavon had a love for the ocean.

I opened the sliding glass door and relaxed a bit, feeling a light breeze with a view of swaying palm trees. I glanced up at the stunning sunset thinking I could get used to this.

A glass of scotch was placed in my hand. "I'm going to get this conversation out of the way, Quinn, and give it to you straight."

I swallowed. "I'm ready."

"I'm still angry with you. You hurt my daughter." I stayed silent, letting him say his piece while I stared out into the backyard. This conversation needed to happen. "While it's nice to see Charlotte so happy again, it's going to take you a while to earn my trust back."

I sipped the scotch and continued to stare out the window. "You have every right to feel that way. I messed up, and no one regrets the pain I caused her more than I do." I turned so I could look him straight in the eyes. "However, I can guarantee you that I'm here to stay permanently. I love your daughter, more than my own life. You have my word that I will never leave her again. In fact…" I swallowed the buzz of nerves in my throat. "I want to ask her to marry me, and I was hoping I could have your blessing."

He arched an eyebrow. "We've had this conversation before, and you ended up breaking her heart. What's different this time?"

I thought about how to answer that. I didn't want him to have any doubts about my feelings, or whether or not things would actually work out this time. It seemed like another lifetime ago when I took him out to his favorite hamburger joint and asked for Charlotte's hand in marriage. I was so young and naïve back then, thinking I had the world at my fingertips. "I guess you can say that I reached the point in my life where I understand what I have. If I could go back and do it differently, I never would have left."

He nodded. "The only problem with that, Quinn, is that it's not just Charlotte anymore. You would be signing up for a life raising another man's child."

"Emery is a part of Charlotte, and there isn't a piece of her that I don't love. I'm fully aware of what I'm signing up for, and I can't make it happen quick enough. I want a life with both of them."

We hadn't told her parents about the baby yet. He had every right to doubt me, and I still needed to demonstrate to him that it didn't matter to me if Emery was blood or not. I loved her as my own, and I would take on whatever role Charlotte gave me.

He glanced at me then looked back to the golfers as they hit their drivers toward the green. "I'm happy to hear that, although that's not the only obstacle standing in your way."

I understood exactly what he meant. Grant had agreed to the divorce, but until everything was finalized, nothing was guaranteed. I was sick of living in limbo. Sick of him being in my way. "I'm doing everything I can to rid her and Emery of that piece of shit."

He laughed and clinked his glass with mine. "It's good to have you back, Quinn." He set his amber liquid down on the table. "What do you say we go hit a few balls? Just don't tell the wife. I may have been stretching the pain from the back surgery just a little bit." He winked and I laughed. It was good to see some things never changed.

———

It was weird looking at palm trees decorated with Christmas lights, and hearing "Rudolph the Red-Nosed Reindeer" blaring from the red convertible next to us as we cruised down the highway. It reminded me of my time in California. Christmas without the cold and snow never quite felt right. We'd been in Florida for three days, and as much as I was enjoying the warmer weather, I was ready to head back north.

I spread the blanket we had packed and set the picnic basket down next to us. Charlotte and I sat side by side staring out into the ocean. Susan and Ryan had taken Emery to a Christmas play in downtown West Palm. This was the first moment we'd had alone together.

I took her hand and squeezed it. "Let's go for a walk."

Our bare feet sunk in the wet sand as the warm sun beat down on our backs. "In case I forget to tell you," she tipped her head back and smiled, "thank you for this."

I kissed her forehead. "No need to thank me. I needed this too. I forgot how much I missed the smell of fresh saltwater and the sound of the ocean."

"Do you miss living in California?"

For a minute, I let my mind wander back in time. I was so focused on work and trying to prove myself that I never had the chance to enjoy the experience.

"The only thing I miss about LA is seeing the sun shine every day."

She bumped my shoulder. "You never talk much about that time in your life."

Charlotte was one of the most confident women I knew. But it was no secret that leaving her behind for my adventure had her questioning her self-worth.

"Honestly." I looked over at the sky. The beams of light from the sun had me squinting my eyes. "There's not much to tell. I spent my time there working and when I wasn't, I was missing everything I threw away."

"Quinn, you thought you were doing the right thing. As much as I hated it, I understand why you did it."

"It's just a time of my life that I don't want to think about." Her green eyes grew soft with understanding. I brushed back a piece of hair that had blown in her face. "I don't want to think about the past. I just want to focus on the future."

Even though there were parts of our past that were memorable, there was also a fair share of heartache. I wanted our future to be brighter and stronger. It wasn't just about us anymore. We would always have our past, but our future belonged to our children. I just wanted to look forward with hope instead of backward with regret.

She stepped forward. "We can do that, but I want you to know one thing."

"What's that?"

She rested her head on my shoulder. "If you ever leave me behind again, I will hunt you down and you better hope that I never find you."

My lips quirked up. "Oh really. Why's that?"

"Because you may carry a gun, but it was you who taught me how to use it."

I placed my chin on top of her head and laughed. "Sweetheart, I took you to the shooting range once and it was ten years ago."

"Exactly, which means my aim won't be very good which would be unfortunate for you."

"Wouldn't missing your target be a good thing for me?"

"Nope." She shook her head. "Because while aiming at your leg, I might end up shooting you in the balls instead."

I leaned back, placed my hands on her hips and tried to keep a straight face. "That sounds painful."

"I imagine it would be. It would also be a lesson you would never have to learn twice."

Leaning forward, I pressed my lips to hers. "My days of walking away from you are over. So, hopefully, my legs and balls are safe for now."

She placed her hands around my neck and stared at me. "You know that I can be frustrating and stubborn sometimes, right?"

I rolled my eyes. "Sweetheart, I've known you for over a decade. Trust me when I say that I know exactly what I'm signing up for. Now let's go eat, I'm starving."

I led her back to our little spot on the beach where our cooler and blanket were set up.

The water washed against the shore as I set my sandwich down in my lap. There were a few beachgoers scattered around in their beach chairs, and an older man playing fetch with his golden retriever.

"What are you thinking about?" I asked, taking a bite of my roast beef sandwich.

She shifted to face me. "I'm thinking about how lucky we are that we got a second chance, and that we are finally going to have that family that we always dreamed of."

I set my plate down and dusted the sand off my legs. The sun was shining down on us when the thought struck. "I couldn't agree more." I leaned in and dipped my mouth to hers. "I'd like to think of this as a new beginning, one where there is no end in sight for us. Marry me."

I've always considered myself a level-headed guy, but I was too caught up in the moment. I didn't care if I had an hour left, a day, a month, or fifty years. Whatever time I had left on this earth, I wanted it with her.

She pulled back and stared into my eyes. "Quinn..."

I'd taken her by surprise. I didn't plan this, but when it came to matters of the heart, there was no logic or reason.

And there was no way to explain or define the need I had to finally make her mine.

"I know this isn't a big grand proposal like last time, and I don't even have a ring. I wasn't planning on asking you today. I wanted to wait until the divorce was final, but Charlotte," I pulled her onto my lap, "I don't want to waste another second. Life is too short. And you're right, we are lucky that we got a second chance. Not everyone gets those. We need to take advantage of the gift we've been given. Let's make it count. Let's do it better than before. Be my forever. Be my wife. Say yes."

Tears flooded her eyes. "People will think we are crazy."

My pulse raced with anticipation. It seemed like it was taking her forever to answer me. "Is that a yes?"

She slid her hands along the back of my neck, her touch was soft and reassuring. "Yes, Quinn. My answer is and always will be yes. Even though you just proposed to me in between bites of your roast beef sandwich."

I grabbed her face and swallowed. "I promise, I'll get you a ring."

Her smile was blinding. "I don't need a ring. I already have everything I've ever wanted." She brought my hand down to her stomach.

I stroked her cheek with my free hand. "You have no idea what this baby means to me. It was always supposed to be you. There isn't anyone else I could ever imagine having a family with."

Since I was twenty years old, I knew that she was the one. I may have let her slip through my fingers before, but I was holding on tight now. Maybe she was right. There would be people who didn't understand, but I didn't give a fuck what anyone else thought.

"I'm sorry that you weren't the one to give me my firstborn." The guilt and regret in her voice was heavy.

"Hey." I brushed a fallen tear off her cheek. "No regrets. I want this life with you and Emery." I kissed her lips, savoring the moment.

Everything in my life was finally aligned. She was going to be my wife, and I was going to be a father.

This kiss was the official start of our new beginning. There was nowhere for us to go from here but up.

EPILOGUE

"Santa came. Santa came!" Emery screamed, running into our room.

"What time is it?" Quinn asked, glancing at the clock on my nightstand.

Sitting up, I rubbed the sleep from eyes as my very anxious little girl landed on the bed, falling right between us.

"Emery," I said, noticing the ring of chocolate smeared along her lips. "Did you empty out your stocking already?"

Her grin was wide and her eyes were alive with excitement. "I did. Santa left me Reese's Peanut Butter Cups. My favorite…the Christmas tree kind."

"You didn't open any presents though, right?"

She shook her head. "No, but you should see how many he left me. Can we please go downstairs now?" She folded her hands under her chin and pleaded.

I kissed the top of her head. "Sure, just give me a minute to get ready."

"I'll take her down," Quinn offered, pressing a kiss to my shoulder and rising from the bed.

"Yes! Yes! Yes!" Emery chanted, jumping up and down.

Quinn grabbed Emery's hand and looked down at me.

This was our first Christmas together as a family. Never in my life had I ever felt so content.

"I love you both," I whispered, overcome with emotion. My pregnancy hormones were off the charts.

"We love you too, right, Peanut?"

Emery nodded her head enthusiastically. She looked about ready to jump out of her skin. Quinn and I both laughed as she pulled him out of the room.

Quinn tucked me against his side, as I sipped on my hot chocolate. Emery's smile was wide as we watched her open gift after gift.

"Thank you," Quinn murmured against my cheek.

I leaned back and folded my toes underneath me. "For what? I haven't given you your gifts yet."

"I don't need gifts. This…" He gestured around the living room. "Is all I need. This is perfect." The Christmas tree sat in the corner, and the stockings with our names on them hung from the fireplace. He was right, it was perfect.

Our moment was broken when Emery got to her final present. I brought the fleece blanket up to my chin, while Quinn grabbed his camera off the table and got it ready.

"This is the last one." She sighed, clearly not happy about that. I swear, she got more enjoyment from opening the packages than the gifts themselves. I looked around the floor to all the clothes, books, crafts, and toys scattered amongst the torn wrapping paper. Quinn and I had gone overboard, but we wanted to make this holiday as happy as we could for her. These past few weeks have not been easy, but we were slowly finding our footing.

"All right." Quinn held up the camera. "Let's see what Santa left you."

Emery tore into the red wrapping paper and held up the wicker basket. She looked confused as she inspected the contents one by one. We watched in amusement as she pulled out a leash, a dog collar, puppy treats, and chew toys.

Her face dropped. She looked puzzled and a little disappointed. "I think Santa made a mistake."

Quinn acted shock. "What? Let's check outside and see if there is anything else. Maybe he left your gift out there."

Quinn handed me the camera so I could capture the moment. He walked over to the door and swung it open. There on our front porch step was a yellow lab with a big, red bow on top of his crate.

Emery's eyes grew wide as saucers she ran over to the door. She looked up at us and gasped. She started jumping up and down, the short strands of her ponytail coming undone. "A puppy! A puppy! I got a puppy! This is the best Christmas ever!"

After snapping a few pictures, I sent a quick text to Brody, letting him know that it was safe for them to come in now.

No sooner after Emery snatched the puppy from his crate and started playing with him, the doorbell rang.

I walked over to answer it while Quinn sat on the floor helping Emery fasten the dog collar.

"Well, look who's here." I acted surprised as Quinn's family stepped inside.

I took their coats, hats, and mittens, and helped them carry their gifts inside.

Brody came up and whispered in my ear, "My brother owes me. That little shit pissed all over my carpet last night."

I giggled. "You were supposed to keep him in the crate."

"I tried, but he kept whining and Gretchen felt bad, so we let him out."

I patted his arm. "You're such a softy. You're going to make a great dad."

"Shhh…" He placed his finger over his lips. "Remember, Mom doesn't know yet."

"My lips are sealed." I playfully pushed on his chest and ushered him into the kitchen. "Come on, I have a couple breakfast casseroles that need to be put in the oven."

———

After breakfast, Quinn's parents took Emery along with our new puppy, Oakley, over to their house to play before dinner. Quinn said he had a present for me. So I hopped in his truck and we drove through town with light snow falling around us. It wasn't enough to stick to the roads, but it was still pretty watching the snowflakes touch the ground.

About twenty minutes into our drive, we pulled onto a private street, passing a newly developed neighborhood being built on the right. We drove farther down the road until we hit a more secluded section of the development.

Quinn pulled into a driveway and put the truck in park. A beautiful brick colonial with black shutters and white trim stood in front of me. It was new, yet had an old Southern charm to it.

"What is this?" I asked, feeling my heart pick up speed. I had a pretty good idea, but I wanted to be sure. He'd been dropping hints here and there about wanting a place of our own.

He picked up my gloved hand and planted a kiss. "Come on, let me show you. I haven't signed anything yet, so if you don't like it, we don't have to buy it."

I trailed behind him in shock. He bought me a house. A freakin house for Christmas.

He walked over to the two-car garage and punched a code in the side panel while we waited for the door to slide fully open.

"What do you think?" he asked as we walked through the foyer leading to a huge open floor plan. The kitchen opened up to a large family room with tall ceilings. To the left was a set of French doors that led to a cozy den.

"It's beautiful." I looked around taking it all in. The kitchen was lined with long white cabinets and a gray-tiled backsplash that matched the slate-colored floors. There was a farmhouse sink in the middle of the kitchen that overlooked a huge backyard, perfect for a growing puppy.

I strolled farther into the room and ran my hands over the black granite countertop looking over the white trim along the windows.

Quinn pointed to the sliding glass doors that led out to the stone patio. "The house was a custom build, but the owners never got a chance to move in because the husband's employer just relocated them to Chicago. We have about an acre of land to work with. I have a lot of ideas for the backyard." He turned and pointed to the staircase on the left. "There are four bedrooms and two full baths upstairs as well as a finished basement downstairs."

I looked around taking it all in. There was a large brick fireplace sitting against the middle of the exterior wall, with long paned windows resting on either side. There was a bay window on the opposite side of the room with a bench seat.

All thoughts stalled in my head when I was hit with a memory.

This was the house we talked about owning one day. I remember laying in the hammock with him all those years ago. He asked me to describe my dream home. I don't know how he found this place, but he managed to find exactly what I'd described to a T. And now I couldn't wait to bring this place to life. To fill it up with laughter and make memories.

This house was ours. All ours.

"I can't believe you did this. This is our dream house." I glanced around, impressed that he remembered every little detail.

Quinn stepped up and his eyes dropped to my stomach. "I told you. I remember everything." He reached over and held two flute glasses in his hands. "Sparkling cider."

I accepted the glass and raised it in the air. "To new beginnings."

"To my amazing fiancée," he said, taking a sip. "I hope

this house is everything you ever imagined it would be and more, because that's the life I promised to give you."

"It's more than enough." I smiled, looking over to the bumped-out sunroom that would be perfect for family gatherings.

He set his glass aside and went down on one knee. My hand flew to my mouth. He reached into his pocket and pulled out a small black box.

"I've come prepared this time." He winked, and then his face turned serious. "The first time I asked you to marry me, I wasn't ready. I was a young, dumb kid who didn't know what he wanted." Tears started to flow down my face as I stared at him in disbelief. "I didn't deserve you then, but you loved me anyway. Even though we were apart for too many years, there was never a time when I didn't love you." I slid my hand to his cheek as he shook his head. "There will probably never come a time where I will feel worthy of you, but if you give me a chance, I will promise you until I take my last breath, I will try."

He opened up the box. I leaned forward to see the sparkling diamonds in a white gold band dancing in the light. There was a large oval shaped diamond in the middle, with two smaller round stones on either side. It was beautiful.

"This ring represents the past, the present, and the future. The first diamond is from your original ring."

"It's perfect," I said in between sobs. Seeing my old stone sitting next to my new ones had everything coming full circle.

He pulled the ring out of the box and slid it onto my shaking finger. His smile was big. "Now, we are officially engaged."

My heart hammered in my chest feeling overloaded with happiness. I was also in shock. Even though he proposed on the beach a few short weeks ago, I wasn't expecting this.

The house, the ring, the baby, my thoughts were endless and excited about what the future held.

My tears were so heavy, it was a miracle that I could even see. "I love you, Quinn. Thank you for bringing out the best parts of me. Thank you for giving me more than I had ever dreamed of." I brought his face to mine. "And thank you for making me see that I didn't have to settle for less. Not when I could have something much greater. You, this house, a family together…It's everything."

He captured a few tears and stared down at my hand. "You finally have my ring back on your finger."

I reached up and threaded my arms around his neck. "Everything is finally right where it belongs."

He lifted me up and spun me around before bringing me back to his arms. He held my hand out and tilted it to the side, staring at the ring in awe. "Promise me you'll never take this off."

The vulnerability in his voice had me choking back another sob. "I promise for better or for worse. You're stuck with me forever."

He took my face in his hands and kissed me. My heart was overflowing with happiness. I'm so glad that he never gave up on me and that I followed my heart. Because this single moment right here was the happiest day of my life.

TEN MONTHS LATER

I walked up the steps to the courthouse with my head down, trying not to draw attention to myself. There was a large crowd gathered outside. It had been eleven long months since Grant was captured, and today was the day he would learn his fate. Quinn held my hand in a firm, supportive grip. His posture was stiff as we made our way into the courtroom.

While the crowd was there to ensure that Grant got what was coming to him, there was still an uneasy air of judgment that followed us. I could almost hear the whispers and the sneers.

The comments online were out there for the whole world to see. About how convenient it was that I moved on so quickly. That I gave birth to another man's child two months after my divorce was finalized. That I was already engaged to be married and that my son was born out of wedlock. But I didn't care. These people didn't know me. They didn't know about all the sleepless nights that I spent crying into my pillow. They couldn't comprehend the hell that Grant dragged me through or all the times where I held my daughter, doing my best to reassure her that everything would be okay in the end.

Most of all, they didn't know that being with Quinn was my destiny.

These past few months had been one thing after another, and it was a miracle that I was still standing.

We walked up the aisle in the courtroom and took our seats behind the prosecutor's table when Grant entered the room.

The crowd began to whisper in a collective rumble as unease grew in the pit of my stomach the moment our eyes met. As much as I wanted to pretend that seeing him didn't faze me, I couldn't control the shiver that ran up my spine.

Grant's eyes shifted from mine to the man sitting next to me. His steps faltered and his lips tightened. His normally warm brown eyes turned to cold steel. The sheriff guiding him into the courtroom had to use his muscles to push him past the prosecutor's desk where he seemed to just want to pause and glare at the two of us.

After a brief hesitation the officer guided him to the defense table where he pushed down on his shoulders, forcing him to take a seat.

His parents and brother were seated directly in back of him. Their faces bore a look of worry only a parent who loved their child could give. I knew how painful this was for them, to sit quietly, wondering silently how things could have gone so wrong for the son they raised.

The crowd grew quiet when the judge entered the courtroom.

The bailiff spoke in a loud, clear voice. "Please rise, the courtroom of the Honorable Judge Bednarski is now in session."

With three taps of the gavel, the judge asked everyone to be quiet and be seated.

The next sound was the squeak of the hardwood chair dragging across the floor as Grant's defense attorney moved to stand in front of the judge.

"Your honor, on behalf of my client, Grant Anderson, we have accepted the District Attorney's plea offer of guilty to five counts of First-Degree Vehicular Manslaughter."

A collective gasp came from the audience, and I heard Grant's mother quietly start to sob.

Grant knew the odds of successfully winning a jury trial, so in order to avoid a prosecutor's threat, a potential legal maneuver that could have landed him a life sentence, he agreed to plead out.

After the judge asked Grant to confirm his plea, and after the families of his victims read their statements, Grant was sentenced to twenty-five years behind bars, until he would be eligible for parole.

Quinn squeezed my hand, and I closed my eyes, thankful that this chapter of my life was over.

———

Thank you so much for reading Quinn and Charlotte's story. I hope you're ready to read the next book in the series because you won't want to miss it. It's a one-night stand gone bad, with a pair of handcuffs that involves a hero with a badge. You can download

Whatever You Need (Marco and Amelia's story) here: https://geni. us/qyBBZ6z

However, I'm not done with Quinn and Charlotte yet. I wrote an EPIC bonus scene that gives you a glimpse into Quinn and Charlotte's future 20 years later!! Click on the link below and sign up for my newsletter to access this fun bonus scene and meet all three of their kids.

Sign-up HERE
Already Subscribed? CLICK HERE

Or Scan:

ALSO AVAILABLE BY S. JONES

THE HARD SERIES

Hard to Love (Chase & Emily)

Hard to Stay (Brad & Lexi)

Hard to Leave (Jack & Chloe)

THE PROTECTIVE SERIES

Whatever It Takes (Quinn & Charlotte)

Whatever You Need (Marco &Amelia)

Whatever You Want (Logan & Ava)

THE ATLANTA ARROWS SERIES

Fumbled Love (Maverick & Kinley)

Fumbled Beginning (JP & Rylee)

Fumbled Arrangement (Rhett and Natalie)

ABOUT THE AUTHOR

S. Jones is a contemporary romance author from Upstate New York. She has a strong passion for writing and reading stories that will rip your heart out before it's put back together again.

If she's not buried in her writing cave, she's usually reading or planning out her next vacation.

She loves to travel to different places and spends all her free with her husband, and two college age children.

When the weather permits, you can find her outside walking her golden retriever, or enjoying a nice cocktail by the pool. She loves cooking and entertaining for her family and friends.

When she's not holding a glass of wine in one hand and her kindle in the other, she loves to hear from her readers at:

authorsjoneswrites@gmail.com